If there was some way...

"Stop." Jeff spoke the word aloud, opening his eyes to stifle the images forming in his head. He and Maggie had no reason to give things another try. Not even the lingering shades of love were enough to dispel the fear and doubt. And neither of them was willing to enter into another possible failure.

Too many miles and too many years separated him and Mags.

He pushed to his feet and headed back to the house. He would enjoy the time they'd been given. He would facilitate fun memories. He would be Mags's sexual fantasies come to life... and let her be his.

And Sunday, when they parted ways, he would leave a part of his heart behind—the part that lay deep in the pit of his stomach right then. The part that ached from its burden.

Dear Reader,

I'm a sucker for "how we met" stories. I enjoy coming up with creative ways to bring the heroes and heroines together that first time. But I'm an even bigger sucker for reunion stories.

Couples who enter a relationship with a history hanging over them jerk our heartstrings. From that instant they see each other for the first time in years, we feel the pull of that old attraction, but with it comes the stomach-churning fear of repeating past mistakes. We want so badly to believe they've learned and have changed enough to make things work this time.

We want them to prove true love *is* forever.

Making a new start isn't easy for Maggie and Jeff—their history is riddled with mistakes. The Kentucky woman and California man aren't the kids they once were, and they're miles apart in more ways than the distance between their homes. So when history starts repeating itself? Well, I hope you laugh, cry and cheer them on as much as I did!

Until next time,

Pamela Hearon

PAMELA HEARON

My Way Back to You

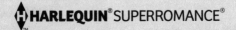

HARLEQUIN® SUPERROMANCE®

Recycling programs
for this product may
not exist in your area.

ISBN-13: 978-0-373-60905-5

My Way Back to You

Printed in U.S.A.

www.Harlequin.com

Pamela Hearon grew up in Paducah, Kentucky, a place that infuses its inhabitants with Southern values and hospitality. Here she finds inspiration for her quirky characters, her stories' backdrops and her narrative voice. Pamela was a 2013 RITA® Award finalist and a Maggie Award finalist for her first Harlequin Superromance story, *Out of the Depths*. *The Summer Place* was a 2014 National Readers' Choice Award finalist. Visit Pamela at pamelahearon.com, and on Facebook and Twitter.

Books by Pamela Hearon

HARLEQUIN SUPERROMANCE

Out of the Depths
The Summer Place
Moonlight in Paris
His Kind of Perfection

Visit the Author Profile page
at Harlequin.com for more titles.

To Nathan and Misty, whose love for each other
is the stuff of romance legends.

Acknowledgments

Many thanks to the people who willingly share ideas
and nuggets of insight, which give my characters
depth and realism. I appreciate how they allow me to
"pick their brains" when I'm writing a story—and I do it
often. With that in mind, a special thanks goes out to
certain individuals: my daughter, Heather Blackston,
and my friend, Rita Dodd, for their help with Chicago
locations; my friends, Dishona and Wesley Wright for
the inspiration behind a particularly fun plot device;
and my critique partners at WriteRomance—
Sandra Jones, Maggie Van Well and
Angela Campbell—for their time,
influence, suggestions, encouragement
and belief in my writing ability.

Thanks to my editor, Karen Reid,
at Harlequin Superromance,
for her generous time and patience,
which transform a good story into a great one.

Thanks to my agent, Jennifer Weltz
of the Jean V. Naggar Literary Agency,
for her perseverance on my behalf
and her guidance along this journey.

And thanks to my husband, Dick,
whose love and encouragement keep the belief
of forever love strong in my mind and in my heart...
and keeps these stories coming.

CHAPTER ONE

NINETEEN DOLLARS...AND a divorce.

That was what the green jersey knit palazzo pants outfit ended up costing Maggie Russell in the long run, even though it had been on sale.

Of course, the purchase was frivolous. But, at the time, it represented the chance to step out of motherhood for a night and feel sexy again, an opportunity to celebrate turning twenty-one and finally reaching legal age despite the fact she was already married and the mother of a one-year-old.

More importantly, it was the perfect way to shove in Jeff's face that he couldn't control every single teeny tiny aspect of her life—and every penny she spent.

He couldn't control *her*.

At least, that had been the plan.

Instead, they'd gotten into a hellacious argument because her purchase overdrew their account. Jeff had yelled about her irresponsibility. She'd cried about his insensitivity. He'd stormed out, and she'd taken little Russ and run home to Mama and Daddy—all the way next door.

That fight had been the one that put her and Jeff over their limit—not that they'd ever specified a number. In fact, it was actually the same argument rehashed so many times they had the lines perfected and didn't need to go through the whole thing again. Everything had been said countless times before. And nothing said was heard. Nothing said was listened to. Not even fabulous makeup sex could assuage the deep-seated anger, frustration and hurt of not being understood. Not this time.

Two months later they filed for divorce. Six months after that, the decree was finalized—three weeks after Russ turned two.

Sometimes, during flights of fancy, usually during the summers when Russ left her in Taylor's Grove, Kentucky, to visit his dad in California, she'd allow herself to wonder what would've happened if she'd never spent that nineteen dollars? What if she hadn't accidentally gotten pregnant at nineteen? What if…?

"Mom, you need to get over. You're about to miss the exit." Russ's impatient tone jerked her back to the present *and* across two lanes of traffic. She may have taught their son to drive, but the backseat stuff was all Jeff, the control freak.

"Jeez, where were you, anyway?" A grin accompanied Russ's eye roll, the combination perfected by the time he'd turned eleven.

"Just thinking about when you were little." She reached out and ruffled the top of his wavy black hair, a mournful sigh escaping her lips. "Here you are, going off to college, but in my mind's eye you're still eight instead of eighteen."

A brief look of panic shot from his black-as-coffee eyes. "You're not gonna cry again, are you?"

"Only about this traffic." She flipped on the blinker and nosed the car into the bumper-to-bumper line of vehicles inching down the ramp to Chicago's O'Hare International.

Russ's panicked look may have been an overreaction but not totally ungrounded. His senior year of high school had been a rough one for Maggie. As each of his activities came to an end, she bawled her way through the ordeal of Senior Nights, and when his name was called at graduation she blubbered aloud.

Her baby. Seven hours away from home. All by himself in this city of three million people. Her heart squeezed, and she felt the familiar pang she'd first noticed when she read the positive pregnancy test nineteen years ago and had reiterated itself on a daily basis ever since. Her dad's sage words followed on its heels. *The nine months before aren't the problem,* he'd say. *It's the ninety-nine years after that kill you.*

No doubt about it, saying goodbye once parent orientation ended two days from now might just do her in.

The only good part about that ominous event was that it made today's excursion to pick up her ex-husband, whom she hadn't seen in person since Russ's kindergarten graduation, pale in comparison.

Russ's phone beeped, and he glanced at the text. "Dad says he's curbside at Terminal 1."

"Tell him traffic's awful, and we'll be there as soon as we can."

"You gotta be more aggressive, Mom." Russ's thumbs flew on the tiny keyboard as he talked. "Quit letting people in ahead of you. We could be there by now."

Quite a way up the road, Maggie spotted the Terminal 1 sign and started easing her way over to the far right-hand lane. "Two months of driving in San Diego each summer makes you the expert in city traffic, huh?"

"Well…yeah, actually." Russ shrugged and shot her a mischievous grin. "Or maybe I'm just more anxious to see Dad than you are."

"I'm sure you are, but I'm still getting there as quickly *and safely* as I can."

While it was true she wasn't exactly looking forward to the reunion, she wasn't horrified by the idea, either. Picking Jeff up from the airport on their way saved him the expense of renting a car. And since the next couple of days would require a lot of togetherness, it seemed like the easiest, most practical solution for everybody.

For sixteen years, they'd made joint custody work despite the distance and the expense.

They could survive this.

"There he is!" Russ rolled down his window, and the ensuing gust of heat caused a burst of perspiration to break out across Maggie's forehead, cheeks and chin.

She grabbed a tissue and dabbed her face, careful not to smudge her lipstick, as she searched the throng of faces lining the curb of Terminal 1, looking for the one that would hold a vague familiarity. Eagerness marked the faces as they waited for the ride that would take them from this temporary gathering place to their next destination, making it all the more fitting she and Jeff should be together again to cross this milestone.

Surely it was that thought—not the sight of her ex standing at the curb, looking trim and fit, white teeth shining against his tanned face, and dark eyes glowing with joy at the sight of their son—that caused her stomach and her heart to clench involuntarily…along with various other parts of her body.

"Dad!"

His son's voice, which had grown so deep over the past few years, still took Jeff Wells by surprise. Especially as he tried to connect the masculine sound with the juvenile antics of the kid hanging out the window of the black SUV, wildly waving his arms.

By the time the car rolled to a stop, Russ was out of the car and had Jeff locked in a bear hug that squeezed a laugh from his lungs. His son would never be one of those hands-off macho types, thank God.

The excitement of seeing Russ made Jeff momentarily forget the awkwardness about to descend on them. But when his eyes caught the hesitant smile of the woman standing beside them, it crashed down with full force.

"Jeff."

"Hi, Mags." The nickname fell from his lips as if he'd last seen her only yesterday.

He fought the urge but lost the battle as his eyes dropped for a quick scan of the woman next to him. The color and short haircut was different, and the body a bit fuller and rounder...curvier. The voice had grown a tad throatier, but the green eyes with their amber flecks remained untouched by time... as gorgeous as ever.

And those full lips. How well he remembered...

The image faded as Maggie thrust her hand forward in a gesture much too formal considering the shared intimacies that had created the fine young man standing between them. "Um..." The green eyes flashed with some kind of emotion as a deep pink flush imbued her fair complexion. "It's good to see you, Jeff."

"You, too."

He ignored the extended hand and felt her stiffen as he pulled her into a hug. He'd been planning this moment for some time and had long ago decided to get past the cumbersome hellos and move into the we've-done-a-helluva-job phase as quickly as possible.

She didn't give any ground. Keeping her feet firmly planted, she bent at the waist and leaned into him—a hug befitting the awkwardness of the moment. They straightened, and he saw his own wariness reflected in her eyes. But then their smiles collided, genuine and relieved they'd shared and lived through the moment.

Russ grabbed Jeff's one piece of luggage. "I'll get this, Dad." He pointed toward the front seat he'd vacated. "You sit up front with Mom."

Maggie's eyebrow and one side of her mouth rose simultaneously. "That'll give his backseat driving more authenticity."

"Want me to drive?" Russ leaned to the side to flash her an impish grin as he slid the duffel into the back compartment.

"Emphatically no." Mags hurried around to claim control of the driver's seat before Russ could get there.

Jeff was already seated and buckled by the time his ex-wife climbed in, so he had a chance at another good look at her without gawking as she got situated. The years had been kinder than he'd expected, especially considering what she went through with Zeke two—no, make that three—years ago.

Fact was, she looked good.

Damn good.

"We're meeting with Coach Brimley at four, Dad,

at the Water Tower Campus. That's downtown, close to your hotel. Tomorrow and the day after, we'll be at the other campus—Loyola Lake Shore." Russ's chatter filled the car, as it did any space when the boy was around. "He said today's session wouldn't be very long. He just wants to meet the parents of the new guys before the official stuff starts tomorrow."

Jeff checked his watch—12:52 p.m. "Plenty of time. Have you checked in yet?"

Maggie shook her head but kept her eyes glued to the windshield. "We came straight to the airport as soon as we got into town."

"Mom's afraid of the traffic. She puts her blinker on and thinks the lane next to her will just magically open up and invite her in."

Mags peeled her eyes away from the road in front of them long enough to flash Russ a look in the rearview mirror. "I got us here right on time, didn't I?"

Russ snorted in return. "We could've checked in and had lunch by now if you'd been driving, Dad."

"You haven't had lunch?" Jeff nudged the conversation away from the direction it was taking.

Maggie and Russ both shook their heads.

"I have some snacks in my bag." Jeff pointed to the backpack he'd tossed into the backseat, and it took Russ no time to find the mother lode of trail mix, snack bars, peanut butter and crackers and mixed nuts he'd stashed.

"Cool!" Russ tore into a package and held it across the seat. "Want some, Mom?"

"No, thanks."

Jeff couldn't help but notice the white-knuckle grip Maggie had on the wheel. She was creeping along, obviously uncomfortable with city driving and they weren't even out of the airport yet. At this pace, they wouldn't get checked in until tomorrow.

"I'd be happy to drive," he offered, and saw her jaw tighten in response.

"Thanks, but I've got it." Her cool tone said she was already pissed, and they'd barely been together fifteen minutes.

Just like old times.

It was going to be three long days.

Three *very* long days.

CHAPTER TWO

IT HAD BEEN the afternoon from hell.

A wreck on the Kennedy stalled traffic for over half an hour, and Michigan Avenue had been like a parking lot, which was ironic because an actual parking lot with any available spots wasn't to be found. Finally, Maggie opted to park at The Drake Hotel since they were staying there. Then the three of them practically jogged the few blocks to Loyola's Water Tower campus, Russ pulling the luggage that would get him through the night, Maggie's sandals slapping against her soles in a rhythmic fashion that mimicked the clip-clop of the horses pulling carriages along the Chicago downtown streets. The trio slid into their seats just as Coach Brimley welcomed everyone to the Windy City.

Maggie ran her fingers through her hair and found her previously fluffy do plastered to her scalp. Speed walking in the heat and humidity had wilted her humidity-control hairspray, and she was certain the makeup she'd so carefully applied that morning had vanished also. Her feet ached from the hard walk in the stylish-but-not-made-for-running leather thongs with kitten heels. To make bad matters worse, she hadn't eaten since five that morning, and her stomach had been so tight then that she'd only managed a few bites. So throughout the meeting, her stomach gurgled often enough to cause the other parents to throw glances her way and Russ's elbow to stay set in continual nudge mode. The lady next to her offered her some mints, which she accepted, but they just made her stomach work harder.

The only one who didn't seem fazed by any of it was Jeff. After one particularly loud rumble that probably registered on the Richter scale, his eyes crinkled with mirth and the corners of his mouth twitched, but nothing more. She supposed Mr. California Cool was used to seismic activity.

"We've gone a little long here," Coach Brimley said. "I didn't mean to keep you into the dinner hour." A titter of laughter moved through the group. "Any last questions?"

Maggie's stomach chose then to emit a gargantuan rumble, which caused her face to heat to frying level.

The coach nodded her way. "Okay, then. The tour of the undergraduate campus will start at nine tomorrow. See you then."

"Jeez, Mom." Russ gave a relieved laugh as everyone stood and started to mill about. "Go get something to eat, will you? I don't want my teammates thinking Kentucky's a Third World country," he said before turning to mingle himself.

Russ's easy manner pulled people to him, just like his father's had always done. Soon he was making introductions to her, and the names Maggie had heard so often of late materialized into real people.

And then, much too soon, Russ and his teammates were saying goodbye, heading to their new rooms at the residence hall on the Lake Shore Campus. Tomorrow they would officially move him in, but tonight was a chance for the members of the golf team to bond, solidifying the special friendships that would stay with them for the next four years—and for some a lifetime.

Or, at least, that was Maggie's dream.

She looked at Jeff's wistful expression as he watched their son walk away with his new friends, most of whom Russ had gotten to know via the internet. Was he sad their time as the major influences in Russ's life was coming to an end? Or was he remembering that other kid who came to Kentucky from California on a golf scholarship and ended up having to forfeit it in order to work his way through the last two years of school while supporting a wife and baby?

Unlike the rare bad haircut she gave that could always be fixed one way or another, life didn't give do-overs.

Even after Russ disappeared around the corner, Jeff continued looking. She saw his Adam's apple bob as he swallowed hard, then he turned to her, dark eyebrows and sculpted shoulders rising and falling in a connected movement. "You ready?"

Her voice remained trapped deep in her chest, but she managed a nod.

He stayed quiet, too, until they got outside, where the suffocating early August afternoon heat had started giving way to the evening breeze. "Now, that's more like it." Jeff slipped his sunglasses on, looking every inch like a movie star.

Maggie, on the other hand, felt like a contestant at the end of *Survivor*. "Can we walk slow?" she pleaded. "I can't take another run in these shoes."

Jeff pointed to her feet as he slowed his step. "Women and their sexy sandals. It's a wonder your feet last your entire lifetime with the torture you put them through."

Had he just referred to her footwear as sexy? Some spring returned to her step. "I didn't realize we were going to be participating in a cross-country event, or I would've opted for something flatter and fully attached."

He snorted. "Being from Kentucky, you could probably get away with going barefoot."

"Don't tempt me."

Jeff gave her a look that said *you wouldn't dare*, and she arched an eyebrow in response.

He changed the subject. "Are you going to be okay with Russ's living up here?"

The people and traffic on Michigan Avenue had thinned some since two hours ago, but it was still difficult to imagine Russ enjoying this crowded place for very long. A weekend was one thing, but four years was entirely different.

"I don't like it," she admitted. "I would've preferred the University of Kentucky. But we both know the scholarship was the key factor. He thinks he's going to love it, but he hasn't experienced a winter up here yet."

"I don't think I could stand the cold." Jeff pointed to a café they were passing. "Want to grab a snack? I know you're hungry."

His familiar grin brought a strange tightening to her chest that stalled her breath for a second. She shook her head and kept walking, waiting for the air that was slow but finally returned. "Everyone from here to Navy Pier knows I'm hungry. But I won't be seen in a restaurant on the Magnificent Mile looking like this."

"Oh, for God's sake, Mags. You look great."

Her stomach flip-flopped this time at the compliment...confirming the extent of her hunger. "Well, thanks, but I've promised myself a hot shower and a nice relaxing room service experience tonight."

Entering the hotel lobby brought a sudden chill as the cold air met her damp clothing. She shivered in response as they hurried to grab the elevator. Oddly, in the crowded elevator that was quite warm, Jeff's arm brushing against hers brought another shiver, deeper and more pleasant—though vastly disturbing. It was as if her body remembered things she wouldn't allow her mind to think about.

They retrieved their luggage from the car, keeping the chatter to innocuous talk as they returned to the lobby, checked in and gave their luggage over to the bellman.

Jeff finished first but waited for her at the elevator. "I'm in seven fourteen," he told her as they stepped in.

"Three eleven for me."

He punched the floor buttons, and they stood alone in awkward silence for a moment as the elevator started its ascent.

It occurred to her they hadn't made plans for tomorrow yet. "I guess we'll need to leave about eight-fifteen tomorrow morning. Want to just meet me at the car?"

He nodded as the door slid open on her floor.

"Okay, then." She flashed him a smile. "See you later." She stepped out.

"Mags."

Jeff followed her out of the elevator, allowing the door to close. "I thought…uh…why don't we have dinner together?"

Her stomach squeezed at the thought. "Oh, wow, Jeff. I don't know…"

He rubbed the back of his neck before shoving his hands in his pockets. "It's been a long time. We have a lot to catch up on." His mouth rose at one corner. "Hell. It might actually be pleasant."

"I…um." Maggie searched for a reason other than the obvious—that they were exes and, as a rule, exes didn't have pleasant dinners together.

"I have a reservation at eight at a fabulous restaurant just across the street. I should be able to add one easily." He nodded toward her feet and grinned. "You won't have to walk far."

Her stomach chose that moment to let out a rumble, and Jeff tilted his head. "Was that a yes?"

She shook her head in resignation. "Oh, what the hell. Okay."

The elevator door opened with a *ding*, and Jeff stepped back inside. "Meet you in the lobby at five till?"

She nodded and waited until the door closed before letting out a verbal groan.

Oddly, her stomach didn't answer back. No, it had drawn much too tight to make a sound.

She didn't have much of an appetite anymore, either.

"FINALLY!" ROSEMARY RUSSELL stopped walking long enough to retrieve her phone from the purse swinging on her arm.

"I told you she'd call." Her husband, Eli, sounded completely cool and unbothered. But all through supper at the diner, she could tell he'd been just as worried as she was about their daughter and grandson's trip today. She couldn't imagine driving all the way up to Chicago with that horrible traffic. They'd expected the call hours ago.

She'd just about worried herself sick.

When she pulled the phone out, the caller ID confirmed it was, indeed, Maggie, thank heavens!

"Hello, sweetheart."

"Hey, Mom." Maggie sounded out of breath. "Just wanted to let y'all know we got here in one piece."

"How was the traffic?"

"Worse than you could ever imagine."

That wasn't what Rosemary wanted to hear. "Oh, dear. And you have to drive in it for two more days."

"I did fine." A door closed and Maggie gave a long sigh. "Jeff offered to take the wheel—I'm sure my driving wasn't suiting him—but I was determined to prove to myself I could do it. I'll be making this trip a lot over the next four years. I might as well get used to it."

"How is Jeff?" Rosemary shot a glance Eli's way and watched his jaw muscle tighten at the mention of their former son-in-law.

"He's fine," Maggie said, then added what sounded like an afterthought. "I guess. I mean, he looks great, but we haven't had much time to talk. I was too nervous to be much of a conversationalist with the traffic and all. Oh, but, Mom, you should hear him and Russ together. It's hard to tell their voices apart."

"Did Russ do okay? With the other boys?" Rosemary had fretted about that, too—that her grandson from tiny Taylor's Grove, Kentucky, would be thought of as a hick by his big-city teammates.

"You should've seen him. Had them eating out of his hand before the meeting was over."

Just like his dad at that age, Rosemary thought wryly. She supposed she should be grateful to Jeff for providing their grandson with a set of extrovert genes.

"I met the coach," Maggie went on. "Seems like a good guy, and—" There was a sharp knock. "The bellman's here with my bag, Mom, so I better go. I'm meeting Jeff for dinner."

Rosemary's heart gave a loud *thump*. "Oh, dear, Maggie. Is that wise?"

Maggie's snort sounded forced. "I'm a big girl. I can handle Jeff Wells just fine."

Rosemary wasn't so sure. She bit back all the warnings suddenly pressing on her tongue. "Just be careful, Maggie. Watch out for…the traffic."

"I will. Gotta go. Love you."

Before she could get out a goodbye, the phone went dead. She slipped it back into her purse. "She's having dinner with Jeff."

"The son of a bitch."

Eli responded to the news exactly the way he *always* responded to Jeff's name when Russ wasn't around. She hoped his blood pressure didn't shoot up. "If Maggie and Jeff can get along around Russ, that's a good thing, right?"

Eli's face flushed bright red. "The son of a bitch left my daughter and his son and moved as far away across the country as he could. There's no forgetting that."

She agreed but didn't say so. Images of the ninety-five pounds Maggie withered to after the divorce still haunted Rosemary. There was no forgetting that, either.

They were in front of their house, but Rosemary pointed toward the end of the block. "It's such a pretty night. Let's keep walking. It'll help us work off that chess pie we just ate."

Eli grumbled an agreement and kept walking, charging up Baxter Hill like he had to put out a fire.

Maggie and Jeff were only going to be together for two days, Rosemary fretted silently. During that time, they had to move Russ into his dorm, go on tours, follow the team on a round of golf, have dinner with the other parents.

There wouldn't be time for sparks to fly.

But they *were* having dinner tonight.

Rosemary tried to relax. Her daughter was now a savvy adult, finally over the man who had shattered her life. A successful businesswoman. A widow. But, despite the eighty-six-degree evening temperature, a shiver ran up Rosemary's spine.

She fought off what she hoped wasn't a premonition, quickening her step to keep up with Eli's long stride.

JEFF HADN'T ANTICIPATED conversation would come so easily. But catching up on their parents' health and Maggie's genuine concern about his sister Chloe's aggressive form of multiple sclerosis had taken them swiftly through cocktails. A lighter mood consisting of stories about Russ kept them laughing through appetizers and salad. So, by the time the entrées arrived, the food and alcohol had loosened their tongues and smoothed the edge of their tension, though it still lurked around their table, in the dark corner.

The food at Spiaggia was even better than he'd expected. He'd done his research online and made the reservations a couple of weeks ago, hoping he and Maggie might have some time alone to discuss a few things he wanted to get off his chest.

But this afternoon, her frazzled manner hadn't been very encouraging. First, she'd turned him down at the café, and if he'd told her the truth—that he'd already made reservations for two tonight— he wasn't sure she'd have agreed. But he'd played it smart and acted as if this was all spur-of-the-moment. An approach that apparently worked because here they were.

"You really do look amazing. Pictures I've seen haven't done you justice." He tilted the conversation toward the more personal side. "I know I said that earlier, but I mean it. And that dress is stunning."

The sleeveless black sheath with the round neck was classy without being overdone. It played nicely against the dark roots of her hair and the blond high-lights and showed just enough cleavage to be entic-ing. Her hair was tucked behind her ears and hefty diamond studs winked at him in the light of the candles on the table.

He wondered if they had been a present from Zeke, which sent a pang of guilt through him. He needed to address that issue. The sooner the better.

"Thanks." She shrugged, her fork paused in mid-air. "I threw it in at the last minute. I'm always afraid of not packing something a little dressy. This one's great because the knit doesn't wrinkle."

Not to mention how it fit those curves.

She took another bite of her gnocchi with wild boar ragù, and his eyes were drawn once again to the full, luscious lips that closed around the fork.

A jolt of stiffness in his groin had him shifting in his seat. He took a drink of wine to ease the dis-comfort. It didn't help much, but, combined with the Crown Royal he'd had before dinner, he found the liquid courage he needed to make the apology he'd been wanting to deliver personally for a long time.

"Mags." He set the glass down and something about his manner must have clued her in. She rested her fork on her plate. "I wanted to apologize for not being there—"

She adjusted her napkin in her lap. "It couldn't be helped, Jeff. Russ understood. We all understood. A ruptured appendix? You could've died."

"Well, yeah, missing his graduation totally

sucked," he agreed. The subject would always be a sore one for him. "But that's not what I'm apologizing for. I want to tell you how sorry I am I didn't come to Zeke's funeral."

"Oh…that." Her voice went small, and she bypassed her wineglass to grab a sip of water.

"I talked myself out of it…thinking about the awkwardness of being there with all your family. But I should've been there for Russ." He reached across the table and laid his hand on top of hers. "I was a coward, and I'm sorry."

He felt her hand tremble before she eased it from under his and rested it in her lap. "It's okay. Really. Having Russ come out and spend that next week with you was smart. It got him away from…from my grief for a little while. It was the best thing for him."

"Zeke must've been a great guy," he continued. "Russ was sure crazy about him."

Her chin quivered, and he could see the glimmer of unshed tears in her eyes. "Yes, he was…crazy about him." She drew a long breath, her breasts swelling, pushing tight against the neckline of her dress. "Russ seemed fond of Jennifer, too." She pointedly dropped the subject of her deceased husband. "He thought she might be the one for you."

Jennifer.

Just the thought of the woman caused Jeff's teeth to clench.

"Hardly," he answered.

Maggie raised an eyebrow in unspoken question, giving him the opportunity to go on or not. "Jennifer was the jealous type," he answered, and took a sip of his wine to get rid of the bad taste talking about the woman left in his mouth.

Maggie gave him a cool look, her mouth drawing into a smirk. "I've found it's usually the man who gives the woman a *reason* to be jealous."

A flare of irritation burned in Jeff's stomach. "Maybe." He nodded and shot her a defiant glare. "Yeah, you're absolutely right. It was my fault, but I don't give a rat's ass. She was jealous of Russ."

Her face sobered. "Oh. Sorry."

"She didn't want our summers 'taken up by him.'" He emphasized Jennifer's phrasing by making quotation marks in the air with his fingers. "Or our Christmases. She decided a two-week visit every other year would be more than sufficient. Can you imagine?"

"No, I can't." Maggie finally took another bite of her food, though with decidedly less enthusiasm than before.

"I'm sorry. I didn't mean to get us off on a bad subject. We were having a good time before we started talking about all this. And it sounds like you do a much better job than I do at picking significant others."

He'd meant to lighten the conversation with his self-criticism, but, to his horror, Maggie's chin quiv-

ered again. And then a tear slid down her cheek…
followed by another…and another.

"Damn, Mags. I'm sorry. I should've realized it
would still be difficult for you to talk about Zeke.
It's only been…what? Three years? Let's just drop
it. How's your gnocchi? Good?"

He was aware he was just talking to hear his
head rattle at this point and not helping a damn
thing. Maggie's tears were coming harder and
faster, though thankfully, silently. The tip of her
nose brightened to hot pink.

"Can I pour you some more wine?" he offered,
lamely, and then convinced himself to shut his damn
mouth before he made things any worse.

Like things could be any worse.

Maggie's body shook with the effort to bring her
tears under control, and he sat and watched, help-
lessly shamed into silence.

When, at last, she could speak, she looked at him
and shook her head. "Zeke wasn't a great guy, Jeff.
He wasn't like everybody thought he was." Pain
flashed from the gorgeous green irises now rimmed
in red. "Marrying him was the biggest mistake of
my life."

CHAPTER THREE

MIXING LIQUOR AND the emotional roller coaster she was on today had been a major mistake. Maggie regretted her words as soon as they left her mouth.

"Did the bastard abuse you?" Jeff's grip on his wineglass visibly tightened.

"No." She rubbed the area over her right eyebrow where a rhythmic throb pulsated. Why had she brought this up now? "Never mind. I shouldn't have said anything."

"But you did." His mouth and eyes narrowed with insistence. "Now you have to finish."

"I've never told anyone. Not even Mom."

"I don't know what this deep, dark secret is." Jeff reached across the table, and this time he didn't just lay his hand on top of hers. He grasped it and held on firmly. "My son was in that environment. I have a right to know what went on."

"It wasn't anything that ever happened around Russ." She tried for an assuring tone, but his touch caused the breath she'd almost gotten under control to quiver erratically again. "You surely can't believe I would ever allow anyone to lay a hand on him."

"For God's sake, Mags, tell me what we're discussing here." His grip became a near-squeeze.

If she'd used her napkin as a gag, which she now wished she had, her mouth couldn't have gone any drier. A sip of water helped lubricate the passage of the words she'd swallowed so many times. "The last week Zeke was alive…two days before he went into the coma…he told me he'd been having an affair for quite some time. Five of the six years we'd been married."

Sympathy softened Jeff's stern look, but his shoulders sagged in obvious relief that this didn't involve Russ. "Wow, that must have been staggering for you."

She nodded. "He told me he was deeply in love with her and had planned to ask me for a divorce. But then the brain tumor was diagnosed, and it seemed foolish to put everyone through that additional heartbreak."

"So why tell you at all?"

Maggie sipped some more water, giving herself time to decide if she could get through this. "He wanted to see her."

Jeff released his hold and leaned back as if he needed to view her from a wider angle. "You didn't…"

"Yeah, I did." The lead brick that had pressed on her heart for three years began to crumble as she finally shared the horrific details she'd kept bottled up. "I called and told her he was asking for her. She took more than a little convincing…seemed bent on the idea that I was luring her down there to make a spectacle of confronting her in front of people. But she finally came, and I gave them several hours alone to say their goodbyes. I put a no-visitors sign on the door so they wouldn't be interrupted."

Jeff closed his eyes, and when he opened them he pinned her with a look that was a mixture of incredulity and disbelief. "Why?"

"Why not?"

"He was unfaithful and you rewarded him?"

"He was dying. I would hardly call that a reward."

"But for you to be civil to her… Kind, even."

She shrugged. It was difficult to explain why she had handled things the way she did. "Something was never right between Zeke and me. We got along. Had a good time together. He was good to Russ. But I think I married him more out of loneliness than love." She stopped short of admitting there had never been the rush of adrenaline for Zeke the way there had been for him—even her reaction at seeing him today. The surge of primal pleasure that time and emotional pain could not erase. She paused for breath and shook some propriety back into her logic center. "I shouldn't be discussing this with you. It's too personal. You and I are practically strangers now."

"We'll never be strangers, Mags."

"Well, maybe not strangers," she acquiesced.

"But thirteen years without face-to-face contact is a long time."

His mouth rose slightly on one end. "Too long." His tone brought a flutter to her stomach that she attempted to stymie with a gulp of wine. "So why didn't you tell anyone? I mean, the sorrow and grief must've been unbearable. It might've helped to talk to somebody."

"I considered talking to Mom, but that felt like a knee-jerk reaction, and it would only upset her. I thought about counseling, but, with him gone, the affair seemed like more of a testimony against *me* than him. It was hard to admit to myself, much less somebody else, that I'd made such a huge mistake. Again." Her voice broke on the last word.

Jeff glanced away, his Adam's apple bobbing as he swallowed hard. She knew that mannerism. It was what he did when he was upset or displeased, and she felt the weight of that displeasure in her stomach.

Yeah, I failed at my second marriage, too. She didn't have to say the words. She knew what he was thinking.

No longer hungry, she pushed her plate back and dabbed her mouth with her napkin.

"Do you want dessert?" Sure enough, Jeff's normally rich tone was flat.

"No. I'm tired. I really just want to go back to the room and relax." She tried not to show how disappointed she was with the turn things had taken.

The pleasant night of catching up and easy banter had morphed into a queasy stomach and a brain that now felt like a tympani being pounded by dueling mallets.

The only relief came when Jeff paid the bill and she was able to escape into the open air. "Thanks for dinner. The food was delicious," she said as they crossed the intersection by Oak Street Beach. The balmy breeze coming off Lake Michigan soothed her frayed nerves. Normally she would have wanted to linger but not tonight. Tonight she'd exposed too much, left herself vulnerable.

"You're welcome," he answered. "But what's your hurry?"

She hadn't realized how fast she'd been walking, not allowing her platform stilettos to hinder her determined gait. She slowed her pace, letting him keep up, not wanting to give the impression she was running from him. But when he drew close enough that their arms brushed, she sped up again—her body's involuntary reaction to a dangerous stimulus.

The hotel doorman saw them coming and welcomed them again into the vast lobby.

"Do you want to have a nightcap?" Jeff indicated the lounge where a few dancers swayed to the beat of the slow, sultry tune crooned by a smoky-voiced singer.

Emphatically no, Maggie thought. *Not with escape so close.* But she managed a smile and a "no, thanks."

Jeff shoved his hands into his pockets and shrugged. "Well, I think I hear a drink begging to be savored."

The *ding* of the elevator provided the perfect opening for a quick good-night. "Have a nice night, then. I'll meet you here in the morning at eight-fifteen." Maggie backed away toward the waiting car. "Thanks again for dinner."

Jeff nodded but stayed where he was, his dark eyes trained on her until the doors closed.

It wasn't until he was completely cut off from her sight that the breath she'd been holding since she'd first glimpsed him ten hours earlier finally made a slow exit from her lungs.

"Macallan 25. Straight." The bartender placed the cut-glass crystal on the bar. The low lighting caught in the ornate design, twinkling like captured stars.

Jeff lifted the heavy glass and swirled the dark amber liquid, hesitating long enough to enjoy the smoky essence before the burn hit his lips, then his tongue and his throat. He usually went for the less expensive Scotch, but he needed something to help get the night back to the perfection it had started with. It had disintegrated quickly with the first mention of Zeke.

The bastard. Putting Mags through that kind of hell in addition to everything else she was going through at the time.

She'd shown remarkable fortitude. Admirable. And to never have told anyone—not even her mother—showed how much she'd changed since they'd split up…how little he knew about her now. It seemed odd now he thought about it, but he and his son rarely discussed the boy's mother.

There was a time when Mags went straight to her mother with everything, which was convenient as her parents lived right next door. The arrangement had continually made him feel ganged up on. Whenever he and Mags argued, she always sought out her parents to support her side. And they never failed to take it.

"You get the prize for having the best taste."

Jeff turned to the voice beside him. A guy, vaguely familiar and big enough to have been a linebacker for the Chargers, settled on the bar stool beside him.

"Nothing quite like The Macallan," Jeff agreed, and held the glass up to admire the color again.

"Crown Royal on the rocks," his companion said to the bartender and then turned back to Jeff with a sly grin. "I'm sure the Scotch is good, but I was referring to your wife. She wasn't just the best-looking mom at the meeting today, she was also the youngest. Must've had your son when she was fifteen."

"Nineteen," Jeff corrected him. "And she's not my wife. We've been divorced a long time."

"Even better."

The next sip burned Jeff's mouth for an exceptionally long time.

"Spike Grainger." The newcomer held out his hand. "My son Matt's a freshman on the team, too."

Jeff shook his hand. "Jeff Wells, Russ's dad."

The bartender set Spike's drink in front of him, and he reached for it with his left hand. No wedding band.

A trickle squeezed through Jeff's constricted throat muscles.

"Yeah, Russ's mom—what's her name?"

"Maggie."

"Cute. The way she kept blushing when her stomach was growling." Spike gave a hearty chuckle. "I saw you guys coming in together a few minutes ago. I assumed you'd been to dinner."

The reminder of dinner sent Jeff's mood further south. "We had." He was being curt, but he already didn't like Spike, whose presence was flavoring his Scotch in an unpleasant way.

"Been divorced a long time, yet you're here together, making it work for Russ." Spike took a gulp and smacked his lips in appreciation. "Good for you."

"You divorced?" Jeff changed tactics and tried to shift the attention away from him and Mags.

"Three weeks. Married for twenty-four years. She's on her honeymoon."

Spike became as transparent then as the crystal in Jeff's hand. The man was trolling—and Mags was in his sights. Hell, he'd been there himself. That giddy feeling of freedom came edged with loneliness and even a sense of desperation. For the first couple of years, he'd swung from woman to woman like a monkey making its way through the jungle.

Had Mags done that, too?

He shouldn't care, but the idea pricked at his heart just the same. She was, after all, the mother of his son. He didn't know much about her and those first two or three years. They'd talked every day, but her reports were always simply that—reports on Russ. They never just chatted about what was going on in their lives. He'd found out a little more, but not much, about Mags through Russ once their son had gotten old enough to make the daily calls himself. He was a talker, that one.

A sudden image of the drive from the airport flashed in his mind—Russ keeping up the constant chatter and Mags with her white-knuckle hold on the steering wheel. And her tearful confession at dinner.

She may be a grown woman, but, in a myriad of ways, she was still that small-town girl he'd known...and loved.

A long-dormant protective instinct kicked in as he swallowed the rest of his Macallan in one gulp and set the glass down on the bar. "Nice meeting you," he lied as he pulled enough bills from his wallet to take care of his bill and a hefty tip.

"See you tomorrow." Spike saluted him with his drink.

The irony of the situation struck Jeff full force as

he walked to the elevator. He was here in Chicago to move his eighteen-year-old son into the thick of the metropolis. Russ had spent the past thirteen summers of his life in San Diego, along with various other times such as spring and Christmas breaks. The kid took to city life like a native, never the least bit fazed by the crowds or the traffic. Jeff had no qualms whatsoever about Russ's being here.

Mags, on the other hand, was a different matter completely.

ROSEMARY COUNTED SILENTLY. *Twenty-nine elephant, thirty elephant, thirty-one elepha—*

Eli gave a gasp and started breathing again, falling quickly into his deep, rhythmic, room-shaking snore.

She closed the book she'd been reading and rubbed her tired eyes. Well, actually, she hadn't been reading. She'd been turning pages for two hours, but the progression of the story hadn't imprinted on her memory. Eli's long periods without a breath had consumed her attention. The snoring wasn't so bad. She'd gotten used to that forty years ago. But the snorting and the gasping, and the long periods of silence freaked her out. She was aware of the dangers of sleep apnea—had read on the internet how it could lead to all kinds of nasty stuff, including heart disease and stroke. Coupled with the high blood pressure her husband already took medication for, he was a heart attack waiting to happen.

And she wasn't prepared for widowhood.

She saw what it had done to her daughter.

Poor Maggie. Her chest tightened at the thought of how much her daughter had already been through.

And now Russ had gone away to college—another reason to worry. And, of course, there was the Maggie/Jeff dinner that had niggled at the back of Rosemary's brain all night.

She'd hoped Maggie would call back and tell her what had transpired, but she didn't, and Rosemary wasn't surprised, although it hurt a little.

She tossed the extra pillow onto the love seat and turned out the light, sliding down in the bed to get comfortable. Maggie used to talk about everything with her. But her daughter had become so withdrawn since Zeke's death that she didn't recognize her at times. Closing herself off from the world, grieving for Zeke in such a vastly different way than she had for Jeff. When Jeff left, she'd cried for days on end. Refused to leave the bedroom. Refused to eat. Talked about him incessantly—so positive he would come back, and they would start again.

She'd kept up that nonsense for years.

But losing Zeke affected her differently. She'd quickly sold their beautiful home on Kentucky Lake, and rather than moving back to Taylor's Grove, she'd bought the old Morris farmhouse outside of town. She would talk about Zeke only if someone brought up his name—and then reluctantly. She never brought him into the conversation on her own.

She had seemed angry, which Rosemary knew was one of the stages of grief. She'd read that on the internet, too. But it certainly had gone on for a long time now. Too long. Maggie didn't date. Didn't do much of anything except work and spend time with Russ.

What would she do now that he was gone?

Eli's breathing stopped again, and Rosemary began her ritualistic counting. She wasn't sure why she counted. He was never impressed with the numbers she spouted the next morning. Tomorrow, over coffee, she would report to him that he'd held his breath for almost thirty-five seconds. He'd shrug and say, "So which do you want—snoring or silence? Because you complain either way."

Her retort would be that she wanted him healthy.

What would she do without him? The previous question echoed in her mind. Maggie was young—could easily start over. But she herself was sixty-one and had been with the same man for forty years. She had no desire to start over. She could never love another man the way she did Eli. Could never love again, period. The thought made her shudder.

Was it her imagination that Eli's color was off?

She slipped her phone from the bedside table and turned on the flashlight app, shining it down on his face—the man could sleep through a rock concert once he got horizontal. He looked so peaceful and relaxed but definitely a little grayish in pallor.

One eye winked open and glared at her. "What are you doing, Rosie? Checking me for fleas?"

"You've been holding your breath."

"And you're getting back at me by shining a light into my eyes? You trying to make me think a train is coming through our bedroom?"

"I wanted to check your color. You look kind of gray."

"You'd be gray, too, if you had to live with you. Now turn off the damn searchlight."

She turned it off and placed the phone back on the table, but not because he told her to do it. She was finished looking... Definitely gray. They would resume this conversation in the morning. She settled under the covers again.

"Rosie." Eli's tender whisper shimmied through the darkness. "Slide back over here, and I'll make *you* hold *your* breath."

She laughed and did as he asked, snuggling into the crook of his arm. He kissed her sweetly a few times then with more purpose, and her tiredness got tangled among the sheets as their excitement rose and the pace of their movements accelerated.

They didn't take long. After forty years, there was no experimentation and nothing new. The new had been sorted through years ago. What worked was kept and had now become part of the routine. What didn't work had been lost with no remorse.

What remained was the best of the best, carefully chosen, deeply intimate and immensely satisfying.

Their sighs mingled as they held each other in the afterglow, and soon the familiar rumble that would become Eli's snore began to take form.

Rosemary changed her tactic and began counting the breaths rather than the non-breaths. It made more sense to pay attention to what gave life to this man she adored.

She'd only gotten to seventeen when drowsiness caused her to lose interest. With his body spooning her back and his arm across her front, she felt warm and complete.

Life without Eli?

The thought induced another shiver.

She snuggled closer against him.

CHAPTER FOUR

"WE COULD'VE *WALKED* faster than this." Maggie blew out a breath and cut her eyes toward Jeff in the passenger seat. "It's only seven miles."

He pressed his lips together as if he intended to give that some serious consideration, but then he shook his head. "I'm not about to walk seven miles in this heat unless I have a golf bag over my shoulder."

Maggie snorted. "Some things never change."

As on the previous afternoon, heavy traffic lumbered its way up Lake Shore Drive. Though she'd added the grumble for effect, Maggie didn't really mind the slow ride. The morning sunshine and the excitement of being in the city—not to mention the company of the man in the car with her—had her blood pumping. She'd allowed herself plenty of time to relax this morning, eaten a hearty breakfast to chase away any growls her stomach might consider making and had chosen a pair of shorts she could wear with sneakers.

Yeah, she'd prepared herself for moving day and the ten thousand trips they would make back and forth to the car with Russ's things.

What she hadn't prepared for was the slam to her stomach brought on by Jeff's smile when she'd stepped off the elevator. Or the delicious tingle his presence gave her in the close quarters of her car. She should find some comfort, she supposed, knowing a part of what they'd had still remained—a kind of validity that what they'd felt for each other years ago had been real. And maybe he felt it, too. The smile that had greeted her this morning had seemed genuine.

"Spike Grainger was in the bar last night," Jeff said.

The comment came out of nowhere as the light turned green and traffic started moving at a faster but steady pace.

"Who?"

"Spike Grainger. His son Matt is one of Russ's teammates. Anyway, he was pumping me about you."

Oh, Lord! "You were discussing me with someone in the bar? Why?" She flipped the air conditioner to high and directed the vent toward her heated face.

"I didn't bring you up. He did. I think he's interested. But you need to be warned that he's only been divorced for three weeks and his ex is on her honeymoon."

Her ex-husband was trying to fix her up with somebody? Maggie bristled, not exactly sure why she found this extremely irritating—except that she'd shared some things with him last night that had left her feeling vulnerable. She certainly hoped she hadn't come across as desperate. "Thank you, Mr. Matchmaker, but I don't need your help finding a man."

"I wasn't helping you find a man," Jeff bit back. "I'm helping you *not* find a man. The guy's needy and on the prowl. I suspect he's going to put the moves on you today, and I wanted you to be aware."

"I told you about Zeke, so now you think I'm some pushover where men are concerned?"

"I didn't say that, Mags."

"You didn't have to."

"I think Zeke was a bastard."

"Let's drop the Zeke subject, okay? I'm good. Things are good." Her hands were aching again from gripping the steering wheel too tightly, just like yesterday. She let go with one and stretched her fingers as the silence continued for a couple of minutes.

"You dating anyone?" he asked.

When she'd first found out Jeff was coming to this orientation, Maggie vowed she wouldn't get into all the subterfuge some exes seem to find necessary. She pretended to focus on the traffic as her mind contemplated whether or not this was something worth lying about to him. She decided it wasn't. "No. I haven't been out with anyone since…you know." She stopped herself short of the conversation topic she'd just banned. "Oh, guys have asked," she added. "I've just been too busy."

"How is business, by the way?"

"Fabulous." Not having to exaggerate about the hair salon she owned in Paducah brought a smug smile to her face. "I have ten stylists and four nail technicians now."

Jeff's eyebrows shot up in surprise. "Wow, impressive."

She'd always assumed Russ kept his dad as informed about life in Kentucky as he kept her about life in California, but maybe she'd assumed too much. "My best friend Emmy's my assistant manager, so everything runs smoothly even when I'm not there. Time with Russ has been my top priority the past few years."

"He's a great kid, isn't he?"

She glanced away from the traffic long enough to share a proud, tender smile. "The best."

The car went quiet again, and then Jeff gave a cough that sounded forced. "Did you...um..." He gazed at Lake Michigan on their right. "Did you date much after we split up?"

"Not for years," she admitted. It was the first open reference either of them had made to their divorce, and her heart squeezed in response. "And only a couple of guys before I met...Zeke." *Grrr!* How many times was he going to come into the conversation? "What's with all the dating talk this morning?" The question flashed in her brain, but she didn't mean to verbalize it. Still, there it was. And there was the university, as well. She moved into the left-hand turn lane and miraculously caught the green turn signal.

"I never questioned Russ too much about you… or your personal life. Didn't want him to think I was prying."

Maggie nodded as she pulled into the parking lot and headed for a spot.

"But, now we're together," Jeff continued, "I realize how much I don't know about your life, so I'm trying to catch up on those lost years. I figured the best place to start was the beginning."

The beginning.

Dread dropped into her stomach.

"Those first few years after we split up may have been a beginning for you." She cut the engine as her fingers found the door handle. "To me, they felt more like the end."

THE WEIGHT OF Maggie's last words stayed with Jeff all day. And while he tried to imagine that weight being carried on his shoulders, it sure as hell felt more like it was hanging somewhere inside his chest.

Years, she'd said. Not weeks or months. It was as if that one word had been engraved on a stone tablet and hung on an iron stake driven into his heart.

As soon as she'd uttered her comment, she'd leaped from the car and joined the other parents arriving for the tour. She'd also volunteered to join a different tour group than the one he was in—on purpose, he suspected. It was as if she didn't want to be anywhere in his vicinity. And it wasn't lost on him that Spike Grainger volunteered for the same group Mags had, taking up the last spot.

Everyone came back together for lunch, and Matt and Spike joined them at their table. As Jeff predicted, Spike grabbed the chair next to Mags. All through lunch, he laughed too loud and too long at her jokes, flirted outrageously and made a complete ass of himself.

Mags was friendly with the big brute, but she didn't return his flirtation. In fact, Jeff thought he could almost read a hint of sympathy in her manner, but he wasn't sure.

Time was when he would've been sure. He'd been intimately familiar with her every mood and every nuance of every mood. If she bit her bottom lip while they were making love, she wanted to play, but if she chewed her bottom lip while they were making love, she wanted him to take the lead and explore. And explore he always did.

The memory brought on an erection that came and went throughout the afternoon, springing to life at Maggie's throaty laugh, lessening when he-man and his son came to help after getting Matt "all moved in in no time flat."

They'd finally left two minutes ago, and their leaving had brought relative quiet to the room—

although the hallway was still crawling with boisterous teenage boys.

Thank God he's gone. Jeff tightened the last nut
on the bunk/futon combo unit Russ and his room-
mate Blake had decided on. The kid from Des
Moines seemed nice enough, but Russ's loud-mouth
ways would likely take some getting used to for
the quiet kid. Of course, that went both ways. His
son, an only child his entire life, would have to get
used to sharing a room with someone. Jeff smiled
at the thought.

"You look happy we're almost done." Mags shot
him a grin as she unrolled a circular rug in the center of the room.

"I am that," Jeff agreed. "I was also thinking
about the learning curve our son will have to go
through beginning tonight."

"Yeah." Her chuckle had a wicked edge that
brought him to life again despite his fatigue. "He
thinks it's going to be like summer camp. He doesn't
realize how hard it can be to live with someone day
in, day out…" She glanced away as her voice trailed
off. "The room looks good, though." She wiped her
forehead with the back of her hand as she made a
slow, tight circle, inspecting the afternoon's progress. "Never thought we could make it look like this
considering how it was when we started."

Her tired eyes met his, and for a moment he
thought she was going to say something else, but
her gaze darted to the top bunk. "But that ghastly

sleeping bag is a travesty when there were all those cute sheet sets to choose from."

"This is easy to make up. No fuss. And just as easy to wash." Jeff captured her gaze again and returned her tired smile. "And he couldn't care less if his bedding is cute."

Just then, Russ bounded into the room. "Look what I just scored out of the garbage!" He held up a leg lamp of *The Christmas Story* variety, except in miniature, tabletop size. "Gort says it works and everything."

"Ick." Maggie's mouth creased sharply downward.

"Ah, c'mon, Mom." Russ rubbed his hand delicately down the leg. "It's a conversation piece."

"Like conversation is something you need more of?"

"She has a point." Jeff eyed the strange object that had his son captivated. "If it works, why would he throw it away?"

Russ shrugged. "Girlfriend gave it to him. Then she broke up with him yesterday, so he says he doesn't want the reminder." He set it on the desk and plugged it in. A flip of the switch and the fishnet-covered leg glowed dimly. "*Fra-gee-lee!* That is rich!" A couple of posters he hadn't decided on yet lay rolled up on the desk. He grabbed them and tossed them onto the top shelf of the closet. "Oh, yeah. Hey, Matt was down at the garbage, too, so I asked if he and Spike would like to have pizza with us tonight. Hope that's okay. I figured we owed them for all their help. They're meeting us at the hotel."

Jeff grimaced, but neither Maggie nor Russ noticed his displeasure. They both seemed fine with the idea of more time with Thor and Company.

"Besides, Mom." Russ swung around and caught Maggie playfully around the neck—standing a full head taller than she—and gave her a soft nuggie. "Matt says his dad thinks you're hot."

"Damn it." Jeff swore under his breath.

"I am hot...and sweaty." Maggie's swift poke at the ticklish spot in Russ's ribs efficiently broke his hold. She stepped away and wrinkled her nose. "He's pretty basic."

Jeff wasn't sure what that meant, but it didn't sound like a compliment so it gave him a reason to chuckle.

"Go easy on him, Mom." A movement in the hallway caught Russ's attention. "Hey, Steeger," he yelled, and bolted that direction.

Mags watched him and then turned to Jeff, eyes wide with wonder. "I've never seen him so hyper. It's like he's five again."

"Basic?" he asked.

"Tries too hard...easy to see through."

"Ah." Jeff tossed his wrench back into the tool bag Spike had provided. "So you prefer the guy who plays it cool."

She gathered up the stack of towels she'd folded

and started toward the bathroom. "I prefer no guy at all."

The heaviness in his chest became apparent again. "Mags—" He wasn't sure what he was going to say—only knew he needed to say something, but Russ bounded back into the room.

"Can we go eat now? I'm going to gnaw on that leg lamp if I don't get some food pretty soon."

Maggie handed over her armload to him. "I can't go eat like this." She pointed at her top, which sported a dirty tread mark from where she'd moved an armload of sneakers. "And neither can you, Russ. Go shower. Now. You can make it a quick one." She picked up one of the boxes that needed to go back to the car.

"I'll get that, Mags. It's too heavy for you."

Jeff reached for it, but she held on and rocked back on her heels. "I've got it. Russ can get the big one after he showers, and you can bring the other small one. I'll have the car by the front door in ten minutes. And don't forget Spike's tools." She disappeared into the crowded hallway.

"Spike has her thinking all the rest of us are wusses," Russ grumbled as he headed for the bathroom.

"*Humph.* I was thinking the same thing," Jeff answered, though too low for his son to hear. The bathroom door closed and he finished what was on his tongue. "I wonder which ranks lower in her estimation—a wuss or a basic?"

DID CHICAGO HAVE a downtown salon that stayed open late? Maggie glanced down Rush Street. With all the testosterone she'd been exposed to over the past three hours, her upper lip probably could stand a good waxing.

"So I see the puck headed right toward us." Spike was in the middle of one of his many tales of heroic deeds. "And I throw myself in front of her and catch the damn thing in the back, right below my shoulder blade. Luckily, with all the layers I had on, it didn't break anything. But I ended up with a bruise this big." He held his hands out and cupped them to form a circle the size of a salad plate. "The doc said if I was an average-size guy, like you—" he gave a curt nod in Jeff's direction as they walked "—it might've paralyzed me...or worse, if it had hit my temple."

A hit to the mouth might not have done too much damage. Maggie kept her thought to herself.

"Oh, hell, Grainger." Jeff pointed his arm in silent direction to make the turn onto Walton. "If the damn puck had hit you in the head, it would've ricocheted off." The tightness in his jaw told Maggie he'd said it only half in jest, but Spike guffawed.

"Good one, man."

She felt certain her presence—walking between the two men—was the only thing that saved Jeff from a hearty pounding on the back.

"I'm glad we decided to walk." She changed the subject, trying to move the two fellows beyond the juvenile pissing match they'd fallen into somewhere around the time the salad had arrived. "Giordano's has to be the best pizza I've ever had, but—"

"You think Giordano's is good?" Spike's mouth was moving again. "You ought to taste the pizza at this little tavern down the street from where I live. They have this one that's loaded with all kinds of meats and cheeses…"

Maggie allowed her mind to race a half block ahead to the stoplight. And the lovely sign atop The Drake that screamed *Freedom*!

She glanced at her watch. They'd put the boys in a taxi back to their dorm right after they left the restaurant. Since traffic was light, Russ might be back at his place already.

Tomorrow wouldn't be quite so busy, thankfully. Hot dogs and burgers at 11:30, followed by a four-man golf scramble. And in the evening they'd have a light family dinner sponsored by the team. Then she'd say goodbye to her precious boy-child until his first trip home, which wouldn't come until Thanksgiving. Her eyes blurred, and she blinked away the tears.

"—carriage ride, Maggie?" Spike was pointing to the horse-drawn carriage stopped at the corner they were about to cross.

She rewound his question in her head. He was asking if she wanted to go on a carriage ride. And, while the idea was appealing, she couldn't bear to stay in Spike's company any longer than she had to.

"It sounds lovely," she answered. "But I don't think I'm up for it. Thanks, though."

He shrugged.

The walk signal came on, and they stepped off the curb. She felt both men's hands touch the small of her back at the same time. She also felt the simultaneous jerk when their fingers touched and their hands dropped back to their sides. She made it all the way across the street unassisted…and somehow managed to contain her laughter.

Considering how talkative he'd been all through dinner, Jeff had become uncharacteristically quiet as they neared the hotel, uttering only that one cut-down to Spike. Something was bothering him. Probably tomorrow's goodbye, if she were guessing.

Spike was never at a loss for words, though. Her dad would describe him as the type whose *"mouth runs like the clatter bone of a goose's ass."* As soon as they entered the hotel lobby, he pointed to the lounge. "How about a drink?"

"Not for me," she answered. "I left my phone in the car, so I'm going to go get it, then head for my room."

Jeff's head jerked toward her, and he gave her a hard look. "You can't go to the garage at night by yourself. I'll go with you." He slapped Spike on the arm. "And then I'm going to hit the sack, too. Enjoy your Crown Royal, man. See you tomorrow."

Alone with Jeff? Gah! She'd seen this coming and tried to avoid it all day. Sure as shootin', he was going to ask her about her answer this morning. She'd seen the next question in his eyes all day and had been careful not to be alone with him. She needed to have her answer formulated.

He was going to ask why she waited years to date after their split. Not that it was any of his business. But this was Jeff—telling him that would only make him suspect the worst. Of course, the worst was the truth. But how could she admit she'd carried the torch for him far too long? That she'd made a fool of herself—so certain he'd come back and want to be a family again? Had worked long and hard to get over him, and yet she had only, during the past few years, finally felt free of him?

"You don't have to go with me," she said as they waited for the elevator.

"Yeah, I do."

The doors opened and relief flooded her to see several people headed the same direction. But it ended quickly as the small crowd dispersed in different directions when they reached the garage level. Her large SUV wasn't far from the door, so maybe, if she walked fast, she could keep a light chat going until—

"Mags, you ran from the car this morning because you knew what I wanted to ask you." Jeff took her elbow and pulled back to slow her pace.

So much for light chatter.

"No use in dredging up the past, Jeff." She hit the button on her key fob to unlock the car door.

"But I need to know. Did you not date for years because of me? Did I make you distrust men?"

He didn't suspect…which, of course, could only mean he hadn't gone through what she had.

That realization pinched her heart enough to leave a bruise.

She gave a thoughtful pause as she opened the door to retrieve her phone from the console. She slipped it into her purse and closed the door, then turned to meet his earnest gaze. "You didn't make me distrust men," she answered honestly. "I distrusted myself."

A flicker of relief shot from his dark eyes, followed quickly by a shadow. She nodded toward the elevator and started moving in that direction. "I couldn't risk failing again." Keeping control of the conversation before he could ask any more questions seemed like her best option now. "Too much depended on my being successful. I had a child to take care of and a career to think about." She stopped as the elevator door opened, relieved to find the car empty this time.

A short ride to the third floor, and this would be over.

They stepped in and Jeff punched the buttons as she continued. "I wasn't sure I was capable of handling those things, so I couldn't even think about throwing a relationship into the mix." This wasn't as difficult as she'd thought. Everything she was saying was the truth—she was simply leaving out a few details.

"And once I opened the salon, there was yet another thing demanding my time." Her stomach gave a jolt as the elevator came to a stop on the third floor. Jeff stepped out with her, just as he'd done the previous afternoon, only this time he started walking with her to her door.

"Something you said last night at dinner kept me awake." His voice was low as they made their way down the hallway. "And, coupled with what you said this morning, it's bothered the hell out of me all day."

"What did I say?" Her spine had pulled into a tight curve at the touch of his hand, pressed absently to the small of her back as they walked. When they reached her door, her shoulders were squared as she turned to face him.

"It was the part about admitting to yourself you'd made a huge mistake. *Again.*"

"O-kay...?"

His hands gripped his hips, and he shrugged. "You can't think we were a mistake, Mags. If *we* were a mistake, that makes *Russ* a mistake."

She leaned against the door, closing her eyes to the raw emotion in his. "You're right. Zeke was a mistake, but referring to us that way was a poor choice of words."

She heard the rustle of his movement and opened

her eyes to find him pressing a forearm against the door frame, his eyes hooded with doubt.

"Russ is the best thing that ever came into my life." His voice was heavy with emotion. "And I know it's been difficult for you. But I want you to understand that it's not been easy for me, either. Being so far away from him—not being able to see him every day—has been hard on me."

The sincerity in his eyes pulled at her heartstrings. She reached up to touch his face in a motherly fashion, to console, the way she would with Russ when she saw that same expression on his face. But as soon as her palm connected with his cheek, the touch became something else entirely— something not at all motherly. It became a lover's caress as his heat scorched her, sent tingles through her arm and into her chest...down into her belly and lower.

The look in his eyes changed in an instant.

He felt it, too.

Electricity charged the atmosphere around them, encapsulating them in its trembling heat. Her eyes held to his steely gaze like a magnet. He leaned in slightly, and she pressed her back against the door but found no escape. Her hand, still on his cheek, should be pushing him away. So why did it slide around to the back of his neck and pull him closer?

The world slowed as his mouth neared hers, and she licked her lips in anticipation. She closed her eyes at the last second, allowing this moment to take center stage in her mind as it had so often in her dreams. The tenderness of his lips, the familiar sweetness...the flutter in her stomach that all too soon would become an aching need.

She'd entered a danger zone and was much too old and wise now to ignore the signs.

Sliding her hand from the back of his neck to his chest, she didn't push him away, but did apply enough pressure to let him know this needed to stop. In answer, he removed his mouth from hers slowly but didn't straighten, staying close enough that his breath continued to feather across her lips, warming them with the caress.

"Russ was never a mistake," she whispered. "But letting this go any further would be."

She felt the burst of air from his disgruntled sigh, but he stepped back, buckling his chin and giving her a nod.

"Good night, Mags." He touched her cheek with the back of his finger.

"Night."

She made short work of getting into her room, barely making it to the bed before her knees buckled under the weight of the moment.

CHAPTER FIVE

"YOU HEARD ANY more from Maggie?" Eli doused his third cup of coffee with heavy cream and stirred it, changing the hue from black to tan.

Rosemary thought Eli's color seemed slightly better this morning than yesterday. She finished off the remains in her own cup and set it down with a sigh and a shake of her head. "No. And I know she must be upset. Yesterday was the day they moved Russ into his dorm. That had to be hard on her."

"You think being around the son of a bitch is hard on her, too?" The cream must have cooled Eli's coffee quickly because he swallowed half the cup in one gulp.

"Don't drink so fast."

"Don't tell me how to drink my coffee." He picked up the cup and gulped down the rest, just out of spite, she was sure.

"I hope it's not hard on her. She's known for a couple of months she and Jeff would be up there together. That was plenty of time to get her head prepared."

Eli stood, pulled the cap from the pocket of his

overalls and flipped it onto his head to cover the mop of silver hair he still sported. He adjusted the bill so that it covered his heavy, still-black eyebrows. "Not her head I'm worried about," he drawled.

Rosemary pushed back in her chair and directed a withering glare his direction. "Shame on you, Eli Crenshaw Russell! That's your daughter we're talking about."

He stepped toward her and braced one arm on the table and one on the back of her chair. Then he leaned down until his twinkling blue-gray eyes were even with hers. "I was referring to her heart, you dirty old woman."

"Oh." She saw the twitch of a grin at the corner of his mouth right before he kissed her heated forehead.

"Gotta go." He patted the top of her head as he straightened. "Those tractors aren't going to fix themselves."

Rosemary leaned her head back, stretching those darn neck muscles that always seemed so tight these days. "But somebody else could fix them. Let's retire, Eli. Let's take that money we've worked so hard for all these years and spend it seeing some of the world…like we always promised ourselves we'd do."

Eli had started toward the door—her words didn't even slow his stride. They never did. "We'll do that, Rosie. Someday."

"Someday," she muttered as she cleared away the breakfast dishes. "Always someday."

Maggie was so much like her dad. She used to say the same thing to Zeke when he wanted to travel, which he did often. He'd usually end up going by himself while she stayed home and ran the salon. Look where it got her. The money she made and saved? What good was it now? He was gone and their chance of doing things together ripped away in the blink of an eye.

Maggie was too much in her thoughts, and Rosemary wasn't going to get anything done until she talked to her daughter. She chose the wall phone, preferring to use it rather than the cell phone, which she was sure was causing all these tumors in the mouth and brain she'd heard about recently.

"Hey, Mom." Maggie sounded more chipper than Rosemary had expected. Not a good sign. That meant she was forcing it, which inferred she was really upset.

"Hey, darlin'. Just wanted to see if things were going okay."

Maggie's sigh reduced the pretense a smidgen. "Things went all right yesterday. But I'm not much looking forward to today."

"I knew you wouldn't be. That's why I called. To let you know we love you and are thinking about you."

"Thanks. That's sweet."

There was that uncharacteristic silence Rosemary detested.

"And how are you and Jeff getting along?"

"Fine. No problems." Back to forced chipper, which set off alarms in Rosemary's head.

"Well…glad to hear that."

Silence again.

"Russ and Jeff are playing in the golf scramble today. Each team member was allowed to choose a partner. I backed off, figuring Russ would rather have his dad on his team."

"What a shame you can't play, too." Rosemary tried to encourage the conversation by showing sympathy. "You enjoy the game. And you're good."

"Yeah, but this is a competition Russ wants to win. Jeff will give him the best chance. There's this guy Spike—his son's on the team. He's always bragging about how great he is at everything. I think our guys are out for his blood, so I hope they draw a good pair to team up with."

Maggie's short laugh sounded more relaxed, but *our guys* was an interesting word choice.

"So what are you going to do while they're playing?"

"Oh, I'll follow along. I guess that's what all the extra parents will do." Now her voice sounded normal—maybe the mom-call had worked its magic, after all.

Rosemary spied Eli's cash box sitting on the kitchen counter where he'd forgotten it. "Well, I won't keep you. I know you have a busy day ahead."

"Yeah. I need to get moving."

"Me, too. Your dad forgot his cash box. Love you. Give Russ hugs."

"Okay. Love you, too. Hugs to Dad."

They hung up and Rosemary realized she didn't know any more about how Maggie was handling being around Jeff than she had yesterday. Her daughter was being very tight-lipped about her ex, which didn't bode well by Rosemary's way of thinking.

She snatched up the cash box and headed into the August morning air, already heated and damp with humidity. The pole barn Eli used as his machine shop sat at the back of their large piece of property. She was in no hurry as she followed the gravel lane back to it. A chicken snake slithered across the path, several yards ahead, leaving a weaving trail in its path.

"Snake in the grass." She chuckled, remembering the epithet Eli had first used in reference to Jeff before he'd settled on son of a bitch.

She'd been fond of Jeff when he and Maggie were dating, and once they'd gotten married, he'd tried hard to man up. They'd just been too young and had too many things stacked against them. But he'd broken her daughter's heart—*that* she couldn't forgive.

Chicken snakes were easy to piss off and quick to bite.

Yeah, that pretty much summed up the Jeff she remembered.

The shadow of the pole barn brought instant cool to her sweaty back, and she stopped a moment to enjoy the sensation. No sound came from the barn. The eerie silence sent her into a near-jog.

The sight that met her eyes when she passed through the oversize garage door brought her to a complete stop.

"Eli? What are you doing?"

Eli's jumping jacks came to a halt, and he swung around toward her, surprise giving way to sheepish in a flash. "What do you mean, what am I doing?" He was winded and gasping for breath, face red from exertion. "Can't a man exercise without being chastised for it?"

She made no attempt to keep the suspicion out of her voice. "You work hard. And except for walking, you've never exercised a day in your life."

"Well…I decided to add jumping jacks to today's regimen. Now get on back to the house and leave me alone." He took the cash box from her and turned his back in dismissal.

"Jumping jackass, if you ask me." She sneered and headed back to the house.

His low chuckle followed her retreating backside, and she allowed a smile since he couldn't see her face.

Eli partaking in calisthenics?

That dog didn't hunt.

Something was amiss.

MAGGIE'S BODY HAD become a battle zone…courtesy of Jeff's kiss last night. Okay, it wasn't only *his* kiss.

She'd been a more-than-willing participant. In fact, she may've been the instigator, Lord help her.

Had she lost her freaking mind?

Maybe so. It kept wandering off of its own accord, breaking free of the reins she'd held so tightly for years.

Even now, after spending the afternoon traipsing around a golf course with Spike filling her ears so full she thought her head would burst, her brain should've been focused on the upcoming goodbye with her son. Instead, it looped continually back to the feel of Jeff's lips on hers, the sizzle that snaked through her belly at his touch. The scene had become a recurring dream that blindsided her anytime she closed her eyes either last night in the dark or today in broad daylight.

Or even now as the dinner was coming to a close.

"And, of course, the top honors go to the team of Grainger/Wells, coming in with a score of twelve under." Coach Brimley handed out the cheesy plastic trophies to the four-man team. They accepted graciously, then Russ gave his trophy a noisy smooch, which brought a laugh from the crowd. For the millionth time that day, Maggie was reminded of the kiss she and Jeff shared last night.

Definitely trophy worthy.

She had yet to talk to Jeff about it, but she would as soon as they had a moment alone. She'd learned the hard way with Zeke that the things you didn't talk about were the ones that came back to haunt you. And, although her dreams last night and her daydreams today had been much too pleasant to be considered haunting, she knew they would come back to bite her in the ass.

The applause died down, the coach made his final remarks, and when the crowd started moving, Maggie's heart pinned her to her seat and stymied her movements.

Hold yourself together, Mom. She read the unspoken plea in Russ's eyes as he crossed the room to her.

Somehow she found the strength to stand up and meet him. He leaned down and enveloped her in a tight hug.

"I'm proud of you, little man." His hold tightened at her words. "Not because you won today. I'm proud of you every day—of the man you've become."

"Love you, Mom." His voice broke like it had so often when he was going through puberty.

His hold loosened, and he stepped back. She wasn't quite ready to let go just yet, but when a second body pressed against her side, she realized he was making room for Jeff in a three-way hug. She fought back another wave of tears, and for a long moment, they stood holding each other as a family—the way they could've been all along if life hadn't had other plans.

"Y'all gonna walk me to my room?" Russ placed

a kiss to the top of her head, which she shook in answer.

"I think that will be too hard. Let's just step outside and make it quick and relatively painless."

Russ never let go of her or Jeff as they threaded their way through the crowd that now felt more like a funeral than a celebration.

On the sidewalk, Russ let go of his dad and clutched her tightly again. "You going to be okay?"

"I'm okay," she lied. Lord, this was so much harder than childbirth. Back then, she'd been numb when the worst of the contractions had hit. But this felt like someone was digging out her heart with a plastic spoon and no anesthesia. "You be good. Be careful. Play nice and watch crossing." She added the signature line she'd used throughout his childhood, which brought a strangled chuckle from them both. Her nose was clogged with unshed tears, and just when she thought she would suffocate from the high pressure area in her chest, he let go and turned to Jeff.

The pats on the back were much harder between the two of them than previously. She suspected man pats were meant to inflict a touch of pain that somehow reminded them of their manhood...or maybe provided an excuse for a tear to escape.

When Russ wiped a hand down his face, it was almost her undoing.

One more quick hug. A peck to his cheek and a

pat to his belly. She couldn't hold herself together much longer. "See you in November."

"Yeah. And I'll see you at Christmas, Dad."

"Take care." Jeff gave a soft pat to his son's shoulder, then he took Maggie's arm and swiveled her toward the parking lot. "Let's go."

She should be irritated Jeff was taking charge, telling her it was time to leave her son. But her feet wouldn't have moved without his prodding.

"I'm driving." He held out his hand, and she relinquished the keys without dissension. Spike waved to them as he got into his car. He was making the drive back to his home tonight—Maggie wished she could do the same. The hotel room would feel lonelier than ever.

But then, so would home.

She made it to the car, through the buckling in, the starting of the ignition and all the way to the point where Jeff was about to pull out of the parking lot. And then the tears erupted from her.

Jeff whipped the car into the nearest parking place and they came to an abrupt stop. Her sight was so blurred she couldn't see him, but she felt his arm around her shoulders pulling her against him. She sobbed into his chest.

"He's going to be fine, Mags," he whispered. She nodded, but words wouldn't come yet. "You've done such a great job. He's well-adjusted. Has a great personality."

"But the house is going to…to be so…so empty with him gone," she blubbered.

"It's not like he's never coming back," Jeff soothed, stroking her hair. "He'll be home in a little over three months."

"But things will never be the s-s-ame. This is the start of him being…being gone for good."

Jeff dabbed at the tears with a tissue from the box in the backseat. "You know what I think?" She shook her head. "I think we should be celebrating."

She straightened, taken aback by his declaration. He cupped her cheeks, directing her gaze toward his with hands that were warm and gentle. Being with someone at that moment felt nice.

"I mean it, Mags. We've done a hell of a job with this kid. We should be proud of who he is, who we're sending out into the world. He'll make it a better place." Then he released her and shifted the car into Reverse. "We're going back to the hotel and celebrating."

Maggie was in no mood to celebrate and planned on heading to her room as soon as they got there. Surprisingly she was able to get her tears under control during the drive, and by the time they got to the lobby, she was almost herself again—except for the puffy eyes. And the thought of going upstairs to her empty room was no longer appealing. So when Jeff took her hand, she allowed him to lead her into the lounge to a table in the shadowy back corner with a high-backed love seat. It was dark enough she didn't feel conspicuous about her red eyes and nose, and cozy enough to relax.

A few couples were taking a turn on the floor, dancing to the pleasant melodies of the soloist with the smoky voice and her accompanist. When the server came to take their order, Jeff didn't ask her preference.

"We'll have a bottle of Pol Roger Brut Réserve and two glasses," he said.

"A whole bottle of champagne?" Maggie asked as the server walked away. "That's a little much, isn't it?"

Jeff grinned, his white teeth gleaming against his tanned face, made darker by the dim lighting. "Only three glasses each. And we're not gonna gulp them. We're going to sit here and savor them for as long as we want." He cocked his head in question, his gaze flitting over her face. "You better now?"

"I'm okay."

"Good." Her hand lay on the love seat between them and he patted it lightly. A couple of hours ago, that touch would have sent a shock wave through her. But saying goodbye to Russ seemed to have desensitized her, leaving her a little numb. Jeff pointed out the window to the street beyond. "What a shame. You came all the way to Chicago and didn't have a chance to shop the Magnificent Mile."

"I actually had a couple of hours this morning. While you and Russ were playing your practice round, and having man time with Spike, I was hitting the shops." She tried to sound contrite, but she couldn't keep the grin from her face when Jeff cringed at the mention of Spike. "All you two got were sore ears and a plastic trophy. I scored a dress, two pairs of capris and three pairs of shoes."

His face sobered, and he took a long breath. "Kind of like old times. Me slaving in the hot sun while you shop."

What a low blow! Immediately, Maggie went on the defensive, her spine stiffening, bracing for combat. But then she saw the edge of his mouth twitch. He was toying with her. Well…she could play, too. "*Really* like old times. You on the golf course. Me left to my own entertainment."

He pinned her with a hard look, but then both corners of his mouth twitched, and he dissolved into laughter. "We were quite a pair, weren't we?"

She nodded her smiling agreement just as the server arrived with their order. The young woman opened the champagne discreetly—no big fanfare to draw attention to the dark corner—and filled the two glasses.

Maggie leaned forward on her elbows, watching the bubbles as they caught the light and danced their way to the top. "It looks like some kind of magic potion."

"It is." Jeff picked up the two glasses and handed her one. His gaze was direct, his eyes soft. "Drinking this will wipe away all the bad times and help us remember only the good. Like Russ…and last night's kiss."

Maggie's heart skipped a beat—apparently she wasn't so numb, after all.

Jeff raised his glass as one of his eyebrows arched in both question and challenge.

Maggie tipped her glass, touching the edge to his. "To the good times—past and future."

MAGGIE'S WORDS SENT an impact through Jeff that left a crater the size of Lake Michigan, which instantly filled with desire. The kiss last night had lit the fuse, and all day he'd been affected by the slow burn. He'd managed to throw the energy into his golf game, crushing the ball with his driver at each tee box, playing like he'd never played before.

But now, it was Maggie he wanted to crush… in the most tender of ways. But he couldn't simply suggest they go up to one of their rooms and get it on, even if that was precisely what he wanted to do. This was a special night—the kind that came once in a lifetime. He would make it last.

The champagne truly was a magic elixir. He watched it bring a sparkle to Maggie's eyes and a blush to her cheeks after just one glass. But when a girlish giggle bubbled out of her during one of his stories that wasn't *that* funny, it gave him pause. Getting her drunk wasn't the plan. This was a night to make memories—he wanted them both to remember it come tomorrow. He ordered a fruit-and-cheese plate to give them a reason to slow down the drinking.

While they waited for the food, the pianist broke into a jazzy swing tune. Dancing was one of the things they did together in college and were good at—second only to lovemaking. "Want to dance?" he asked, unsure if it was something she still enjoyed.

"Yes!" Her answer was nearly a squeal.

As they fell into the rhythm, the years fell away, and their bodies moved in perfect precision. They swung, they twirled, two hands clasped, then one hand and an underarm turn. Both of them anticipated the movements of the other as if the entire dance had been choreographed. Jeff was vaguely aware they were clearing the dance floor, but he didn't let it stop them—tonight was all about the good times. Besides, he and Maggie had often done the same thing in college.

"Ready?" he asked as the song neared its end, and she nodded.

"Ready."

He sent her into an impressive set of underarm twirls and prayed she didn't get sick like she did that time at the frat house—their first clue she was pregnant. The last notes brought her tightly against him and he dipped her dramatically. The lounge went silent and then a hearty round of raucous applause exploded from every corner. To Jeff's amazement— and slight embarrassment—the open passageways into the lobby had filled with onlookers as people had stopped to watch the impromptu show. With their arms around each other's backs and a couple of waves to the crowd, they sauntered back to their table and anonymity, short of breath, panting and hanging on to each other for support.

"I haven't danced like that in twenty years." Maggie's words were punctuated by gasps as she plopped onto the love seat, sliding over to make room for him.

"Me, neither." The exertion from the dance had given him a momentary respite from the erection he'd sported most of the day, but Maggie's breathless exclamation shifted it back into forward gear. He tried to ignore it as he poured them more champagne and relaxed against the back of his seat.

Maggie stacked some cheese onto a crostini and drizzled it with honey, then held it up in offering. Rather than taking it from her, he opened his mouth and she fed it to him. He closed his lips around the bite, deliberately catching the tips of her fingers in a small suck to gauge her response.

She didn't flinch. Didn't draw back. On the contrary, she allowed the tip of her middle finger to linger a fraction longer before dragging it down the middle of his bottom lip. Her lids drooped to half-mast, and she gave him a smoldering smile as she leaned back against one shoulder, her face and body turned slightly toward him.

His eyes dropped from hers to her mouth, mesmerized by the way her lips parted sensually, her tongue touching them, making them glisten in invitation.

He took a sip of champagne to wash away any of the lingering cracker, then leaned toward her, bringing his mouth to hers in answer. She left her hands as they were—one lying between them on the seat, the other relaxed in her lap. Her lips coaxed him deeper, parting for him, allowing small, sexually charged whimpers to escape, which sounded like both need and satisfaction.

And that kiss was just the beginning.

As they talked and laughed away the rest of the champagne, it was obvious that they both knew exactly how this magical night was going to end.

And so, during the last dance—a slow one that pressed her against him, making her aware of the effects she was having on his body—it came as no real surprise when she whispered to him, "Do you have condoms?"

"That's a loaded question," he whispered back, enjoying the way his breath on her neck caused her to shiver. "If I say no, where does that leave us? But if I say yes, it's as good as admitting I went to the drugstore in anticipation of this after last night."

Her cheek rested against his as her fingers played softly with the hair at the nape of his neck. "I hope the answer's yes."

"Then it's yes."

Her response was a contented sigh as she pressed her body closer to his.

CHAPTER SIX

KEY CARDS WERE such wonderful inventions. No
fumbling with locks—just a smooth transition from
outside to inside, public view to privacy…exes to
intimates.

Somewhere deep in her mind, a voice screamed
that she was making a huge mistake, allowing this
man to crack the safe place she'd built to contain
her feelings for him.

But she couldn't hear the screaming over his soft
murmurs when his mouth left hers for just a moment. They kissed long and hard, a frenzy of passion and excitement—as if there were no tomorrow.

Because, for them, there wasn't.

Tomorrow wasn't anything that needed to be discussed. Everything they desired had to be acted on
tonight, then tucked away and forgotten.

Clothes came off hurriedly, amid giggles and
kisses, and the condom package made its appearance. But just as she moved for the bed, seeking
shelter under the covers, Jeff stopped her. "Not yet,
Mags." With his hands on her hips, he turned her
to him. "I want to see you."

His gentle tone and the way he nuzzled her neck eased her discomfort some, though not completely. He hadn't seen her up close and personal in sixteen years. What would he think of her now? "I'm not twenty-one anymore," she cautioned.

He tugged her hands away from where she'd positioned them across her breasts. "Neither am I."

True, he'd added a few pounds—a thickness that only made him appear more solid. Her additional weight had become a soft roundness through the belly and hips that had been flat and tight, almost boyish, when last he'd seen them.

He guided her into the shaft of light that shone through the space where the drapes were slightly open. They stood for a while, naked amid the lights of the city, exchanging pleasant touches—he, using the backs of his fingers, she, smoothing her palms across his biceps and triceps, appreciating their toned definition. His caresses heightened the awareness of every nerve ending he touched.

"You don't see how perfect you are." His fingers brushed a path from her breasts to her neck and into her hair. He tilted her face up to meet his gaze. "Firm in the right places. Soft where you should be." He covered her mouth with his in a scorching kiss, stealing the breath from her lungs.

The girl she'd been once upon a time stepped from her hiding place into the light. Beautiful. Cherished. Unlike Zeke, Jeff had never failed to make her feel that way in the bedroom, which was probably one reason it had taken so long to get over him.

But she had.

And now, here he was again.

This time the girl vanished as quickly as she'd appeared.

Maggie wasn't someone who could be charmed into believing anything lasted forever. That girl had been replaced by a resilient woman who knew that some things lasted only one night. And those things had to be enjoyed when they offered themselves.

She consciously gave herself over to the moment, bringing her own heat to the kiss. An appreciative sound rose from the back of Jeff's throat.

He backed up and sat on the end of the bed, breaking the kiss but running his hands over the soft mounds of her rear as he pulled her to stand between his parted legs.

His mouth, still hot from the kiss, burned a wet path across her stomach, pausing to let his tongue explore her navel, and then his lips moved upward to caress the underside of her breasts. He lifted them, kneading them gently as his tongue flicked along the crease.

It was a new touch for her, and she let her head fall back, mewing her pleasure, massaging his scalp with her fingertips, following his head anywhere he moved it.

His hands roamed her back while his mouth explored her front, sucking first one nipple then the other, making her ache in the most delicious way. As his mouth moved downward, she stepped back instinctively to give him access to other areas. He slid to his knees, flicking his tongue across her most sensitive spot, making her gasp in pleasure and thrust against him. But the urgency built up too quickly, became almost painful, and she stepped away suddenly.

Jeff's head shot up, his dark eyes full of question.

"It's been a long time for me. Not since Zeke." She stopped. "Years."

He stood and pressed against her. "What a waste of time."

She smiled at the compliment, the ache between her legs lessening to bearable. This time, when she took his hand and led him to the bed, they lay down together, snuggling under the sheet. She intended to keep things slow. But after a few more deep kisses, his hands in constant exploration, growing bolder with each touch, she abandoned the plan, unable and unwilling to take responsibility for the actions of her body.

She guided his hand to where she needed him most, stroking him boldly to inflame him with the heat she felt until he finally admitted in a ragged breath, "Mags, I can't take much more."

She laughed. "Oh, thank God."

He tore open the condom package he'd thrown on the pillow and made quick work of sheathing himself.

And then he hovered above her. The face she'd yearned to see for so long, positioned exactly where she'd fantasized it would be.

But this was no fantasy.

This was a chance to end things better than they had the first time.

MAGGIE WAS GAZING into his eyes, and damn if she wasn't chewing her bottom lip!

At this point, sixteen years ago, he would've ignored the nuance. His rocket would have been fueled, loaded and ready for blastoff.

He lowered his mouth to hers, catching her bottom lip when her teeth freed it from their grip, then proceeded to nibble and suck on it himself. He felt her position shift slightly, readying for his entry. Then he watched her eyes widen in surprise when he shifted, too...away from the expected.

His lips caressed her neck before traveling to her breasts, devouring each one in turn. Then he continued down the middle of her stomach, across her navel, to the juncture of her thighs. Then lower.

Her gasps of pleasure as she raised her hips to meet him were almost his undoing, but he breathed through the initial panic and retained his control.

Lower he went, his tongue gliding along the inside of her thigh. He paused at her knee, lifting her leg just enough to flick his tongue across the crease at the back. Her pleasurable groan encouraged him to continue. She reached for him but could only graze the top of his head with her fingertips as he moved lower still.

He changed his course slightly, moving to the outside of her calf, skimming his tongue along the indentation of the muscle from the knee to the ankle. He covered her entire foot with kisses, sucked her high arch and each of her toes, before switching to the other foot and repeating the entire process on the other leg.

By the time he returned to the intimate V between her legs, she was panting, clutching the sheets tightly in her fists and thrusting toward him with a body language message he couldn't ignore.

His own body was sending messages of its own, his erection so rigid now the condom might not be able to withstand the pressure much longer.

He eased his tip into her slowly, but she was having none of that. She rose on her elbows and shifted her body in his direction, enveloping him completely in her tightness. Her legs gripped him, pulling him deeper as she danced beneath him, making small circles with her hips as she thrust. She set an excruciatingly appealing rhythm that tore him between wanting to finish and wanting this to go on all night. Fast. Slow. Harder, softer. To the edge and back, over and over.

The feel of Mags and the taste of her on his lips. Their eyes locked. The musky scent of their mingled heat. The bed pounded the wall, percussion backup to their gasps, moans, grunts and pants. The heightened sensory experience was sending Jeff into space—a vacuum where there was no gravity and no time.

Only him and Mags.

Her hands flew over her head to grasp the spindles of the headboard, and he felt her back drawing into an arch as she cried out.

He let go then as his body exploded and imploded at the same time. He wasn't aware he'd shouted until recognition hit that it was his voice ringing in his ears. Mags still held her head and neck in a stiff arch, and he could feel her muscles clenching him in their spasms. He pushed tighter against her, wringing every drip of pleasure for her he could.

Her eyes were squeezed shut, her breathy panting coming in spurts from her sensuous open mouth.

Nothing was more beautiful than a woman enjoying multiple orgasms.

Correction—nothing was more beautiful than Mags enjoying multiple orgasms. He'd never been with another woman who'd had them.

He watched the tension leave her body, mesmerized by the sight. Slowly, her head and neck relaxed, her mouth closed and her eyes fluttered open as if she'd been in a trance. He saw her eyes draw into focus and the languid, sexy smile form on her lips. "Mmm." Her eyes closed and opened in a dreamy blink.

Jeff relaxed, too, lowering himself to the bed, on his side but still snuggled against her. He pinned her right arm under him where it had slid onto the pillow and propped his head on his hand so he still had a good view of Mags's face. He traced her features with the tip of his finger. "God, you were good." He kissed the end of her nose, then her mouth.

Her smile widened, but her eyebrows furrowed slightly and she groaned. "Four years was too long to go without that."

Jeff shifted to let her move her arm, then slid down to rest his head on the pillow, drawing her against him.

He pressed a kiss to the top of her head, then let his cheek rest on the spot.

"Sixteen years was too long to go without that," he whispered.

JEFF'S WORDS CROUCHED in the front of Maggie's mind, ready to pounce as soon as she came fully awake.

Of course, she'd heard him when he spoke them, and her heart palpitated, trying to conjure a reaction. But her body was so mellow after the amazing release she couldn't get worked up about it. Sleep came quickly, hard and deep—mimicking what she'd experienced with him.

But morning broke through the parted drapes, bringing her to full consciousness, and her heart twisted in her chest as soon as she opened her eyes.

What did he mean, sixteen years was too long to wait?

Surely, he wasn't having second thoughts about the divorce.

Oh, good Lord, what had she done?

The two of them still lay as they had fallen asleep. Sometime during the night, she'd turned more toward him, and now his dark chest hair tickled her nose. His free arm draped across her, hand resting at the small of her back.

Mmm—it all felt so good.

Too good.

Memories of what Jeff had done—and what she'd done in return—swirled through her emotions, mixing them into a strange morning brew.

She moved to sit up, but the arm that rested across her tightened.

"Where you going?" He pulled her tighter against him and she became aware of the erection pressing on the upper thigh that she had wedged between his.

She glanced at her watch. "It's almost nine. Time to get up."

"I'm already up."

She heard the grin in his voice. "So I noticed. You always were a morning person." She wiggled her leg only the slightest but felt his immediate response. His grunt of approval made her grin, too.

"And you were always an anytime person." He nuzzled his nose into her hair, his warm breath warming her all over.

He was right. She *had* always been ready for him—anytime, anyplace. Things had been different with Zeke. Once, sometimes twice a week. She'd accepted the decline in her libido as part of the normal aging process. That theory didn't seem to hold up, though, as she was already feeling vibes from simply waking in her ex's arms.

"Do you have anything *pressing* today?" He humped her leg playfully, emphasizing his word choice.

She chuckled at his movements, but then sobered. "Only the long drive home." She sighed. "And starting the process of getting used to being alone in the house for longer than two months."

His hand caressed her rear, fingers dipping low enough to elicit a guttural sound from her. "See there. Nothing that can't be put off for a little while—or until they run us out of here at checkout."

He was spot-on. She had nothing she needed to get home to. But what would another round of sex with Jeff do to her emotionally? Send her into that battle again—the one she'd fought so long to win?

No. This time his leaving wouldn't be a surprise. It was inevitable. She was forewarned and prepared.

And the time to think about the emotional impact of sex with Jeff had passed, barely heeded, hours ago. What difference would one more time make?

Or two?

"You're right." She withdrew her leg long enough to sling it across his and roll on top of him to a seated position. The sheet fell away, and the morning sunshine dispelled any chance of hiding under the cloak of darkness. But she didn't care. She was who she was. And the way his eyes devoured her at that moment made her think who she was was pretty darn hot.

And so was he.

Despite his look of pleasure and surprise, sleep still lay heavy in his eyes and a thick growth of black stubble coated his lower jaw and mouth area. She well remembered the beard burn she used to get from their morning trysts.

So worth it.

She brushed the tousled hair off his forehead and patted his bristly cheek, which did indeed scratch when he turned to kiss her palm. "No use of the mouth until you shave," she instructed.

He sat up, locking his hands behind her back. "Oh, really?" Using his tongue, he teased the tender area along the line of her jawbone.

A delightful shiver coursed through her. "So not fair." She sighed, but leaned her head back farther.

"How about this?" He nibbled along the same path. "Is this okay?"

It actually was quite pleasant, since his tongue had already moistened the area. She moaned in response and dragged her long nails up his back, drawing a satisfying shiver from him. Other areas were becoming moist without any direct touch.

He loosened his grip enough to lean her back slightly, and nipped his way to the peak of her breast.

She arched her back, thrusting a nipple toward him to meet the sweet assault that never came.

He stopped, and the pause lasted long enough to make her aware something was up. She straightened and found him frowning at her chest. "Did I do that?"

She followed his gaze to the red splotches marking each place where his whiskers had made contact with her fair skin. She shrugged. "No biggie."

"Yes, it is." He took her firmly by the waist and tried to set her off his lap. "Let me up, and I'll go shave."

She pushed him back onto the pillow. "No way, bucko. Follow the rules and don't use your mouth, and everything will be good."

His mouth quirked on one side. "Just good?"

"Maybe *just* good." She wiggled against him with her backside, lightly clawing at his chest and stomach. "Maybe worth waiting sixteen years for."

"Nobody should have to wait for sex this good. Just think what a happy state our world would be in if everybody could have it like this all the time. War would be a thing of the past." He grabbed a condom package from the table and ripped into it.

So *that's* what he'd meant last night. He hadn't been feeling any heavy remorse—only making commentary on sex in general. What a relief! Flashing a wicked grin, she took the condom and proceeded to put him through as much agony as possible as she slid the protective covering into place. Then she slid herself into place, as well.

"Oh, baby." With his hands on her hips, he held her firmly and raised his hips to meet her.

The reminder that this morning would be their last time together like this made her want to slow down and make it last, but her body would have none of it. The way he filled every part of her—as no one else ever had and probably never would—gave him total control, and when he shifted into high gear, she went along for one of the greatest rides of her life.

And this time, she cried out his name when the delicious spasms rocked her core.

She collapsed on top of him, sweaty and gasping for air. She could feel their hearts pounding against each other, dancing to the same beat.

A fitting closure.

Her breathing finally righted itself, and Jeff's arms loosened enough to allow him to trace circles on her back. His touch was so soothing and relaxing, she could have lain there all day. But they were on a bit of a time schedule, in spite of pretending otherwise.

"I can take you to the airport if you'd like," she said at last. "What time's your flight?"

"I'm not flying out until Sunday. One of the guys at the dealership is from Wisconsin, and his family owns a cabin on Lake Geneva that they rent out. I'm getting a car and driving up there to spend a few days. Play some golf."

"Mmm." He'd moved one of his hands up to her hair and was brushing his fingers through it. It felt so good she couldn't bring herself to move yet. "Sounds nice."

His chest rose as he took a deep breath, and when he let it out, it fluttered through the top of her hair. "Mags?" he whispered. "Come with me."

HE FELT MAGGIE'S spine stiffen under his hand, then she released what he recognized as a forced laugh. "We're exes, remember? That wouldn't be proper."

"We're consenting adults." He glided his hand down her back to cup her fine ass. "To hell with proper."

She shook her head.

He'd just had twelve hours of the most amazing sex ever, and he wasn't prepared to take no for an answer unless it came with a better reason than being exes. Rolling to his side, he deposited her on the pillow and rose on an elbow to look her in the eye. "You've got to do better than that…and you've already told me the salon practically runs itself, so that one won't fly, either."

Worry clouded her gorgeous green eyes as she heaved a conflicted sigh. "We're being unrealistic. Playing with fire. That sort of thing."

"This has nothing to do with reality, Mags. It's pure fantasy." He watched as the worry in her eyes gave way to question. "Yes, I admit it. I've fantasized through the years about us having sex again."

The admission felt good, perhaps because it was the first time he'd allowed himself to acknowledge it openly...or maybe even more so because he saw the truth in her eyes and the uneasy smile it brought to her lips. She'd fantasized, too. "This could be our chance to have fun, Mags. We'll be able to part company without all the drama of last time." Her chin quivered, and he kissed her to bring her thoughts back to the present. "What do you say? Three days of golf, great sex and no drama."

Her finger traced the outside of his ear. "I'd considered staying up here for a day or two to visit the museums. Even mentioned the possibility to Mom and EmmyLou."

"Who?" He wasn't familiar with the name.

"EmmyLou Creighton, my best friend, and the salon's assistant manager?"

Jeff nodded, remembering the mentioning of the name that first night at dinner.

"She was the first stylist I hired," Mags went on. "It was just the two of us for several years."

She was actually seriously considering his offer! He pressed further and took advantage of his position by toying with her bare nipples, catching them between his fingers and bringing them to hardened peaks. "See there. Your subconscious was making plans to set this up before I even mentioned it."

That brokered no verbal response, but she looked

miserable and still conflicted. A pang of guilt ran through him. "I'm sorry, Mags. I shouldn't be pressing you to do something you're not comfortable with." He sat up, shifting his weight away from her, preparing to make a friendly, unemotional exit and get the hell out of Dodge.

Her hand caught his arm. "Stepping out of my comfort zone might be good for me."

"You want to do it?" This had to be her decision—he wasn't about to talk her into anything she'd regret later. He'd already had to live with that guilt far too long.

She nodded and a spark of excitement glinted from her eyes as she sat up. "It may be crazy, but I haven't done anything crazy in a really long time."

"Me, neither."

Not since letting you go. Whoa! He hadn't spoken that aloud, had he?

Jeff took a couple of deep breaths to slow his racing heart. Where in the hell had that thought come from? This little excursion was a fun trip, and he wouldn't think of it as anything more.

"I do insist on one rule, though." Maggie's eyes were stern, but her grin gave her away. "No more using the mouth until you shave." She cupped his cheeks with both hands and wiggled his head playfully.

He grabbed her hands and held them tightly in his lap, forcing her face close to his. "Oh, really?"

He flicked his tongue along the base of her jawline and up around the back of her ear.

"*So* unfair," she whispered.

CHAPTER SEVEN

"I'M TELLING YOU, Eli...something's up."

Baxter Hill seemed especially steep this evening. Maybe it was the fried catfish, hushpuppies and French fries she'd fixed for dinner that felt so heavy in the pit of Rosemary's stomach. Or maybe it was something completely different—like the nagging feeling her daughter was lying to her about staying in Chicago to sightsee.

"You...don't think...it's the son of a bitch, do you?" Eli's heavy breathing caused his words to come out in spurts.

She'd tried to slow their pace several times on tonight's walk, but her stubborn-ass husband seemed bent on making it home in record time. "My gut feeling is, yeah, he's involved. Probably just being around him for three days threw her into a funk. She might've needed to stay up there as a distraction until she could get her wits about her again."

"Maybe she's...not wanting to...leave Russ."

"That's possible. But, if that's what's going on, I hope she doesn't let him know she's still there. That'd only make things harder for both of them."

Rosemary didn't really believe Maggie would stay in Chicago because of Russ. Time after time, Maggie had talked about how it was best to not let him know how much it was going to hurt her, leaving him so far away. She was resolved, and once she set her mind to it, Maggie always followed through.

Letting go of Jeff had been the exception.

So maybe it was simply that being around him shook enough of those old feelings loose that Maggie needed a big-city distraction rather than an empty house where she was more likely to dwell on it.

Rosemary prayed that was the reason, anyway.

They reached the top of the hill and turned around to head back down. Eli's face looked like it had been rubbed with beet juice. "Good Lord, are you sure you're okay?"

He gave her a hard glare and started down without breaking his stride, not saying anything more until they reached the bottom. "She's been busy with Russ and probably hasn't had time to see the city," he said when he'd caught his breath, his words no longer clumping.

"She does enjoy museums," Rosemary conceded as they turned onto their front sidewalk. "I'm probably reading too much into it."

Reaching the porch a couple of strides ahead of her, Eli plopped down on the steps. He pulled off his cap and ran a hand through his hair, sending drops of sweat flying in all directions. The look he gave her stopped her in midsit. "Rosie, I think I might have a problem."

Rosemary's knees stiffened, lifting her back to fully standing. "What is it?"

"I get pressure in my chest when I go uphill." He pressed a flat palm against his heart. "But not down."

A cold chill gripped Rosemary despite the heat surrounding her. "When did this start?"

"First felt it last week when I lifted Mabel's casket. Pain. Right here." He patted his heart. "I figured I'd pulled a muscle. But I feel it every time I exert."

Things began to fall into place. "So you were doing the jumping jacks…"

He nodded sheepishly. "To test my theory."

"I knew something was wrong." Rosemary thrust her finger at his face and shook out her frustration. "How many times this week have I asked you if you were okay?"

Eli grabbed her finger and stilled it. "And now I'm admitting I don't know if I am. I think I need to go to the hospital and find out."

Eli was suggesting the hospital? He'd *never* done that in all the years she'd known him. The seriousness of the situation sank in. "Oh!" She pressed a trembling hand to her mouth, trying to hold back her distress. She swallowed, and it lodged in her throat, making the muscles constrict and ache, causing tears to well up in her eyes.

"Don't you go crying on me, now." Eli's voice was calm. "Just get the car keys, okay?"

Rosemary stumbled up the steps and into the house, grabbing her purse and feeling around inside it to make certain she had her keys and her phone. By the time she got back outside, Eli was sitting in the passenger side of the truck—another clue this was serious. Eli always insisted on driving.

Because the pain was sporadic rather than constant, they bypassed the county hospital and drove on to Paducah, the closest city. It had two excellent hospitals, but they chose Baptist Health where Maggie had been born and Rosemary had had her gall bladder removed several years ago.

They were moved through the ER quickly once Eli explained his symptoms, and before long he was lying on a bed, wired up to an electrocardiogram machine.

Rosemary had regained her composure…for the most part. She just tried to convince herself Eli was right about the pulled muscle. Mabel's casket *had* been solid oak. Heavy. Eli had no business being a pallbearer at his age. The younger men should take over that job.

"You haven't had a heart attack," the doctor said, at last. "Your EKG looks fine." If he'd been standing on the same side of the bed as she, Rosemary would've hugged him. "But—"

Uh-oh. Buts are always bad.

"I can't rule out that you might have problems.

I'm going to admit you, and we'll keep an eye on you tonight. Tomorrow morning, we'll do a stress test and see if you have any blockages."

"How 'bout I go home, sleep in my own bed and come back in the morning for that stress test?"

"It won't hurt you to sleep somewhere besides your bed this one night," Rosemary chided, but she couldn't stir much anger into her voice. They seldom went anywhere overnight. Had never even been on a vacation. Eli's steadfast rule was that he slept in his own bed.

The doctor frowned. "I'd prefer you allow me to admit you. We can keep an eye on you and make sure you stay comfortable."

Eli's lips pressed together. "I'd prefer to sleep in my own bed. No way I'll be comfortable in this place." He pointed to Rosemary. "She'll keep an eye on me."

"I won't be able to sleep a wink," Rosemary protested.

"See there?" Eli said to the doctor.

"You're refusing admission, then?"

Eli nodded. "For tonight I am. No use sleeping somewhere other than home until I absolutely have to."

"Oh, for heaven's sake, Eli." Rosemary let out the frustration that had built over the past couple of hours. "We go home, you might not wake up at all."

He shrugged like it was nothing, and the firm set

of his jaw told her there was no point in arguing. "That's a chance I'll take."

The doctor moved to the computer on the stand beside the bed and brushed a key to bring it to life. "Well, in that case, let's see about making you an appointment for tomorrow morning. How does ten o'clock sound?"

Rosemary glanced at her watch—8:38 p.m. The next thirteen hours and twenty-two minutes might be the longest of her life.

"You think it's really this peaceful here, or does it just seem that way after three days in Chicago?"

Maggie stopped and listened for the owl again. There it was. She hadn't caught sight of it yet, but it sounded closer.

"I think it's really this peaceful." Jeff stopped, too, and pointed in the direction of the answering hoot. "But being in the city makes you long for the quiet. Sometimes, I just take off and drive to get away from the noise. Even away from the ocean. Just absolute quiet."

Another new factoid to add to her growing list of items she was learning about her ex—such as his passion for soccer and his love of cooking. During the two-hour drive, then the eighteen holes of golf and the steak dinner on the deck of the lovely lakeside restaurant, she'd come to realize her companion had changed in many ways from the boy she'd been married to.

In his younger days, Jeff had always been the party animal, frat boy, in constant search of action. And now he enjoyed quiet. She would've never guessed.

He took a sip of the wine they'd brought with them on their sunset stroll around the south end of the lake. "This place reminds me of our camping trips on Kentucky Lake."

Maggie scratched her nose with a grin and held up her glass. "We'd need to replace these wineglasses with mason jars of Toad's 'shine."

Jeff barked a laugh at the mention of his fraternity brother's nickname. "Toad! Haven't thought of him and his homemade moonshine in years. I wonder what he's doing now?"

"Probably running a distillery someplace, if he followed his passion." They laughed in agreement. "You know," she confided, "I've always figured it was during one of those camping trips that I got pregnant."

Jeff paused to think about that for a minute and then held up his glass toward her. "Then here's to camping on Kentucky Lake."

Maggie clinked her glass to his. "And here's to being much more careful this time around."

They walked in silence as the top of the sun plunged below the surface of the lake, making the blue water deepen to shades of purple. They came around the bend, and the lovely house Jeff had rented—much too modern and chic to be considered a cabin—came into view.

"So you really don't have any regrets?" she asked quietly, and the sad expression he turned her way told her he understood the unspoken completion of that question—*about us.*

He took her hand, interlacing their fingers and continued walking. "I have lots of regrets, Mags." He took a sip of wine, and she wondered if he needed it to give him the courage to be honest. "Marrying you," he continued. "Having Russ. Those aren't part of them. I regret not staying and giving our marriage more time." Her heart did a backflip at his words. "We've obviously become different people from who we were back then. Maybe it could've worked out differently if we'd held on."

"But we wouldn't have become the people we are now if we hadn't gone our separate ways. And I like how I turned out." She took a sip and added, "And I like how you turned out, too." She nudged a grin from him with her elbow.

They walked a little way in comfortable silence before she spoke again. "You know, it surprises me to hear you say you don't regret our marriage. I always assumed you felt nothing but relief to get away from me."

He shook his head. "I was relieved to get away from the pressure. I always felt ganged up on, like it was three against one."

"It was," she admitted. "To this day, my parents place the blame solely on you."

Jeff shrugged off the comment. "My biggest regret will always be the time I lost with my son."

Her hand tightened instinctively at the sorrow in his voice. "I'm sorry you didn't get to see him more often. We did the best we could."

He nodded, and they fell into silence again.

"I'm glad you came with me, Mags."

She smiled. "Me, too." It surprised her that the words came so easily. Having this peaceful time to clear the air with Jeff was something she'd needed badly, without even realizing it. She'd always been so afraid that being around him again would make her fall back in love with him. But it didn't feel that way now. She *did* love him on some level. And always would. Russ gave her a love connection to this man walking beside her. What she was feeling was born of that connection. It was normal and certainly nothing to fear—no matter how hard her heart beat when he touched her.

"What do you have planned for tomorrow?" She steered the conversation away from the serious. They'd pretty much said it all these past few days, and there was no reason to keep rehashing the same conversation.

He gave her a suggestive grin.

"Besides that."

"So I have to think about something else, huh?" They reached the beach area of the rental and each of them claimed one of the Adirondack chairs at the edge of the water where the waves would lap their feet. "How about golf in the morning? Maybe rent a boat and spend the afternoon on the lake?"

"That sounds like the perfect day." She tried to take a sip, but her glass was empty. "I'll get the bottle." She stood, and as she passed between the chairs, Jeff took her hand and kissed it.

There was no reason to get worked up by all this attention. He'd always been demonstrative with his affection. It was one of the things that had drawn her to him. And it was one of the ways she saw his influence in Russ's mannerisms.

She let her thoughts drift to her son and wonder how his day had been. What would he think if he found out his parents were at Lake Geneva together?

She laughed softly. *He'd probably be scarred for life, like every other kid who imagines his parents sleeping together.* Her own parents came to mind, and she pushed the idea away with a silent *ew*!

Retrieving the half-empty bottle, she made her way back down to the beach, but Jeff had vacated his chair. She looked around. Where was he?

"Psst."

The stage whisper drew her attention to the lake. There she could make out Jeff's head, bobbing in the dark water.

"C'mon in. Water's perfect."

She pointed toward the house. "I don't have my swimsuit on."

"Neither do I." His deep laugh came ashore with the next wave.

Sure enough, his clothes were stacked in a neat pile on the seat of his chair.

Not needing a second invitation, she began to rid herself of her clothes very slowly, taking plenty of time to fold each piece precisely and lean over to place it carefully on the chair.

"You were one of those guys who tortured people in another life, weren't you?" His tone was a blend of pleasure and agony.

Maggie shrugged out of her bra, then stepped out of her panties and stretched her arms skyward. "This feels *so* good after playing golf."

"Are you coming in, or am I getting out?" he demanded.

"Isn't there some rule about swimming after drinking?" She eased into the water, which was indeed the perfect temperature.

Jeff met her where the water was waist deep. Taking her hand, he led her a little farther out and then stopped to take her in his arms.

"Not to worry," he said. "I have no intentions of swimming tonight."

JEFF LAY ON his side watching Mags sleep. She looked beautiful and serene, the worry lines that too often creased the area between her brows gone for now. That she'd become a worrier was obvious…and a surprise. When they'd been married, she didn't seem to worry about anything except Russ. Left worrying about everything else to him. A spoiled only child, she never gave a thought about tomorrow.

She'd changed…and that change was making him crazy.

He quietly got out of bed and slipped into the shorts he'd left lying in the chair. Checking one last time to make sure she was still asleep, he padded silently across the room and eased through the sliding glass door onto the deck.

The light breeze was balmy and inviting, and a gazillion stars twinkled overhead. It seemed a shame to view them like this when they could be seen in stereo by the water. He moseyed down to the beach, making himself comfortable again in the Adirondack, letting his senses fill with his surroundings. The scent of the sweet night air found its way to his tongue. Stars reflected in the water, accompanied by a summer chorus of crickets and bullfrogs. The water warmed his toes and ankles.

Ahh. Life was good.

So why wasn't he happy?

He thought about Mags, sleeping peacefully. They'd had a great time together. He'd forgotten how much fun she could be.

But…how could he have forgotten that? And why did remembering it cause an ache so deep it was almost unbearable?

He rested his head against the chair, closing his

eyes, trying to remember what he and Mags had really been like. Over the years, his recollections had dulled or heightened, depending on whether the memory was good or bad.

What had happened to the two of them? Why hadn't they made it? The initial physical attraction had been there. The lovemaking had been outstanding—and still was. Sure, they'd been young, but they'd truly cared for each other. Even that was still evident. A lot of divorced couples could never have done what they did this week—or ended up like this. They were different from the rest. Had always been different and always would be.

So what had made them think giving up like everybody else was the best solution?

Mags asked if he had any regrets. How could he tell her losing her was the one thing he could never forgive himself for? What good would it do to admit that?

He'd come close to saying it. But they were still a world apart. He had the car dealership that supported him, his parents and his sister. Mags had the salon she'd built from nothing—a business that couldn't be picked up and moved, any more than his could. What had she said during the car ride up? *After Russ, and Mom and Dad, the salon's the most important thing in my life. It's my other child. I love nurturing it and watching it grow.*

Too many miles and too many years separated him and Mags.

But if there was some way...

"Stop it." He spoke the words aloud, opening his eyes to try to stifle the images forming in his head. They'd moved the only *way* into a college dorm this week. They had no reason besides Russ to give things another try. Not even the lingering shades of love would be enough to dispel the fear and doubt.

And neither of them was willing to enter into another possible failure.

"So..." He pushed himself to his feet and headed back to the house. He would enjoy the time they'd been given. He would facilitate fun memories. He would be her sexual fantasies come to life...and let her be his.

And Sunday, when they parted ways, he would leave a part of his heart behind—the part that lay deep in the pit of his stomach right then. The part that made him ache from its burden.

It was much too heavy to continue carrying around for the rest of his life.

He'd have to find some way to let it go.

CHAPTER EIGHT

THE TECHNICIAN SHOWED Rosemary and Eli to a small, darkened room with several chairs gathered around a computer monitor.

"Dr. Reeves will be right in," the young man told them, and then disappeared back into the quiet hallway.

They each took a seat, and the chill in the room deepened when she saw the look in Eli's eyes. He took her hand. "It's not good, Rosie."

Her insides started to crumble, but she hoisted herself up on some fake bravado. "Nonsense. You can't know that yet, so don't go borrowing trouble." She patted his hand with her free one.

"I could see it on his face. He didn't like what he saw. Wasn't good."

She started to protest again, but the young cardiologist they'd met earlier that morning hustled in. "Here we are." He laid a hand on Rosemary's shoulder as he stepped by her to his seat. Something about the touch held a warning, and her spine stiffened in reaction.

"I know y'all are anxious, and I don't want to keep

you in the dark." A couple of keystrokes brought the screen to life, shedding some light into the room but not reaching Rosemary's fear. "The stress test shows you have three blockages we need to take care of, Mr. Russell. The good news is they're repairable. The bad news is it can't be done with stents."

His words caused a blockage within Rosemary, as well. Her mind stalled as the image on the screen swirled before her eyes. Her body took the opposite reaction, though, as only Eli's grip kept her tethered to the seat when her every impulse was to flee.

"…cardiothoracic surgeon…bypass surgery…" Fragments floated through her head, some snagging on the jagged edges of her immediate fear, others corralled into a dark place where she could take them out later and examine them one at a time. "…eight to ten hours…surgeon preference?"

Into whose hands did they want to place Eli's life? What kind of question was that? "The best," she answered. "Whoever has the most experience and the best track record of success is who we want."

"Well, of course." The cardiologist's grin irritated her. Did he think she'd made a joke? Eli's thumb brushed hers softly, intercepting her angry retort. "All of the surgeons on staff are excellent," the doctor continued, unaware how close he'd come to experiencing her wrath unleashed. "We'll see who's available."

After a few more questions, he led them from the dark room to the first of many stops. Scheduling.

Dr. Heflin's office—the cardiothoracic surgeon Eli chose. Cardiac pre-op questions and counseling. The lab for blood work. The pharmacy, to fill the prescription of nitroglycerin Eli was given for chest pains he might incur over the weekend.

By the time Rosemary fastened her seat belt for the ride home, her head was about to explode from the amount of information and anxiety she had crammed inside. It pushed at her temples and behind her eyes, making her all too aware of the beating of her heart…and Eli's, as well.

"Monday." She cradled her head against the back of the truck seat, determined not to dissolve into the heaping, quivering mass she was on the inside.

"It is what it is, Rosie." She heard the resolve in Eli's voice, felt it in the touch of the hand he laid on top of hers. "Better to do it, and get it over with."

She knew he was right. But three days from now her husband's heart would be stopped, his life placed in the hands of someone she'd just met and a machine with no capability of knowing the importance of the man it would be connected to. The thought chilled her to the bone.

All the way home, they rehashed what the doctors had told them, with Eli filling in many of the gaps she'd missed. Some of the details were frightening, such as a blockage that had been in his heart so long it had created its own bypass. Others gave her some relief. If they hadn't been avid walkers for all these years, he probably would've had a heart attack.

Rosemary managed to keep her composure for the first few minutes at home as her eyes followed Eli all the way to the machine shop. Then she made her way to the privacy of their bathroom, locked the door and collapsed in a heap on the floor.

She cried until she'd let out as much of the frustration and fear as she could push to the surface right then. There was plenty more in the recesses, awaiting its time.

She rinsed her face with cold water until the majority of the redness and swelling were gone. Then she went in search of her phone to call Maggie and tell her the news.

"GOOD LORD, WHEN did you get so stodgy?"

Maggie shook her head in feigned disgust at the shocked look she'd brought to Jeff's features.

"I'm not stodgy." His tone was both amused and defensive. "But, if we get caught—"

"We're not going to get caught, Jeff." She cupped her hand to the bulge her suggestion had created in his golf shorts. "You saw the course marshal wave to us back on seventeen. He was headed the other direction. And that foursome behind us is so slow we'd have to set stakes to make sure they're moving."

Jeff glanced around from the golf cart where they sat, obviously checking out the layout of the cart path leading up to the eighteenth tee box, which sat atop a high hill. A pergola-type structure with flow-

ering vine-covered latticework for sides had been
built at the base of the hill, probably to give shade
to those having to wait to tee off, as well as protec-
tion from wild drives. He wiped a hand across his
eyes and grinned. "You should've been a lawyer.
You make a persuasive argument."

She could tell he was starting to relent, so she
used the advantage and pressed the point home.
"C'mon. It won't take long, and it will feel *so* good."
She added a sexy moan to her voice. "My mouth…
mmm."

Jeff's laugh, the way he responded to her—had
been responding to her for the past two days—was
giving her a heady feeling of power. She unbuttoned
the waistband of his shorts and had the zipper down
halfway when her phone vibrated against her thigh.

Her first instinct was to ignore it, but it might
be Russ. She pulled the phone from her pocket to
check the ID. "Mom," she read, and started to slide
it back to its resting area.

"Take it." Jeff buttoned his shorts and zipped back
up. "We'll save this for later."

"Chicken," she taunted as she removed the phone
from her pocket again and swiped the screen. "Hi,
Mom."

"Hi, darlin'." Mom's voice sounded thick. "Have
I…" She cleared her throat. "Have I caught you at
a bad time?"

Jeff took advantage of the quiet electric cart and
continued on up the path toward the tee box.

"Just trying to do a few things here I can't do at home." She flashed him a wicked grin when her answer drew a shake of his head and a low chuckle.

"Well, I thought I better call and tell you about a situation we have here."

Maggie felt her smile fade. A *situation* usually meant a death or a fire in Taylor's Grove. "What's happened?" Her tone garnered Jeff's attention, eyes full of question.

"Your dad was having chest pains last night, and we went to the ER at Baptist, but his EKG was fine."

"Oh, good."

"Not so good. He had a stress test this morning. They found three blockages and scheduled him for bypass surgery Monday." Her mom rushed out the last words on one breath.

Maggie's hand flew to Jeff's arm, gripping it tightly. "Dad's having open-heart surgery Monday?" The golf cart jostled to a stop.

Her mom's long breath whispered of despair. "Yeah."

"Oh, Mom." Maggie's heart beat to the rhythm of her rising panic, each pulse pushing a new question to the front of her mind. "Has this been going on long? Why hasn't he said something?"

"He evidently noticed a pain when he lifted Mabel's casket last week, but he thought he'd pulled a muscle. Then last night when we were walking, he had pain going uphill but not coming down, so he figured he might have a problem."

"So, it's been going on a week." Frustration at her dad's stubbornness tightened her jaws. "Is there any damage?"

"No, he didn't have a heart attack. They want to fix it before he does."

Maggie's hope latched on to that bit of good news. "I guess that's something." She didn't know when he did it, but Jeff's arm was around her. She leaned into him, accepting the support and comfort he offered. "How's Dad taking the news? Can I talk to him?"

"He went out to the shop as soon as we got home. You know him. He's acting like it's nothing."

"Well." Maggie turned toward Jeff, speaking as much to him now as to her mom. "I'm going back to the hotel and packing up. Then I'll head home." Jeff nodded in agreement and started the cart again.

"It's already late enough in the day that you wouldn't get home until after dark." That was true. Home was a nine-hour drive from where she was now. "And I don't want to be worried about you on the highway by yourself. Just wait and come home tomorrow or Sunday. You can't do anything here, anyway."

"Except be there if you need me…"

The unspoken completion of that statement hung in the silence a couple of seconds before her mom answered in a shaky voice. "We're gonna be fine, sugar."

"I know." She hoped the conviction she'd forced into her own voice sounded genuine.

"Please don't hurry home. We'll just see you when you get here."

"Okay. Give Dad hugs. I'll be there as soon as I can. Love you." Maggie ended the call and slumped back into the seat. "Guess you heard."

Jeff nodded. "Did he have a heart attack?"

"No." She filled him in on the details as they followed the cart path back to the clubhouse and turned everything in.

She handed Jeff the keys on the way to the car. "If you'll drive, I'll call Russ and let him know what's going on."

"I think that's a good idea. He should at least be aware…"

Their eyes met across the top of the car and they nodded to each other before they got in. It was a little odd that, with everything they had argued about during their years together, they had always seen eye to eye when it came to their son.

"Hey, Mom." Russ sounded out of breath when he answered.

"Hey, little man. You doing okay?"

"Yeah. I love it up here. There's so much to do."

Russ sounded happy, which lifted her spirit some. And, although she wanted to have a long conversation and hear all about his doings, right then she needed to deliver her news and get it over with. "I need to tell you about Grandpa." She went through the scenario again, answering his questions and making a point of staying upbeat.

"I'm gonna talk to Coach, and tell him I need to come home."

Russ and his grandpa were very close—she'd worried he'd want to rush to his side. "No, Russ. I don't want you to do that." She firmed up her voice. "You just got there. I mean, you're hardly even settled in yet, and there's nothing you can do at home except sit at the hospital. I'll call you and keep you informed of everything that's going on."

He paused. "Are you okay? There at the house all by yourself?"

Of course. He thought she was back in Taylor's Grove. "Yeah. I'm good." Not exactly a lie. "But I don't think you should call Grandma and Grandpa just yet. They're still pretty emotional. Maybe wait until Sunday?"

A disgruntled sigh drifted through the phone. "Okay. But keep me posted."

"I will. I promise."

They said their goodbyes, and Maggie leaned her head back to relax for just a minute.

Jeff's phone rang, and he looked at the ID. "It's Russ."

JEFF PULLED MAGGIE'S SUV into a restaurant parking lot and stopped. He had to give his complete attention to this conversation to keep from giving away his and Maggie's clandestine getaway.

"Hey, Russ. What's up?"

"Hey, Dad. Mom just called and told me Grandpa

is gonna have open-heart surgery." His son's tone
was heavily laced with concern.

"Wow. I'm sorry to hear that. When's it scheduled for?"

"Monday." Russ paused, and Jeff waited. "I think
I need to go home for it. I'm gonna go talk to Coach
Brimley—"

"I don't think you should do that." His words
caused Maggie's head to jerk toward him, eyes wide
with concern and question. "Your first tournament
next week is the one that will define your place on
the team for this year. You need to be there."

"But, Dad—"

"I know you're concerned, son. But all you'd be
doing would be sitting at that hospital for hours.
This surgery has become pretty commonplace. It's
not nearly as scary as it sounds."

"I know. But it's still dangerous and Grandpa's
old—"

"He's only…what? Sixty-five or sixty-six?"

"That's old, Dad. And something *could* happen."

Of course, sixty-five sounded ancient to their son.
Jeff remembered when it had sounded ancient to
him. "Nothing's going to happen, Russ."

"You can't be sure. We didn't think anything
would happen to Zeke, either. But it did."

Wow. When had his son become so grown-up?
So knowledgeable about life…and death? "I need
to be there for Mom."

Jeff gave Maggie an everything-will-be-okay nod. "Your mother will be fine."

"You didn't see her after Zeke died." Russ's tone was all mature man, sure of himself and with a take-charge attitude. "She took it hard, and it made her... different. She needs somebody besides Grandma around if something happens to Grandpa."

So even Russ could tell something changed with Zeke, though he'd evidently never let on to Maggie. It seemed so unfair that his son had to take on the responsibility of supporting his mom during that kind of crisis. Somebody else should have taken that burden off the then fifteen-year-old.

Jeff's heart squeezed. *He* should have been there for his son and the boy's mother.

Well, he hadn't been. But he could make up for that, at least in part...and garner a few more days with Mags in the process. "Tell you what. You know I'm in Lake Geneva, right?" He'd told Russ all about his plans when he'd made them.

"Yeah."

"How about I extend my vacation a few more days, and I'll go down to Kentucky and take your place?"

"You'd do that?" Russ sounded pleased, but Maggie leaned away from Jeff, shaking her head in protest and giving him a look that said he'd taken leave of his senses.

"It's the least I can do. I wasn't there when you needed me after Zeke's death, but I can be there for you now. I'll be like your representative, keep you abreast of everything."

"That would be so cool, Dad." Relief gave Russ's voice a boyish tinge once again—the way it should be. "You should totally call Mom. I'll bet she'd let you stay with her. I mean, the house is huge."

Jeff could barely keep from holding back the chuckle. "Yeah, well, I'll talk to her, and we'll see if she offers."

Maggie must have known what he was referring to. She rolled her eyes and gave her head a shake of resignation.

"Okay. Well, I feel better, knowing you're gonna be there. Guess I'll stay here, after all."

"Good decision."

"Want me to call Mom and warn her you're gonna call her?"

"No. A warning might give her too much time to think about it." He reached over and took Maggie's hand, giving her a smile. "I think it'd be better if I just talk to her myself."

"'Kay. Good luck. Call me."

"I will. Love you."

"You, too. Bye, Dad."

Jeff ended the call, then pinned Maggie with a direct look. "So...how would you feel about having a houseguest for a few days?"

He wasn't sure if the heavy sigh that pressed through her lips was pleasure or frustration.

Maybe a mixture of the two.

CHAPTER NINE

ONE MINUTE MAGGIE was having fun on the golf course with her ex-husband, and the next minute her world was careening out of control.

Actually, it wasn't *completely* out of control. It was simply out of *her* control and in the hands of Jeff Wells. How had he managed that? With hardly even a nod in her direction, he'd promised Russ he would be there for her dad's surgery, invited himself into her home, changed his flight to Wednesday and called and arranged with his dad to have a few more days off.

"You're not mad at me, are you, Mags?" He pulled back onto the road.

Oh, so now he was concerned about her feelings on the matter?

"I'm not really mad. I'm stunned. I'm confused. I'm upset about Dad. I…I really don't know how I feel." She massaged her temples, which felt good but did nothing to help sort out her feelings. Jeff in Taylor's Grove. Staying at her house. This would be the biggest news to hit the town since Ollie Perkins came out of the closet last year.

"I can stay at a hotel if you'd prefer."

Was he a freaking mind reader? "It's not that I mind you staying at the house, Jeff."

"I need to make up for not being there for Russ—and for you—when Zeke died."

Her heart stuttered. "You think my dad is going to die?"

"No, of course not." He stole a quick glance her way. "Open-heart surgery is an everyday occurrence now. But it's going to be an emotional time. You've acknowledged you're upset. And your mom won't be in any shape for you to lean on her. You need somebody."

"And I appreciate that. But, can you imagine all the talk it'll stir up? Mom and Dad are already upset. Dad's heart will blow, for sure, when he hears you're staying with me. He's liable to drag out his shotgun."

"Like he did the first time?"

Maggie snorted at the old joke. "This time, he'll be running you *out* of town."

"Just listen to me." He brushed the back of his finger down her cheek. "Take away all the stuff that stems from other people. Do *you* want me to stay with you?"

She considered that. "Well, yeah, maybe. I mean, you're right that it's not going to be an easy time to be alone."

He shrugged. "Then where I stay is nobody's

business. But I told Russ I'd be at the hospital for Eli's surgery. That doesn't broker discussion."

"Don't use that tone with me, Jeff," she snapped. "It's *my* family we're talking about. *Everything* about this situation is open for discussion, and you do not seem to be hearing me. So listen now. Mom and Dad won't want you at the hospital. It'll upset them further. You don't even have a name to them when Russ isn't around. You are the son of a bitch to Dad…and that's when he's being nice."

Jeff seemed unfazed by her revelation. "He just thinks Russ doesn't hear it. It's been a running joke between Russ and me since somebody at school told him what the term meant, but that's beside the point. Your dad's going to be knocked out, so there's no way he'll know who was there and who wasn't, unless somebody tells him. If he finds out after his heart is fixed, it shouldn't make any difference. I mean, I don't plan on going into his room and visiting him. I'm simply Russ's stand-in during the longest hours." He reached over and squeezed the hand lying in her lap. "And I want to be there for you, too."

"But tomorrow and Sunday…" She was thinking aloud. "I'll have to go to Mom and Dad's. And to church. People will come by."

"We'll deal with that when and if it happens."

"Of course, we'll have *some* warning." She grasped for a positive. "I have an alarm system on the driveway."

"Why?" He chuckled. "You hide men often?" She could tell he was trying to lighten her mood, and, darn, if it wasn't working.

"Well, you never know when it might come in handy."

"Like this weekend." He pointed to the empty stretch of highway in front of them. "Looks like all's clear to me."

She leaned her head against the window, out of excuses. "You do have to admit, this is all pretty bizarre. I drop my son off at college, hook up with my ex, go with him on a one-day vacation, take him home with me during a family crisis and stow him away in my house like a wanted man."

"So I'm *wanted* now. Interesting." He patted her leg. "Would you quit worrying? Things like this happen all the time in California."

"Pfft. Hollywood, maybe." She shook her head.

"Hollywood's part of California."

She rolled her head in his direction. "You always make everything sound so simple."

"Nothing about life is simple." He grinned and gave her a wink. "Life's like eating an elephant, Mags. The only way to tackle it is one bite at a time."

"Got any steak sauce?" she asked.

"You don't seem yourself, Rosemary." Sue squinted and peered at her, chin buckled in question. "Is everything okay?"

Rosemary wasn't surprised Sue Marsden picked up on the discomforting vibes coursing through her. The woman could sniff out gossip faster than a bird dog on a covey of quail.

Rosemary hadn't wanted to come out tonight for this very reason, but Eli had insisted on life as usual. Soon enough, his condition would be the talk on everybody's lips. Such was the way of life in Taylor's Grove, where your business was your neighbor's business. There was comfort in that, she supposed. For the most part, people discussed others with an attitude of love and concern. Yet, if malice could be interjected, it was usually Sue who saw that it happened.

The park at the center of town was hopping— typical of summer nights in the village, but especially Friday nights when everybody came to greet their neighbors and start the weekend. Eli and his group of closest friends had gathered in the shade of the giant elm tree out by the curb. Unsure of how to answer Sue, Rosemary glanced in Eli's direction just in time to see Tank Wallis pull her husband into a hug.

So the word was out.

Rosemary shook her head. "We found out this morning that Eli has three blockages in his heart. He's scheduled for bypass surgery Monday in Paducah."

"Oh, dear Lord!" Sue's embrace loosened the angst Rosemary had been holding in. Between her emotional state and the men hugging on the other side of the park, it didn't take long for everyone else to begin gravitating toward one of the two groups, asking questions. The news spread like wildfire through dry brush, and within minutes Sawyer O'Malley, pastor of Taylor's Grove's only church, had convened a spur-of-the-moment prayer service on Eli's behalf right there at the park.

Rosemary no longer held back her tears. She let them flow freely in welcomed release, mingling with those of friends who genuinely cared for her and her family. Afterward, she graciously accepted the hugs and pats and general outpouring of love with a heart full of thanks.

"It's miraculous what surgeons can accomplish these days, Rosemary." Bree Barlow sidled as close as her swollen, eight-months-pregnant belly would allow. "Just look at my mom. She's a walking miracle."

Bree's mom, Stella, who'd suffered a traumatic brain injury a year ago, had recently married and moved to Paducah. "Yes, she is," Rosemary agreed. "I sure do miss her, though." Her own Maggie's absence stung fiercely right at that moment, and she gave Bree's hand a motherly pat. "But I love that you and Kale moved into the house. You're infusing new life into Taylor's Grove, and we sure can use that."

"It's a little bit of a drive for Kale." The young woman's eyes scanned the crowd, and Rosemary could tell by the way her face beamed when she'd located her husband. "But the apartment at the marina was just too small to raise a family there. We've hired a young man to help run the place, and he's thrilled with his new 'bachelor pad.'" She scrunched her fingers in the air to form imaginary quotation marks and shrugged. "Everybody's happy."

IvaDawn Carroll moved in on Rosemary's other side with Nell Bradley behind her. As soon as Bree stepped away, Faith O'Malley stepped in to take her place. And so it went. The remainder of Rosemary's time on the square was like a dance jam session with her in the center, changing partners constantly. By the time ten o'clock rolled around and Taylor's Grove started closing down for the night, she was mentally drained and physically exhausted. She headed straight for bed as soon as they got home.

Eli wasn't too far behind, but far enough that he caught her naked as she changed from her clothes into her nightgown. He pressed against her from behind, kissing her ear and fondling her breasts.

"You can't be thinking about sex tonight."

"Not exactly." He turned her around to face him, keeping her encircled in his arms, and gave her a wolfish grin. "I'm thinking about making love. By my recollection it's Friday night."

"Well, yes, but…" She leaned back to see him better. It was true Friday night was—had always been—*their* night. "Surely, you're not serious."

"As a heart attack." His grin twitched. "Sorry. Bad choice of words."

"No, Eli." She pushed free of his embrace and stepped away, snatching up her gown and moving to her side of the bed. "Not in your condition."

"Dadgummit, Rosie." He glared at her, gripping his hips. "My condition's no different than it was two nights ago."

His words fueled the frustration that was taking the place of her fatigue. "Maybe not, but in my head it's different. I know now that you've got blockages, and they might cause you to have a heart attack."

"Got my nitro right here." He shook the small bottle he'd removed from his pocket and placed it on his nightstand.

She was incredulous. "Right in the middle of your coming, you grab your chest and I'm supposed to have the wherewithal to pop a pill in your mouth?"

He laughed and sat down on the bed, thwarting her effort to pull back his side of the covers. "I expect you'll be coming, too."

"Don't be an ass, Eli. No." She tugged the covers loose enough to slip under them. "I'm too upset."

Sullenly, he trudged into the bathroom to brush his teeth, and she lay there trying to sort out all the emotions coiled in her stomach. What if something went wrong during the surgery and her precious Eli died? Tonight could be their last chance to be together. On the other hand, what if she gave in, and he had a massive heart attack? She'd never forgive herself. Scenario after scenario played in her mind—none of them good.

By the time Eli emerged from the bathroom and turned out the light, she was a quivering mess. As he crawled into bed, she scooted over to meet him.

"I'm so scared for you," she whispered, snuggling into the warm side he presented as he raised his arm in invitation.

"Don't be scared, Rosie." He rubbed his hand down her arm. "I'm not gonna leave you."

"I know." She nodded, feeling sure he meant what he said. "Just hold me."

"I will." He kissed the top of her head. "I've no intentions of letting go."

THE OLD, YELLOW farmhouse at the end of the drive was pretty and quaint with flowering window boxes, white trim and a couple of red rockers on the porch. *Homey* was the word that came to mind as soon as Jeff got his first glimpse. It was also lit up like Times Square.

"Looks like somebody's home," he said, rolling down his window to get a good look at the giant oak trees that were older than the century-old house.

"I have the lights on a timer," Mags explained. "I don't like to come home to a dark house way out here."

That was understandable. The city boy in Jeff was half-appalled she would even consider living here by herself, with no close neighbors. Somebody could be lurking in the barn or one of those other outbuildings. He bit back his comments, not wanting to scare her. But he didn't like the arrangement, just the same.

Even the garage was a separate building. They exited it through a side door that led to a beautiful garden area with a stone path running through it. Their rolling luggage clattered against the uneven pavement. The path split off to a stone patio with a hot tub, a fire pit and plenty of seating. "You entertain a lot?" he asked.

"Russ and his friends were here all the time." He heard the wistful timbre in her voice. This homecoming had to be tough for her, made even more difficult by her dad's situation.

"Our house has always been a favorite hangout, winter or summer." She nodded to the huge swimming pool in the side yard and then pointed beyond it into the darkness. "You can't see it tonight, but over there Russ has started mowing a large area and marked it off himself to use as a driving range."

Jeff chuckled. "He told me about that. Said you weren't thrilled with the setup."

She motioned for him to follow her onto the screened-in back porch, another outdoor living space. "I wasn't thrilled with the balls he would shank over into the yard and forget to look for when he was finished." She punched a code into a panel by the back door and he heard the *snick* of the door as it unlocked. "Run over one of those things with the lawn mower, and it can smash out a window."

She pointed at a window at the back corner. "I have firsthand knowledge of that."

The back door led into a giant room that was kitchen, dining room and great room combined. Much more modern than he had expected. "Wow! Did you renovate, or did you buy it like this?"

"I had it done." She pointed to a couple of weight-bearing pillars. "This space used to be chopped up into small rooms. I wanted it open, so I had walls knocked out."

He did a three-sixty to take it all in. "It looks great."

"Thanks. Sitting at the hospital with Zeke all those weeks, I had a lot of time to look at magazines. That's when I started getting ideas about what my own home might look like."

She led him into the front part of the house through a wide hallway that graced the area around the front door. A stairway climbed the left-hand wall with open doorways flanking it front and back. The one in back opened to a large library that also contained a pool table. The one in front was a small sitting room. To the right of the hall was only one door. Maggie opened it to reveal a bedroom suite that took up the entire front quarter of the house. "My room." She turned and gave him a questioning look. "And your room while you're here...if you'd like."

The weight he'd been carrying in his chest lightened some. "I'd like that very much." He hadn't been sure what the arrangements would be once they got back to Taylor's Grove, especially since he'd invited himself.

They wheeled their luggage into a large walk-in closet, which contained two overstuffed chairs and a lamp. He pointed in question.

"This is also a safe room." She showed him the massive steel door pushed back into a pocket in the wall. "There's one upstairs in Russ's room, too. And the basement has a wine cave that doubles as a storm shelter."

He shook his head in mock wonder. "You're certainly prepared for disaster."

"I try to be. I'm a mom."

A twinge of sadness darted through him—sadness that life had dealt her enough disaster that she prepared for it now. A far cry from the carefree girl he'd known all those years ago.

He reached for her, brushing his fingers down her spine. She leaned in and kissed him softly, chasing away the fleeting twinge.

By the time they finished the tour of the house—two full baths and three additional bedrooms upstairs, and another that had been transformed into a game room—it was after one o'clock.

"You want to see the basement tonight, or are you ready to go to bed?" she asked as they came down the stairs.

"I'm exhausted from the drive, but I don't think I can sleep just yet. I need to unwind."

At the bottom of the stairs, she turned and gave

him an awkward glance. "I'm pretty upset about Dad, Jeff. I don't think—"

"Oh, please, Mags." He threw an arm across her shoulders and directed her toward the kitchen. "You think I'd suggest sex after the day we've had?"

The tension released from her shoulders as they dropped in relief. "How about a Scotch on the patio? It might be a fitting end to this day and relax me enough to sleep."

He lifted his eyebrows. "You drink Scotch?"

"Macallan 25."

"The surprises just keep on coming."

They stopped at the bar on the back porch, and she retrieved the bottle and two heavy crystal glasses. "Ice?" she asked, and he shook his head.

"Me, neither." She laughed quietly. "I can't imagine diluting that fabulous peat flavor."

She poured them each a couple of fingers and then cocked her head in question. "How about enjoying this in the hot tub?" Without waiting for a response, she began taking off her clothes. Watching her undress caused his body to stir in spite of his fatigue, so when he undressed there was no place for his erection to hide.

She just grinned and shook her head slightly as she handed him his drink and led him outside.

The temperature of the hot tub was perfect, and the Macallan was perfect. But it was the twinkling fireflies, like tiny living stars, that caused his breath to catch.

"I haven't seen fireflies since I left here."

"Lightning bugs," she corrected with a grin. "They're one of my favorite things about summer."

He followed one in flight, looking up just in time to see a bright shooting star streak across the sky.

"Ooh." Maggie's face broke into a dazzling smile. "Make a wish." She closed her eyes.

He took a sip of his Scotch. It burned a path all the way down into his chest. He didn't need to wish. The only thing he wanted to wish for could never come true.

It was impossible to rewind the past sixteen years.

But if he could, he would handle things…and this woman beside him…much, much differently.

CHAPTER TEN

"MAGGIE!" EMMYLOU'S EXUBERANCE exploded over the phone line and into Maggie's car. "Puh-leeze tell me you're making a serious dent in your shoe budget and not really spending your Chicago time in museums. You want to look at old stuff? I'll let you wax Hiram Caper's back the next time he comes in. Ew! Ew! Ew!"

Maggie made the expected gagging sound as she pulled from her lane onto the county road. "Aw, c'mon, Emmy. You know Hiram saves his fur for that coat you're weaving." Retching sounds met her ear. "Anyway, I'm not in Chicago anymore. I had to come home early. Remember how you thought Dad's color was off last week? Well, you were right." She went on to explain.

"I *knew* it! But, oh, Maggie, I'm so sorry! How's Rosemary doing?"

"She was upset when we spoke yesterday, but I haven't talked to her this morning. I'm headed over there now."

After stewing about it all night, she'd decided that coming clean with her parents about her houseguest seemed like the best plan of action. Jeff agreed, even suggesting he go with her, but she'd declined his offer. The bomb was hers to drop…but she wasn't looking forward to dealing with the fallout.

"Give them hugs from me. And, gosh, you, too," Emmy went on. "You sure didn't need *this* on top of moving Russ and having to put up with Jerk-off Jeff."

Maggie cringed. Emmy had never met Jeff, but over the years, her friend had developed an intense dislike for him, fueled mostly by Rosemary and Eli's skewed opinions. "Jeff and I actually got along pretty well, considering…" She let her voice trail off. There were a couple of different ways she could finish that sentence. *Considering we've gone through a box of condoms since Wednesday night* or *considering he held me close all through the night,* but she didn't want to open up any of that for discussion. Sometime later…not now. It was a conversation that required time…and alcohol…and was sure to be more fun than the version she planned to have with her parents in a few minutes.

Emmy completed the thought. "Considering he's the jerk-off who left you brokenhearted and leery of relationships for years."

Yeah…and that.

"I hope you weren't *too* nice to him," Emmy continued. "Just enough to send him back to California with a painful hard-on every time he thinks about you."

"Well…let's just say I tried." Maggie caught a glimpse of her grin in the rearview mirror.

"Good girl. You want to go out tonight? It'd be good for you. Get your mind off your dad."

"I don't think so, Emmy. After the bustle of the city and the long drive yesterday, I'm ready for a night at home. Maybe watch a movie or something." Sharing part of her actual plans with her friend helped to alleviate some of the guilt she felt for her duplicity. Steaks on the grill, a bottle of wine, maybe a movie, maybe a swim—those were the ideas she and Jeff had tossed about in bed this morning. A nice, quiet evening at home.

"I understand, girlfriend. You need anything from me?"

"Just keep the business out of bankruptcy." Maggie threw up a hand and waved to Nell Bradley as their cars passed.

Emmy snorted. "No chance of that. We've been full to the gills with that back-to-school special. If I have to tell one more kid to sit still, I'm gonna consider adding a Taser to the end of my comb."

"You can't use a Taser on a kid!"

"Not for the kid. I'd zap the mamas. If they'd go sit down and shut their traps long enough for me to do my job, the kids wouldn't be so squirmy."

"Or we could start serving martinis and wine. Jeff told me a lot of the salons in California do that."

"Well, do tell." Emmy gave a boisterous laugh.

"Kentucky bourbon would be more appropriate, I think."

"Or moonshine." The turn onto Main Street came into view, and Maggie flipped on her signal.

"Speaking of which, I've got a new batch made. I'll bring you a jar."

"Apple pie?"

"Yes, ma'am, with whipped cream vodka."

"Mmm. Can't wait." Maggie's mouth watered just thinking about Emmy's spicy, homemade, deliciously deceptive concoction. It tasted nothing like the stuff Jeff's friend Toad used to make in the still he'd built in his barn. But like Toad's, Emmy's could knock a mule on its ass in no time flat. "I'm in Taylor's Grove now, Em. I'll talk to you later, okay?"

"Call me if you need me."

Emmy dropped the call on her end as Maggie made the curve around Yager Circle and turned right on Walnut. A short distance up the road brought her to Baxter Hill and her childhood home. Her mom must've heard her pull up. She was waiting at the door, face furrowed into a frown by the time Maggie made it to the top of the steps.

"You didn't do like I asked, did you? You drove all the way home last night."

Maggie shrugged. "I was anxious to get here."

"I would've been worried sick if I'd known you were out on that highway at night all by yourself."

Maggie wondered which would have actually worried her more—knowing her daughter was on the highway alone or knowing she'd made the trip with her ex in the car with her?

Maggie gave her a quick hug. "And yet here I am, all in one piece. Where's Dad?"

"Here." His signature growl came from the kitchen.

She leaned over and whispered, "How's he doing?"

"Better than me," her mom whispered back as they entered the house.

She found her dad standing at the sink with a cup of coffee poised at his lips. She kissed his cheek and then stood back to take a good look at him. "You look like the picture of health to me." She opted for the lie, trying to contain her fear. Both Mom and Emmy had commented on his color during the past few weeks, but Maggie hadn't seen it until now. *Death warmed over* was the horrifying term that came to her.

He winked, closing a lid over a bloodshot eye that obviously hadn't rested much through the night. "Nothing wrong that getting away from your mom's nagging won't help. I'm kind of looking forward to the vacation." He slurped his coffee noisily.

So he wasn't ignoring the elephant in the room, merely downplaying its size. Whatever device he needed to use in order to cope was okay by her.

"Bet Mom feels the same." She got a cup from the cupboard and poured some coffee. "But I want to hear the details of what's going to happen Monday."

Her dad's grin faltered. "Lots of time to discuss that. First things first. Tell me about my grandson's new home, then you can fill me in on how the son of a bitch is doing."

The way his face flushed to bright red wasn't nearly as alarming as the movement of his hand to the area over his heart. Had he felt a twinge? Merely at the mention of Jeff?

The gesture caused a stall in Maggie's own heart as well as her tongue…and shot her good intentions of a conversation with her parents all to hell.

A heart-to-heart conversation about Jeff was unthinkable until her dad's heart got fixed.

ROSEMARY WATCHED THE subtle changes come over her daughter's face. The normal ivory complexion fluctuated to deep pink while the tension around the eyes softened. Her lips puckered as if kissing an unseen entity.

Oh, dear. This was bad. Very bad.

Rosemary didn't need this on top of everything else she had to worry about. Her breakfast pulled on its army boots and started marching a cadence inside her stomach.

Just as quickly as the changes on her face occurred, Maggie seemed to catch herself, covering her momentary hesitation with a gulp of coffee.

"Russ is in love with Chicago and Loyola, both. He's already made lots of friends, and he and Jeff and another boy and his dad won the parent/child tournament, so he's established a bit of a name for himself." She laughed and wrinkled her nose.

"Mom, you should've seen the ugly lamp he fished out of the trash bin. It's a leg lamp and it's hideous, so, of course, he thought it was the greatest find ever." She laid her hand on her dad's arm. "He wanted to come home for your surgery."

"Dadgummit!" A disgruntled sigh exploded from Eli's lips. "Y'all are trying to make this into a much bigger deal than it is."

"It *is* a big deal, Dad." Maggie's tone sharpened. "And there's no use acting like it isn't. It's open-heart surgery and it's serious. But I did some research yesterday on the way home—"

"How could you do research while you were driving?" Rosemary watched her daughter's eyes widen, and she looked like she had when she was three years old and had just cut her own bangs to a quarter inch.

"I…um…well, not actually *while* I was driving. But I had my tablet with me, so I read about the surgery when I made a rest stop. And this morning." Her eyes darted away as she took another sip of her coffee.

She was lying. Her discomfort niggled at the base of Rosemary's instincts. *Why* would she lie about something so minor?

"Anyway, I didn't want him missing his first match." Maggie shifted the conversation back to Russ. "I promised we'd keep him informed during the surgery."

"I have confidence the doctor knows what he's

doing." Eli stuffed his hand into the pocket of his overalls—his signal that the conversation was over. "Now fill us in on the son of a bitch."

That odd expression flickered across Maggie's face again. It was gone in an instant, but it *had* been there.

"Jeff's fine." She nodded as if agreeing with her own statement. "We got along well. No arguments. No bickering. In fact, being around each other after all this time was probably good for us. We made our peace."

Something in Maggie's tone caused a prickle to tiptoe across Rosemary's scalp, and she realized it was her daughter's *lack* of emotion. The words were too modulated...too controlled.

She tried to ignore the way her gut twisted "What does he look like now?"

A shrug. A sigh. "Handsome as ever. The years have been good to him."

Yes, her tone was too casual. Shouldn't there be *some* disgust or peevishness...something?

Realization dawned and words poured out on a wave of motherly incredulity. "Oh, my Lord, Maggie. Don't."

Maggie's hand trembled as the cup paused halfway to her mouth. "Don't what?"

"Don't be taken in by that boy again."

"He's not a boy. He's thirty-eight."

Aha! A defensive tone. Rosemary's jaw and fists clenched simultaneously. "I don't care *what* he is.

He broke your heart once, and he'll do it again if you let him."

"Oh, for heaven's sake, Mom."

"Dadgummit, Rosemary. I've told you before." Eli's arm swung up to rest on their daughter's shoulder. "Our Maggie wouldn't fall for that lying son of a bitch again. She's too smart. Give the girl some credit."

"I'm not a girl anymore, either, Dad. I'm thirty-seven." Her eyes shifted between them, giving each a level look. "I divorced one husband and buried another, so it's not like I've been living in a cave somewhere."

Worry continued to pummel Rosemary's insides. "I hear your words, but I don't hear any denial."

Maggie rolled her eyes and let her head fall back in exasperation. "Mom, you wear me out."

"See!" Strong alarms were going off now. "Still no denial."

"You just have to ignore your mother right now, Maggie." Eli feigned a sad look and shook his head. "She's had a bad case of optical rectitus ever since we talked to that doctor."

Maggie leaned away from him with a questioning look. "What's that?"

"Optical rectitus?" He grinned. "That's an inflammation of the nerve that runs from the eyeball to the asshole and gives her a shitty outlook on life."

Maggie had chosen the wrong time to finally take a large gulp. As she burst out in laughter, coffee spewed in all directions—including down the front of her dad's favorite overalls.

Irritation bubbled up in Rosemary. Not from the mess—Maggie began cleaning that up immediately—but from the fact they were siding against her, trying to act as if she was way out in left field when every instinct in her told her she was right.

She knew Maggie better than anybody…maybe better than Maggie knew herself.

She glared at Eli, and then a movement outside caught her eye. Stella Fremont was headed up the front walk. Bree Barlow must have called her mother and filled her in on the news of Eli's surgery. It looked as though Stella had a basket of her friendship bread with her.

"Y'all quit your nonsense now. We've got company."

She hurried to greet her friend, glad for the chance to step away from the scary subject for a while.

Even more glad that Jeff Wells was all the way across the country…far away from her daughter at this time when she was especially vulnerable.

FOR THE five-hundred-and-twenty-seventh time, Jeff glanced out the window, hoping to see Maggie's car coming up the driveway, and then chastised himself for being so excited about being with her again. It had been a long day, filled with plenty of activity, so he couldn't really say he was bored…just restless.

Maggie had assured him before she left that no one would come out to her place today because she was still supposed to be in Chicago. Making her appearance in town would be like hanging out a visitors-welcome sign, though, so tomorrow they might have company.

But by then, Eli and Rosemary would know he was here.

He'd set out to clean the house but found very little that needed doing except a bit of dusting. A set of old golf clubs in the garage—Zeke's maybe?—provided a morning of practice on his son's home-made driving range. It occurred to him while he was taking some swings that, if he lived there with Russ and Maggie, he would have built a putting green, as well. But the thought reiterated itself that he *didn't* live there with them, and with that his enthusiasm for using the driving range vanished. He returned the clubs to where he'd found them.

He swam for a while. But soon, his memory had turned to skinny-dipping with Mags two nights ago. Suddenly being in the pool alone wasn't much fun, so he went inside to fix some lunch, settling for a can of soup.

The well-stocked wine cellar was impressive. He recognized some of the vintages as really expensive and rare. Maggie had told him Zeke was a wine snob. She'd made a wise choice hanging on to these bottles. Tonight, they would enjoy the perfect wine to go with whatever she brought home—and he would secretly gloat that he, rather than that bastard Zeke, was getting to share it with her.

Wandering around Russ's room had been a bittersweet self-guided tour. His heart swelled with pride at the ribbons, certificates and trophies proudly displayed. But that same heart also ached because he hadn't been there for the presentation of any of these awards.

Not even the diploma proudly displayed on the desk. That nicked his heart more than any of the rest.

A photo album lay beside the diploma—one of those professional-looking, hard-bound books made available to anyone these days with a computer and a little patience. Russ's senior picture graced the front along with the words *Happy Graduation* at the top and *Love, Mom* at the bottom. The first page contained photos of his son as a newborn with his head full of black hair. Jeff's breath caught and held at a photo of him and Mags holding their new baby boy. So young...so happy. So in love.

Where did the time go?

Russ turning one, his face covered in blue icing from his Cookie Monster cake. Jeff laughed aloud. His parents, the proud grandma and grandpa, were in this photo. Gosh, his mom and dad looked so young there. And Chloe, so beautiful as a young teenager—ten years before the MS started eating away at the nerve coverings in her body, confining her to a wheelchair, slurring her speech to the point few people other than he and his parents could understand her wants and needs.

He didn't begrudge his dad's early retirement to help Mom take care of Chloe in their own home. He didn't begrudge having to step in and run the dealership and the pressure of making sure the profit could sustain the entire family.

But he did begrudge the damn disease that had limited how his sister could live her life when she should've had the freedom to soar.

And he begrudged all those times he'd wanted to spend more time with his son but keeping the family financially afloat had taken priority.

The next page showed Russ at two. The divorce hovered unseen in the background but was evident. No more pictures of him and Mags together. He moved on through page after page, year after year. No more pictures of him at all.

Eighteen years of his son's life, and he was only present for the first four pages.

An anguished cry rose into his throat and seeped out of the corners of the mouth he tried to keep closed.

Oh, he had his own photos of Russ's birthday parties—the ones they celebrated when he came to California, which were never actually on his birthday. Instead, most of them took place in August before he'd have to return to Kentucky to start the school year. But it wasn't the same.

And it wasn't the birthday photos that bothered him the most. It was Russ playing soccer, shooting a basket, giving it his all at Little League football, participating in the junior high spelling bee, eating ice-cream cones with his friends in the back of a pickup truck. Fishing with Zeke. Enjoying watermelon on Rosemary and Eli's porch.

The everyday photos laid his heart wide-open, but he looked at them, anyway. Slowly he made his way through every page, memorizing the little details so he could pretend he'd been there, too.

By the time he got to the end, he felt drained. Maybe time for a nap? He couldn't recall the last time he'd lain down in the middle of the afternoon.

He started down the steps when a light buzzing noise sounded. An alarm of some kind. Mags had mentioned an alarm that let her know when a car had turned into her driveway. She was home! He took the remainder of the steps two at a time, fully awake now and ready to welcome her.

Oh, hell! The car that passed the window on its way to the back of the house wasn't the one he'd been expecting—it was a red Scion FR-S.

He ducked into Maggie's bedroom and peeked out the window as the car came to a stop.

A redhead emerged with huge white sunglasses and hair held back with a wide black band. She went straight for her trunk on legs so long they must've

started at her armpits and were made even longer by
the short shorts and high wedge sandals she wore.
When she leaned over to retrieve the items from her
trunk, her more-than-ample cleavage threatened to
spill out of the formfitting top with the low, low,
low neckline.

EmmyLou Creighton. He recognized her from
Maggie's vivid descriptions of her best friend.

She straightened up with her arms full of bags.
Groceries? It ran through his mind that she could
just be acting as a thoughtful friend, stocking Maggie's fridge with some items to tide her over. But
she might also be planning on dinner.

Damn! What should he do? Had she talked with
Mags yet? Did she know he was here? She was a
blabbermouth. He could tell that from the stories.
Could he risk her knowing he was here before he
was sure Maggie had told her parents? He sure as
hell didn't want them hearing it secondhand.

He patted his pockets, intending to text Mags and
ask for guidance. Where was his freaking phone?

Damn it! He'd left it by the pool.

Just to be on the safe side, he ducked into the
closet Mags had shown him last night. If Emmy-
Lou knew he was here, she would probably call out
his name. And, if she didn't know, he could wait
here until Mags got home and either got rid of her
or explained the situation.

He heard the back door open and close, so she
knew the combination. She was singing—well,

bellowing—a Katy Perry song at the top of her lungs, which made him doubt she knew he was there.

He flopped down in one of the chairs, irritated by the situation. Surely, Mags would be home soon.

With no phone and no books or magazines, the singing soon became his only source of entertainment, and even that quieted some after a while. He started to doze and closed his eyes, giving in to the nap he'd considered earlier.

A shriek startled him awake!

He jumped up just in time to catch a heavy shoe box slung against the side of his face. The corner caught him in the eye, and he grunted in pain. "Wait! Stop!" He flung up his arms to ward off the next hit, but she fooled him and came in with an underhand to his genitals. He crumpled over in a defensive move. "Don't! EmmyLou!"

Hearing her name brought her up short. She paused and gave him a wary look. "Do I know you? How do you know my name?"

He held his hands up in surrender, trying to catch his breath between the streaks of agony pulsing through his groin.

"I'm Russ's dad." He leaned his hands on his knees and managed to get to a standing position. "I'm Jeff Wells, Maggie's ex."

"You're Jeff Wells?"

"Yes." He gave a relieved laugh and wiped his hand down his face. His focus returned just in time to see the fury that lit the redhead's eyes right before she hauled back and boxed him again...this time in the stomach...with her fist.

CHAPTER ELEVEN

MAGGIE'S SHOULDERS SLUMPED in defeat when she spotted her friend's car in the driveway.

Here comes another lecture.

Emmy would be all over her because she hadn't told her about her houseguest. She blew out a long breath at the irony. Her mom would have been all over her if she *had* told her the truth. Damned if she did; damned if she didn't. That pretty much summed up the way her life had been going of late.

She pulled into the garage and retrieved the groceries from the backseat. The homegrown tomatoes from the region used to be one of Jeff's favorites. She'd bought enough for him to enjoy the entire time he would be here.

Angry shouts met her as she opened the back door.

Emmy's voice! What in the world…?

She followed the sound toward her bedroom.

"…not to mention all those years she spent waiting for you to come back."

Oh, Emmy, please shut up!

But she didn't.

"How do you walk out of someone's life like that—someone you made a vow to stay with forever and had a child with? How do you live with yourself? You're the kind of guy who gives all the rest of them a bad name!"

Maggie found them—or at least Emmy—standing in the doorway of her bedroom closet.

"What in heaven's name is going on here?"

Emmy spun around, eyes wide in surprise. "I... um..." Then the eyes narrowed suspiciously. "Why didn't you tell me the jerk-off was here?" She threw up her hands and stomped past Maggie, out of the room.

Maggie stormed after her, talking to her back all the way to the kitchen. "Emmy. Calm down. I didn't tell you because I haven't told anyone. Russ was upset about Dad's surgery, and he wanted to come home for it. We didn't want him to do that, so Jeff promised him he'd be there in his place."

Emmy leaned a hip against the kitchen island and crossed her arms. "And, of course, he talked you into letting him stay here." Her eyes shifted and focused above Maggie's head.

"Yes, I did. And maybe that was a mistake."

Turning at the sound of Jeff's voice behind her, she gasped at the sight. "Oh, my God! What happened to you?"

The area around his left eye was an angry red, and it was swollen enough that the eye was closed.

"I hit him with those boots I borrowed." Emmy

didn't sound the least bit contrite. "I went to put them in the closet, and he scared me—hiding in there like a pervert burglar—so I let him have it with the box to his face."

"And the nuts," Jeff added, eliciting another gasp of horror from Maggie.

She'd left her house six hours ago as a peaceful sanctuary and returned to find it a free-for-all.

"And then I punched him in the stomach." Emmy shrugged. "Just for general purposes."

"You've got quite a punch." Jeff rubbed his stomach and the side of his mouth twitched with mirth. "Ever think of going into the ring?"

He was acting like this was a big joke? Maggie was aghast. The skin around his freaking eye was beginning to turn blue.

Emmy's hands went to her hips, and she struck a pose. "Ever hear of kickboxing, jerk-off? How do you think I got a smokin' body like this?"

Oh, good Lord. Maggie yanked open a drawer and pulled out a plastic storage bag to fill with ice.

"In California, it generally takes several surgeries to achieve those results."

That brought a snicker from Emmy, and the tension in the room kicked down several notches.

Maggie handed Jeff the bag of ice. From another drawer Emmy pulled out a dishcloth to wrap it with and tossed it to him.

"Thanks." He nodded to both of them.

"Well." Maggie clapped her hands together. "I

realize this is a tad late, but Emmy, this is Russ's dad, Jeff Wells. Jeff, my best friend, EmmyLou Creighton."

Jeff grinned and stuck out his hand. "Glad to make your acquaintance, EmmyLou."

Emmy grinned back as she took his hand. "I'm still reserving judgment. But you only grunted when I hit you in the balls instead of squealing, so I'll give you that."

Jeff laughed, probably not realizing Emmy actually meant what she said.

Her friend's eyes came to rest on Maggie then and her face sobered. "So you want to fill me in on all the specifics now? You went to Chicago to move your son to college and finished that by hooking up with your ex?"

Heat flashed in Maggie's chest and started creeping up her face. "I…um…" She didn't want to lie to Emmy, but how would Jeff feel about her discussing it just yet?

His arm came around her shoulders and gave her a squeeze. "Yep. That's pretty much the way it happened. We discovered the attraction was still there, so we just decided to go with the moment."

"Really?" Emmy squealed and danced in place a few steps, drumming the granite countertop with her fingers. "That is *so* cool! Just like in the movies!"

"Now, Emmy," Maggie cautioned. "Don't go letting your imagination run away with this. We simply decided the grudge match had gone on long enough, and it was in everybody's best interest— especially Russ's—to let it go."

"So you've buried the…*hatchet*, so to speak?" Emmy's eyebrows shrugged to emphasize her meaning.

Maggie rolled her eyes. Only then did she take a good look around the kitchen. "Did you bring food with you?"

Her friend sniffed. "The makings for tacos and margaritas. I thought you were going to be lonely."

"Tacos and margaritas sound great."

Maggie caught the genuine enthusiasm in Jeff's voice.

"Well, I'll just leave this stuff with y'all, then." Emmy waved a hand toward the items she'd brought. "Enjoy."

Maggie shot Jeff a questioning look, and he responded with a nod. "Stay, Emmy," she said. "We'll fix the tacos and have a nice supper out on the patio."

Emmy paused and shook her head. "Y'all probably want to be alone."

"You might as well stay." Jeff snorted. "You've probably put me out of commission for a few days, anyway." They all laughed together, and then Maggie felt Jeff's hand on her shoulder again. "C'mon, Emmy, stay," he insisted. "I need to find out if all those tales Maggie told me about you are true."

Emmy directed a pointed look Maggie's way, and Maggie nodded.

"Well, okay. You talked me into it." She shifted her gaze to Jeff and arched an eyebrow. "And I intend to find out the same about you, so just get yourself ready."

"CALL ME EVERY couple of hours Monday, you hear?" Emmy shifted her car to Reverse and continued talking as she backed around Jeff and Maggie. "And if you need me to take you to the airport Wednesday, Jeff, let me know. I love Nashville. I'll use any available excuse to spend some time there."

"Thanks, I will." Jeff hoped Maggie could take him, but it would depend on how well Eli was doing by then. Emmy volunteering as his backup ride relieved him of *that* worry.

But right then, a different worry inhabited prime residence in his mind. What had started as a niggle with their first ride to Loyola last Tuesday had blown into a full vexation during Emmy's tirade this afternoon. He would have to broach the subject carefully and not give Mags the chance to dismiss it. And if she did, he would insist.

He needed an answer.

Emmy threw a wave out the window as she stepped on the gas, and they waved their goodbye to her taillights.

"Whew!" Jeff ran his hand across the back of his neck. "Does her mouth ever close?"

Maggie shook her head. "Dad says Emmy is probably incapable of farting because her mouth doesn't stay closed long enough to build up any pressure."

Jeff guffawed. Only Eli could come up with something that outlandish. "I'll bet she and your dad are a hell of a mess when they get together."

"I get stomach cramps from laughing at them."

He rested his arm around her waist as they walked, subtly directing her toward the patio where they'd been relaxing all evening. He wanted to keep her that way—relaxed and open.

"I'm sorry about your eye." She glanced up and protruded her bottom lip in sympathy. "Does it hurt much?"

"Naw," he lied, and then thought better of it. If he wanted complete honesty from Mags, he needed to set the tone. "That's not true. It hurts like hell." The swelling had completely closed the eye, which made his depth perception wonky, and the bruise reached from his eyebrow to his cheek. "But I'll live."

"I'll get you more ice." When Maggie pulled away toward the house, he caught her and pushed her gently into a chair.

"You sit. I can get my own ice."

He went in and filled the bag again. Spotting the mason jar of Emmy's moonshine, he grabbed it and a couple of shot glasses from the bar.

Mags turned at the *clink* of the glassware on the

table and raised an eyebrow. "That stuff will rid you of any pain you might be feeling."

"That's what I'm counting on." He started to pour.

"Half shots. And sip. Don't gulp," she warned as he handed her a glass.

He followed her lead and took a small sip, expecting a punch to the stomach similar to the one Emmy gave him earlier. What he got instead was a burst of cinnamon, sweet and satiny. "Wow!" He drew back and looked at it through his good eye. "That's smooth."

"Hence the danger." Mags wagged a finger at him. "I'm telling you, it's a wolf in sheep's clothing. Two shots deep and you can't keep your head up. Despite the yummy taste, the main alcohol ingredient is still Everclear."

A heron glided overhead in the direction of the pond at the back of the property. Jeff watched it, feeling the warmth of the drink starting to work its magic. He laid the ice pack to the side and reached out to take Maggie's hand.

She started to smile but it quickly faded. "What?" she asked.

"Emmy's last punch—the one to my stomach— came *after* she knew who I was. She said some things…"

The deep breath left her lungs on a slow, audible sigh. "Yeah. I heard."

That sounded like a confession, and the truth pressed against his chest wall. "She said *years*,

Mags. That you waited for years, expecting...hoping I'd come back."

"Yes, it's true. I was still in love with you long after we split up."

"I thought you hated me." He worked hard to isolate his frustration and shove it out of the conversation. "When I left, you didn't even come out to say goodbye. You sent your mom out with Russ."

"Because I didn't *want* to say goodbye." She glanced away, searching the darkness. "Don't get me wrong. I wanted you to go." Her eyes came back and rested on his. "I needed some peace in my life. What we were doing to Russ with the constant arguing terrified me. He'd started to stutter, if you remember..."

"Yeah, I do." Jeff had tried hard to forget that, but he'd watched his son's speech patterns cautiously until he was in the fourth or fifth grade.

"That was my breaking point." Mags got the shot glass halfway to her lips and then put it back down. "I'd already failed as a wife, and I was failing as a mother, too. Something had to give. I thought you and I were too far gone to fix. Letting you go seemed like the only answer."

Jeff's attention caught on the regret implied by the word *seemed*, but before he could question it, she went on.

"After you left, I slept for days. Didn't eat. Didn't bathe. Refused to see anybody...including Russ. Until Mom finally shamed me back into the world of the living. But, even after everybody else thought I was okay, I still cried myself to sleep at night for a long time. Letting you go physically was one thing, but letting you go with my heart…that took years."

His heart compressed. "But you did? Right?" He held his breath, not sure which answer he wanted.

"I finally decided I was making myself crazy, and I needed to move on. I went to Pastor Sawyer for counseling."

Jeff remembered the kind pastor. They'd gone to him, two kids scared out of their wits, and he'd immediately agreed to marry them. No lectures… no condemnation.

"He convinced me to give myself permission to love again."

The air stuttered in Jeff's lungs.

"Zeke came along about that time. He was fun… very indulgent, like Mom and Dad. He treated me like a queen and adored Russ. I jumped in with both feet, thinking it was my new acceptance of myself that I was celebrating." She paused. "Later, I realized I was trying to make up for lost time. Trying to get my twenties back as I approached my thirties." She shook her head. "I think he saw me as a challenge—someone who needed to be shaken out of her lethargy—and he thought he could be what I needed, only to realize too late that he couldn't. I was way past believing in the fairy tale."

And what about now?

The question was poised on the tip of his tongue.

He took a sip to dislodge and wash it away, yet it remained even after he swallowed.

But he saw the look in Maggie's eye, understood that she'd correctly deciphered his unspoken message. She paused and leaned toward him slightly, preparing to speak again, pinning him with her direct, unblinking gaze, and his body became all ears, open and ready to absorb what she said.

She licked her lips, and then her mouth formed sounds he heard and understood.

"And you should be, too," she said.

WHAT WAS HE EXPECTING?

Jeff was far from being drunk, but he'd had enough alcohol for his defenses to be lowered. Disappointment flashed in his eyes, and her gut twisted with panic, away from that corner he was trying to push her into.

She jerked her hand from his grasp. "We had an agreement, Jeff. This week was supposed to be fun and relaxing. A time to clear up lingering issues, not create more."

"I just thought—" He reached for her hand again, and she pulled it from his reach to rest it on the arm of her chair.

"What? That a few nights together would change everything? Fix everything that was broken?"

"Well." He shrugged. "They have, haven't they? I mean, I feel like we've made a lot of progress."

"We've managed to spend six whole days together

without having a big fight, if that's what you mean…
unless, of course, this escalates." She crossed her
arms over her chest.

"I'm not trying to start a fight." He pointed to
his eye. "One is plenty, thanks. But I'm trying to
be honest with you about how I feel. And how I feel
is that maybe the two of us gave up too quickly."

No, no, no!

"Did you not hear anything I just told you? I
didn't give up quickly. It took me years to give up,
and I'm not about to open myself up to the possibility of falling back in love with you. We've moved
on—literally. We live all the way across the country from each other. This—" she wagged her index
finger between them and then caught it with her
thumb to form an O "—has a zero percent chance
of becoming anything more than great sex with a
former spouse." She pushed out of her chair and
paced to the edge of the pool, needing distance and
breathing room.

Jeff followed, obviously not understanding why
she moved…or not caring.

Why was she not surprised?

His hands rested on her shoulders, and he tried
to turn her toward him. "Mags—"

She wheeled around and flung his arms away
from her. "I mean it, Jeff. I don't need this. I moved
my son to Chicago last week. I came home to find
my dad facing major surgery. I don't need anything
that adds pressure to my life. I have plenty as it is.

And, if that's where you're going with this, go get your bags 'cause we're driving to Paducah and getting you checked into a hotel right now."

"Mags." His hands came back to her shoulders with a firmer grip, and he bent down to look her in the eyes. "I'm sorry. You're right. I lost my senses there for a moment. I'm not trying to add any more pressure to your life. I came here to be supportive— someone you could lean on during a difficult time." He dropped his arms to encircle her and pull her close. The fingers of one hand crept into her hair and coaxed her head against his chest while the other made slow circles on her back. "I want to be the safe room where you can go and not be afraid. I'm sorry if I upset you."

She closed her eyes and relaxed against him, feeling all the pent-up emotion of the day drain away. It had been forever since she'd leaned on anyone, and it wasn't something she did easily. But it felt pretty good.

"I'm sorry, too," she said. "I should take it as a compliment that the idea of reconciliation would enter your mind. Most couples find it hard to even speak to each other after divorce."

"We were never like most couples." He kissed the top of her head and tightened his hold, and she allowed herself, at last, to hug him in return.

"Not sure if that's a good thing or a bad thing."

His hand came around and a finger nudged her chin up, bringing her eyes to meet his. "Why?"

"Society sets the rules for most couples. They spend the remainder of their lives nursing an intense dislike for each other. We're winging it into uncharted territory."

Jeff smiled and gestured toward the sky with a dramatic, sweeping motion. "'To boldly go where no man has gone before.'"

Maggie sighed in relief. The playfulness was back. She shrugged her eyebrows suggestively. "Want to go do a little role-playing in bed? You can be Spock and I'll be Lieutenant Uhura?"

Jeff's face turned somber. He held up his hand and parted his fingers in the Vulcan salute. "'Live long and prosper.'" He closed the salute by caressing her nipple through the top she wore.

And if she had any lingering doubt about his answer, he closed his mouth to hers in a kiss that carried her far out into space.

CHAPTER TWELVE

AT SIX-FORTY-FIVE Monday morning, Maggie pulled up in front of the Twenty-Four Hour Café in Paducah. Always open and about a mile from the hospital where her dad's surgery would be performed—the perfect rendezvous point for her and her ex.

"By the time you eat and make the walk to the hospital, they should've taken him back." She put the car in Park and turned toward the passenger seat. "I'll text you if they're running late."

He nodded. "Okay."

As soon as her dad was out of danger, she'd tell her mom about Jeff. Probably not until tomorrow. But any hope of pulling off this silly—but necessary for now—charade rested in the details. "Where are you staying, if she asks?"

"Out by the mall," he shot back the rehearsed answer.

"And when did you get here?"

"Late last night. I drove in from Lake Geneva after talking to Russ, but I'd advised him not to say anything to his grandfather, so Eli wouldn't get upset."

"We'll be cordial, but not overly friendly…"

"So any talk about having sex the past four nights is off-limits."

"Jeff, I'm not in a joking mood." Her breath pushed out in a huff as he leaned over and brushed a kiss to her lips.

"He's going to be fine, Mags. I'll see you in about an hour."

He left her with an assuring nod, and she made the short drive to the hospital.

Her parents were just checking in when she joined them. An onlooker would have thought her mom was the one facing surgery. She looked as sickly as Maggie had ever seen her, and Maggie realized she was indeed sick—with fear. Her face was pale without makeup, and her eyes were red and swollen likely from crying or lack of sleep—or both.

Her dad on the other hand was the picture of calm. Smiling and joking as if he hadn't a care in the world—a bravado Maggie recognized as fake but appreciated just the same.

They took him back for prep work, which didn't take too long. And then Maggie and her mom were allowed to wait with him as the first drugs began taking effect, and he became groggy. His mouth drew up in a loopy grin. "When this's done, gonna retire, an we're gonna travel the world, Rosie. See the sigh's."

"That'll be fun, Eli." Her mom's smile wavered,

and Maggie wondered if her dad could see the lack of belief in her eyes as she smoothed her fingertips across his forehead, readjusting the cloth surgery cap. "Always wanted to see the Grand Canyon."

"We'll go an' ri' one of them donkeys to th' bot'm." Raising and lowering his eyelids seemed to be an effort. "Then we'll hel'copper out."

Maggie squeezed his hand. "You be good in surgery, Dad. Don't give them any trouble."

"Jus' hope th' doc ain't a damn Yankee." His eyes closed, and she thought it was for good this time, but he surprised her by cracking the right one just a little. "If I coul' kee' my eye ope', I'd tal' to ya through m' eye." Maggie chuckled at the nonsense, glad it meant he was relaxed and feeling no pain. "See ya la'er, ladies." The eyelid drooped again. "Love ya."

"Love you, too." Her mom laid her hand over his heart for a moment, then gave him a pat. Her shoulders rose and fell with a shudder as the nurse came to take him back to surgery.

"We'll call the waiting room and let you know how he's doing," the young man assured them. "But this surgery takes a long time, so don't get nervous if you don't hear from us for a while."

They watched until the last corner of the bed conveying her dad disappeared around the corner of the long corridor, then she gave her mom a reassuring hug. "It's going to be a long day. Did you eat breakfast?"

Her mom shook her head. "I couldn't eat anything."

"Do you feel like eating now? Want to go to the cafeteria and grab a bite?"

"No. Maybe later."

They entered the waiting room, leaving their names with the elderly volunteer at the desk who was manning the phone, and staked their claim in an unoccupied corner, away from the other four groups of families gathered in small clusters.

Maggie had brought a book and several magazines, which she offered, but again her mom shook her head. "I can't concentrate right now."

Pastor Sawyer and his wife, Faith, showed up a few minutes later. Their calming presence acted like a soothing balm for which Maggie was immensely grateful—especially when Jeff walked in and she heard her mom bristle, "What in the world is *he* doing here?"

Maggie was fairly certain *world* would have been replaced by *hell* had Pastor Sawyer not been there. She herself let out a surprised gasp that could have won an Academy Award. "I have no idea."

Jeff spotted them, sauntering over with his hands in his pockets. "Hello, everyone." He nodded as he made eye contact, not lingering on Maggie any longer than anyone else.

"You're not welcome here, Jeff Wells," her mom snapped, and jerked her head around to cast an accusing glance at Maggie. "Did you talk to him?"

Before she could answer, Jeff spoke up. "Russ

called me. He was upset and wanted to come home for his grandpa's surgery. I was in Lake Geneva playing golf, and I had a few more days off, so I volunteered to be his substitute. And before anyone has to ask—" he pointed to his black eye "—I got clubbed by a guy trying out a new iron in the pro shop."

"Man, that's a shiner!" Sawyer shook his hand warmly and clapped him on the shoulder. "It's good to see you again, Jeff. We'll consider your presence here a blessing on your son's behalf."

Her mom gave a disgruntled humph.

"It's been a long time." Faith hugged him but threw a questioning look toward Maggie, who gave her an assuring nod.

"How's Russ doing?" Maggie asked. "I've been trying not to call him."

Jeff nodded. "He's okay. Worried, of course."

Maggie glanced at her mom, noting how the muscle twitched in her jaw. "You want to join us?" She motioned to the vacant chair beside her mom, who shifted as far toward Maggie as the chair arm would allow.

"Sure." As he sat, he threw a surreptitious wink Maggie's way, and she blinked in return.

Her mom stared sullenly out the window, too much of a lady to make a scene but not trying to hide her fury. One thing was for certain, though— Jeff's presence had brought color back to her cheeks.

They burned fiery red.

ROSEMARY KNEW THE earthquake was only inside her, but it seemed as though her whole world was being shaken apart. At the same time, the entire situation felt like an out-of-body experience—as if she'd somehow escaped the ludicrous position and could float above it all and look down on its absurdity.

Jeff Wells, the person from their past she most wished never to see again, was sitting next to her, chatting as if he hadn't been absent from their lives for more than a decade. Older, still handsome, though not nearly so cocky, which was a terrible thing now she thought about it. Losing that king-of-the-world attitude made him all the more desirable, which might cause Maggie's head…and heart…to turn toward him again.

Bad. Very bad.

On the other side, Maggie read, aloof and uninterested, practically ignoring him except when he pulled her into direct conversation, which generally focused on Russ and last week's move. The lack of emotion on Maggie's part was the scary thing.

Curse at him. Throw books. Scratch his good eye out, Rosemary wanted to say. *Just give me a glimpse of the old Maggie. I don't trust this one who acts untouched by anything that happens. The one who suffers in silence. She's the one most likely to withdraw from the world again…because she's already halfway there.*

"Mom." Maggie nudged her with an elbow and nodded toward the old man at the desk. "He's paging us. We're here!" She waved.

"Russell family?"

Rosemary nodded and hurried over to the phone he held. "Hello? This is Rosemary Russell."

"Hi, Ms. Russell. Are you Eli's wife?"

"Yes." Her pulse thrummed in her ears.

"This is Diane. I'm assisting with Mr. Russell's surgery. I wanted to let you know he's on the cardiopulmonary bypass machine now. I'll call you when they take him off, but that won't be for a few hours. He's doing well."

Eli's heart was stopped, his life cradled in the tubular arms of an uncaring machine.

Her own heart did a somersault. "I'm—I'm glad to hear that," she lied. Gladness was not an emotion she could apply to the most terrifying words ever said to her. "Thank you."

Back at her seat, she gave everyone the news, which was received with enthusiasm. Sawyer led them in a brief prayer, and then all her companions got on their phones and spread the news of Eli's condition.

Let them take care of it. She didn't want to talk to anybody—except Eli.

"Now might be a good time to get something to eat." That was Jeff…taking control.

"I'm not hungry." She refused to look at the interloper.

An awkward moment followed and then Sawyer said, "That's a good idea. I'm getting hungry myself."

"Why don't you go, too, Maggie," Faith suggested. "I'm not hungry just yet. I'll stay here with Rosemary."

Maggie gave Rosemary a questioning look, and she gave her daughter a reluctant nod.

"We can bring you something if you like," Jeff offered.

"I *said*, I'm not hungry." She gave him a glare that should've withered a hardened criminal.

Not this one. He shrugged and had the audacity to allow the corner of his mouth to twitch. "Maybe later, then."

She watched them out the door. "I don't like this, Faith."

"That's obvious." Faith moved over to the chair beside her and took her hand. "I imagine you don't like anything happening today, though."

"You know, he and Maggie were in Chicago together all last week, and now he shows up here this morning out of the blue. He hasn't been back to Kentucky since Russ was five, yet he's here today. It just smacks of…of…something I don't like."

Faith's laugh was light as she squeezed her hand. "I'll tell you the same thing I told Stella last year. Let's accept those healing vibes whatever direction they come from."

"I saw the vibes Jeff gave my daughter when they

split up." Rosemary shuddered at the memory of Maggie in her dark bedroom, drapes drawn, blinds closed, as if letting light into the room would make the pain more visible...more acute. "They weren't the healing kind, trust me."

"I remember."

Of course she would. *Everyone* in Taylor's Grove would remember.

"Things change, though."

Gah! Faith seemed determined to talk about this.

"Maybe some healing *did* take place last week, Rosemary. I mean, they seemed to tolerate each other pretty well this morning. And Maggie didn't turn down the opportunity to go eat lunch with him."

"I don't want things to heal between them." Rosemary bristled. "What I want is for Jeff Wells to go back to California and leave my daughter alone."

"That's your head talking. Your heart knows it would be better for everybody—especially Russ— if those two could forgive and move on."

The mention of Russ shot a pang of guilt through Rosemary. Her grandson had always been such a trouper when it came to his parents. He loved them both equally. Worshipped his mom. Idolized his dad. And the Wells family never shirked in any responsibility when it came to Russ. They lavished him with attention and gifts. If possible, he'd been even more spoiled than Maggie.

"It's the moving-on part I want to see happen," she answered.

"Well, then..." Faith leaned her head against Rosemary's. "Let's just hope everybody's heart heals right along with Eli's."

The mention of her husband brought Rosemary back to the present and today's worry. If Eli came through this okay, *maybe* she would work on forgiving Jeff Wells.

But it wasn't going to happen today.

Or anytime in the near future.

JEFF'S PHONE PINGED.

On my way.

He caught the waitress's eye and signaled for the check, which she brought to him along with the sack of carryout. He paid the bill and went outside the café to wait for his ride.

When Maggie pulled up, he went around to the driver's side and opened the door, holding up the bag. "The burger and fries are still hot. Let me drive, and you can eat."

"Ooh, thanks." She snatched the bag and relinquished the driving duty without a fuss. Once she got buckled in on the other side, she unwrapped the sandwich and flipped back the bun, flashing him an astonished grin. "I can't believe you remembered!"

"Mustard, pickles, lettuce and onion." He laughed. "Burgers were our staple back in the day. How could I forget? So how's your dad doing?"

The nurses' reports throughout the day had been good. Eli had done well and the surgery had been successful. When the family was told he was regaining consciousness and they could go back to see him, Jeff had decided it was time to make his exit. He'd walked back to the café where Maggie had dropped him off that morning and waited there for her to come pick him up.

"He looks great." She dove into the burger with gusto, filling him in on her dad between bites. "He was alert and not talking out of his head. The doctor said he'd probably move into a regular room tomorrow. And Mom asked about a cot to sleep on. He said there'll be a recliner in the room that goes all the way down into a bed, so she can stay as many nights as she wants."

"How many do you think that will be?"

"As long as he's in here, probably." She juggled the cheeseburger to the other hand so she could pat his leg. "But getting that guest room for her tonight was a stroke of genius. I can't believe I hadn't thought to check on the possibility."

"When my uncle had his heart surgery, my aunt stayed in one. I figured other hospitals had them available, too."

"Well, it won you some hard-earned brownie points, that's for sure. From Mom *and* me."

"That's not why I did it. I couldn't stand the thought of her sleeping on that couch in the waiting room after enduring such a long, exhausting day." He smiled to himself at the small victory, though. Throughout the day, Rosemary had turned down everything he'd offered from food and drinks to magazines and newspapers. But when he'd inquired about available guest rooms for the family of patients and secured her the last one, her shocked gratitude had been genuine.

"When Dad talked to Russ, I nearly lost it." Maggie fished a French fry out of the sack and held it to his lips. He took it, letting his teeth graze her fingers. "Don't bite the hand that feeds you, mister."

"Not biting. Just nibbling," he corrected. "And yeah, when I talked to Russ he was pretty excited his grandpa sounded so good, but he got a little choked up."

Rather than heading straight for the highway, which would have been the fastest route home, Mags directed him through town, pointing out things that had changed since he'd last seen the area. Paducah had always seemed like a nice, small city, and he'd often lamented that they hadn't moved there rather than staying in Taylor's Grove next door to Eli and Rosemary. A little distance from her parents may have been all they needed to give them a fighting chance, but now, they'd never know.

They rode in amiable silence for a while, and he didn't try to push her into conversation. The day had been physically and emotionally tiring. A good, long soak in the hot tub with a wee bit of Scotch was on his agenda.

"Do you think we pulled it off?" She broke the stillness, at last.

"I think so."

They laughed and talked the rest of the way home about the close calls they'd had throughout the day, how they'd covered well and agreed no one seemed the wiser.

"Thank goodness Sue Marsden was busy today." Mags finished her burger, wadding up the paper it was wrapped in and tossing it back into the bag. "I'm not sure we could've fooled her. She has a knack for rooting out gossip, even when there isn't any."

Jeff remembered Sue's vicious reputation for spreading the word. That was one thing he didn't have to put up with in San Diego. Living in the city afforded him a nice bit of anonymity.

He made the turn onto Maggie's lane. Through the foliage of the trees, he saw the lights of the house—a welcoming sight. He could almost feel that hot water surrounding his body and the Scotch burning his tongue.

He'd just made the turn into the driveway when Maggie let out a shriek.

"Oh, no!"

A car was headed toward them up the drive.

"Switch seats with me, Jeff!" He could hear the panic in her voice. "Get down!"

"It's too late for that, Mags."

The words had barely left his mouth before the headlights of the approaching car flashed to high, nearly blinding him with their close proximity.

"It's Sue." Maggie's voice was flat, as if shock had knocked all the emotion from her.

The car rolled toward them slowly as he brought Maggie's car to a stop and put down the window.

Sue Marsden, looking a little older than he remembered but still sporting the same hairdo, gaped at him, not even trying to hide her surprise. "Why, Jeff Wells! I thought you were Russ."

"No, I'm me. How are you, Sue?" He tried for casual, as if seeing him shouldn't be the shock she was treating it as.

"Well, I'm just fine. What in the world brings you way out here?" Her eyes darted back and forth from him to Maggie, who was now leaning toward him.

"Jeff was here for Dad's surgery. He's staying in Murray, so he rode to Paducah with me this morning."

Wow, Maggie was a quick thinker.

"No use having two cars going the same direction," he added.

Sue stuck her head out the window, craning her neck to look back at the house. "I didn't see your car."

"Oh, I put it in the garage when we left. You never

know when a hailstorm's going to pop up around here this time of year."

"Mmm-hmm." Sue's smile had a smirking quality about it. "I heard Eli came through the surgery with flying colors, Maggie."

"Yes, he's doing great."

"I was sorry I couldn't get to the hospital, but I canned some chicken vegetable soup last week, so I brought a couple of jars for you. Thought you could use them for a quick meal after long days at the hospital."

"That's very kind of you, Sue. Thank you so much."

"There's a loaf of homemade bread and some chocolate chip cookies, too. I left it all in a basket on the bar on your back porch."

"I'll make good use of it," Maggie assured her. "Thanks again."

Sue was obviously not in any hurry. "If I'd known you were entertaining, I would've brought more."

"No entertaining going on here," Jeff interjected. "Just switching cars. Then I'm on my way."

Sue's head tilted in question. "Where are you staying in Murray?"

Damn! "A hotel out by the mall." God, he hoped Murray had a mall. He watched her brows draw in. "Not too far from the football stadium."

"Oh, you mean the strip mall. I'm sure you could've found *other* accommodations closer than that." She shifted her gaze back to Mags, who was gouging her knuckle into his leg. No one said anything for a moment, so Sue let her eyes drift back to Jeff. "Well, it's good to see you again. I gotta tell you, that's something I never *dreamed* would ever happen." She shifted her all-seeing eye toward Maggie one last time. "I'm planning on visiting Eli tomorrow, Maggie, so I expect I'll see you there." She smiled sweetly. "Bye now."

As the car rolled away, Maggie groaned and sank back into her seat. "I am so screwed."

"What? You don't think she believed us?" Jeff thought it had actually gone pretty well.

"Not a chance." Her head rolled from side to side on the seat back. "But what if…" She pulled upright and lifted her chin defiantly. "What if we beat her at her own game and *really* give them something to talk about."

She had his full attention. "How?"

She laid out what she had in mind and then waited.

Instead of telling her she was certifiably crazy, he gave her a nod. "I'm in. Let's do it."

CHAPTER THIRTEEN

OH, GOOD LORD, what was she doing?

What was this strange power Jeff Wells had over her, which made her think that some of the most preposterous things she'd ever done were good ideas? Getting married at nineteen. Having a fling with her ex-spouse. And now…this.

Maggie filled her lungs with what would probably be her last good breath for the next half hour and slid slowly out of her car.

On the way there, she'd tried to downplay the impact their appearance would make. But she'd obviously misled herself…and Jeff. As they crossed Yager Circle to the crowded park at the center of Taylor's Grove, all conversation came to a halt. Eyebrows raised, eyes widened, jaws went slack and mouths gaped. It was as if some alien life form had materialized in the midst of the townspeople.

Of course, Jeff *was* from California.

"Maggie!" Faith O'Malley came toward them, arms outstretched. "I was just telling everyone how great Eli did. Come fill us in on the latest." She patted Jeff's arm affectionately. "And I'm glad to see you took us up on the offer to visit Taylor's Grove. The people who couldn't come to the hospital have been dying to see how you look now."

IvaDawn Carroll rested her palm against her cheek and sighed. "I'll s'wan, Jeff Wells, you are just as handsome as ever. And Russ is the spittin' image of you at that age."

People clustered around, and, while everyone was within earshot, Maggie decided to unload her news. It was a bit like plunging into Kentucky Lake the first time each spring. Easing in wouldn't do. You just had to jump in and get it over with. She took a gulp of air and dove in headfirst.

"I decided it was silly for Jeff to be out the money for a hotel when I have that big house with all those empty rooms. He's staying with me until he leaves Wednesday morning."

There were a couple of audible gasps—not as many as she'd expected—and what seemed like a long period of stunned silence. Then Ollie Perkins clapped Jeff on the shoulder.

"Glad to hear that, Maggie. I worry about you being way out there all by your lonesome. Seems I can put my fretting off a couple more days, at least. Then I'm gonna have to talk you into a dog."

"What's Eli think about this?" Tank Wallis's deep voice boomed from behind her, and Maggie turned to meet his concerned frown.

"Dad doesn't know yet, Tank." She grinned sheepishly. "And I would appreciate it if nobody told him before he gets home. I want to make sure those stitches up his sternum have healed enough to hold good and tight when he blows that gasket."

Tank guffawed and most of the others laughed with him. Most…but not all.

"He's doing well, though," she finished.

For a little while, all attention drifted from her and Jeff to Eli. Then the current changed, pulling Jeff into the gang of men and she into the circle of women, where she met much more personal questions.

"What does this mean?"

"Are y'all getting back together?"

"Whatever has gotten into that brain of yours because you sure can't be thinking clearly? Have you forgotten what it was like…before?"

Maggie fielded the questions like a major leaguer, throwing out answers as if she'd practiced them for months. Most she simply answered honestly.

"This doesn't mean anything.

"Heavens no, we're *not* getting back together.

"We figured it was time to put the past behind us and behave like adults. We can be friends, and Russ can benefit from our ability to get along, at last."

She tossed away any suggestions of impropriety as if the very notion was unthinkable and, therefore, unworthy of an answer.

By nine-thirty, the crowd had started to thin. The people had been treated to a feast of gossip and could go home full as a tick—and Maggie knew full well it was her blood they were engorged on.

She yawned, exhausted. Jeff caught her eye, indicating he'd picked up on the signal with a nod over the heads of the group of men still surrounding him.

"It's time to go home before I fall asleep on this bench, ladies." Maggie excused herself, and the women who remained either went to locate their husbands or headed home alone.

Faith slipped a hand through Maggie's arm and walked with her to the car as Jeff finished up the last bit of a story that had all the men chuckling.

"Promise me you'll be careful, sweetheart," Faith whispered, and Maggie turned to see the concern in her eyes. She knew then that Faith knew the truth, but it was okay. She also knew Faith understood.

"I will," she answered, the words landing deep in her belly.

"This was a smart move." Faith gave her a knowing smile.

Maggie shrugged and grinned back as Jeff joined them. "Sue met us in my driveway tonight, so we decided if people were going to hear, anyway…"

Faith nodded her approval. "And Rosemary?"

"Tomorrow."

"She already suspected today."

"Then we'd better get there early."

Jeff opened the car door for her and handed her the keys.

"MOM, WE NEED to talk."

Maggie's tone brought Rosemary's heart to a standstill.

Her daughter had been uncharacteristically chatty all morning, pleasantly reminding her of the girl she used to know. The ICU waiting room had been filled to capacity, so most of the visitors from Taylor's Grove came in small groups and stayed only a few minutes.

To her surprise, everyone acted as though Jeff Wells's presence in place of his son's was a fine thing and was to be expected. She guessed those who came yesterday had filled in the rest of the community about Jeff.

But why in the world was everyone so nonchalant about it?

Something in Maggie's tone told her she was about to find out.

"I wanted to tell you earlier, but the waiting room was too crowded. I thought it best to wait until we got a private room."

As the doctor had anticipated, Eli was doing well enough to be released from ICU to a room on the cardiac floor. They'd sent the family ahead, confirming he would be there within the hour. Thank goodness Maggie had insisted Jeff stay in the waiting room.

Rosemary eyed her daughter warily. "This has something to do with Jeff, doesn't it?"

Maggie nodded. "He stayed with me last night."

White-hot anger flashed through Rosemary, singeing away any filter that might have guarded her tongue. "You've done some pretty foolish and irresponsible things in your past, but this beats them all."

Maggie's eyes widened slightly. "Maybe not. You haven't heard all of it."

Rosemary waited, steeling her spine for the next slicing blow.

"We thought we could keep it a secret. Figured it was nobody's business, honestly." She drew a long breath. "But then Sue was in my driveway last night when we pulled in."

Rosemary's heartbeat shifted from idle to overdrive.

"She would've told everyone, anyway, so we went to the park and beat her to the draw."

So *everybody* knew, which meant it was only a matter of time before Eli's fragile heart would be split wide open by the news. "How could you do this, Maggie—knowing what your father and I are going through right now? Don't you even care how this is going to rip him apart?" Her mouth became the catapult for her feelings. "Being nineteen and a silly teenager is one thing. Your dad and I accepted your foolishness back then and did everything we could to support you. But now you're a grown woman, and you ought to have learned your lesson about Jeff Wells."

Tears welled up in Maggie's eyes. So her feelings were hurt? Too bad. Better to have hurt feelings than a twice-broken heart.

"He's just feeding his ego with you—making sure he can still make you jump at his command. Have you forgotten who was there to help you pick up the pieces of your life and glue them back together after he left you high and dry?" Rosemary knocked her fist against her chest, mimicking her heart's intense rhythm. "I was. Your dad and I. Jeff Wells was long gone, but we were there. We supported you and Russ, making sure you had a life like you'd always been used to."

"And I'm grateful for all that, Mom." Maggie's voice was quiet and tight. "This has nothing to do with that. This is just me wanting to feel alive...like a woman again."

"You never think of anybody but yourself," Rosemary snapped. She knew that wasn't really true; Maggie had a kind heart. But it seemed that, too often, other people were on the receiving end of that kindness, and right at that moment, she wanted it to be *her*.

"I asked everybody not to say anything to Dad until we knew he was well enough to take it."

"Like that's supposed to make all this okay? Listen to yourself, Maggie." Rosemary was on a jag now. The frustration that had been building since last Thursday night came pouring out. "Just sit back and hear what you're saying. The person who ruined your life—the person you finally got away from—has stepped back in for a week, and you're already opening yourself up to let him in again." She threw up her hands in disgust and backed away, then came back with a vengeance, thrusting a finger toward Maggie's visibly shaken face. "Well, you're on your own. You're going into this with your eyes wide-open as a grown woman, and I won't try to stop you. But find somebody else to lean on when you start to fall apart, because your dad and I have quit that business."

The door swung open and the orderly started backing into the room, bringing Eli to his home away from home for the next week.

The discussion had to stop, and it was just as well. Rosemary had said everything she needed to say. And if her daughter had anything else to add, she didn't want to hear it.

"Anybody home?" Eli called.

With a look of understanding passing between them, she and Maggie stepped up to greet him, happy-face masks pulled securely into place.

"I'D NEVER REALLY thought about the embarrassment they went through back then." Her mom's harsh words had echoed over and over in Maggie's mind since that morning.

Sitting in the chaise with Jeff at her back, she found the courage to explore the subject a bit more. "Having to face everybody in town with the news I was pregnant. Can you imagine the things Sue probably said to Mom...*and* behind her back? They'd always doted on me. Treated me like I could do no wrong. It must've been quite a shock to admit their precious baby girl had screwed up royally."

Jeff's hand rubbed her arm. "I don't remember it as all that bad. I mean, I remember *telling* them. I thought your dad was going to kill me—and I do believe it ran through his head. But when I told him I loved you and wanted us to get married, he calmed down...some, anyway."

His phrasing brought a lump to her throat. *I loved you and wanted us to get married.* Over the years, people—well, specifically her mom—had tried to tell her what she and Jeff had back then wasn't the real thing. Sure, it might've been undeveloped and immature with a load of lust mixed in, but this week convinced her it had been real. She turned her face and leaned to the side to watch his reaction. "How would we react if it were Russ?" Living so far away and having so little contact with each other, this was one of the many things they'd never discussed.

Jeff's eyes held hers steady. "We would be supportive of whatever he wanted to do."

"But what if he wanted to marry her, and we realized she was some gold-digging bimbo?"

Jeff's arms came around her front to press her closer. "A gold-digging bimbo who would be carrying our grandchild," he reminded her as he kissed her forehead. "We would have faith he was making the right decision and support whatever he decided."

Maggie turned and faced the pool again. "Did you ever have 'the talk' with him?"

"Every time he visited, starting when he was twelve."

"Twelve!"

Jeff's laugh vibrated against her back. "As soon as he started noticing the bikinis on the beach, I started talking. How about you?"

"As soon as he started car dating. Before every date."

"Man, he must've thought we were paranoid."

"We were."

They laughed together, and the question niggling at her brain broke loose. "So…did your parents think I was a gold-digging bimbo?"

"No." Jeff rested his chin on top of her head. "They loved you, and you know Chloe idolized you. But they did realize you were spoiled rotten, and they warned me you weren't going to be happy living on my paltry minimum wage salary."

"And they were right."

"Yep."

"Admitting our parents were right. Examining their side of the situation." Maggie faked a shudder. "Gosh, we've gotten old."

Jeff ran his hands under her blouse to fondle her breasts. "Maybe we should go to bed before we get over-the-hill."

Had the situation been different, she would've said to heck with going to bed and would've insisted on making love right there in the chaise by the pool. But tonight was their last night together—*ever*. And while she didn't want to get maudlin about it, she also wanted to acknowledge it and draw it out as long as possible.

She stood and held out her hand. When he took it, she pulled him out of the chaise and led him to her bedroom.

Unlike the night in Chicago, tonight there was no haste in their movements. They undressed each other slowly, covering each newly exposed area with kisses that seemed almost reverent. Knowing it was their last time made such a difference, and Maggie wondered how that could be applied to everything in life.

How differently she would've behaved if she'd had warnings of the last time something would happen. The last time Russ sat on her lap. The last time she threw the ball for Snickers, her old collie.

The last time she and Jeff made love back then…

If she'd known it would be the last time, what would she have done differently?

She took that question to heart and answered it with her actions. Back then, she would've done everything she could to satisfy him enough to want to stay. This time, she wanted him satisfied enough to have good memories of her the rest of his life.

She sought to give him perfection, and he answered in kind. Every kiss, every nip, every lick, every touch was perfectly timed…perfectly placed. They moved forward and retreated, two steps forward, one step back, in a perfectly choreographed dance that was bittersweet and intoxicatingly erotic. Time became a nonentity—an invention thrust upon the human race that had no place in *their* world. Their passion deepened and carried the night along for the ride.

When he loomed over her for the last time, their eyes met and held, hearts acknowledging the importance of the moment, minds tucking the image into the deep recesses of those things never to be forgotten.

She raised herself on her elbows, capturing his mouth as he entered her. Then she shifted her arms to grasp behind his neck, pulling him down onto her as she arched up into him, aching to touch every inch available.

She met his thrusts with a heat that fused their bodies, made them one…one last time.

She cried his name, willing the walls to catch the sound so that every night thereafter she could hear it if she listened closely. Her head and eyes rolled back, and she lost focus as the exquisite spasms erupted from her core and spread outward. But her name bursting from his lips brought her back to the moment, and she rode it to exhaustion.

Jeff collapsed and rolled to his side, pulling her to him in a fierce embrace she couldn't have broken from if she'd wanted to.

But she didn't want to. She stayed in the same position all night, content to be sleeping in his arms this one last time.

"DO YOU FIND this entire situation as frustrating as I do?"

Jeff had avoided the obvious throughout the two-hour drive to Nashville, acknowledging the futility of their situation. But with the airport exit looming, he'd lost the urge to be careful and wanted to speak what was on his mind...and in his heart.

Maggie didn't try to play coy. She shrugged, not taking her eyes off the road. "A little."

"Only a little?" he pressed.

"I'm forcing myself to think about the positive aspects—like how much easier it'll make things for Russ now we're getting along. And how much easier it will be to call and talk to you about things—things about Russ, I mean. Just because he's in college doesn't mean he won't still need parenting."

"You can call me to talk about *anything*—not just Russ. I mean, we could chat about stuff happening in our lives, you know? Even everyday stuff."

"You mean like who we're dating? I could call and ask for advice?"

His stomach flip-flopped at the thought. "Sure," he answered, and she flashed him a wary glance. "Yeah, maybe not."

She snorted. "Didn't think so."

Departures. He glared at the sign. Damn!

"You could come to California on vacation. It's changed a lot since you were there last. You could stay with me, and I could show you the sights."

"Hmm. A sex vacation. I've never thought of taking one of those."

"Stop being so damn flippant about this, Mags."

"There's no other way to be. We knew what this was going into it. Yes, it's been wonderful. Yes, it's been exciting and fun, and, yes, even comforting. But it's over." She pulled to the spot on the curb marked Unloading—Ten Minute Parking.

"It'll never be over. You know tha—"

She hit the button to raise the cargo door and climbed out of the driver's seat.

He hustled to meet her at the back of the car and threw his bag onto the walkway, grabbing her hand before she could scurry away. "You will give me a proper send-off this time."

A long blink accompanied her sigh. "Thanks for being here for Russ and for me." She tried to hold a smile but it wavered with emotion. "It's been… nice. All of it. I'm glad we had this time."

"Me, too." An easy tug brought her willingly into his arms. She lifted her mouth to his in a kiss, scorching in its tenderness. Her eyes glistened when they broke apart.

"See ya." She patted his back and stepped away.

"Call me," he instructed, and got only a shrug in response. "I'll call *you*," he called to her back, but he wasn't sure if she heard. She was already getting in the car. He waved as she pulled away and thought he saw her wave in response. But he couldn't be sure.

In fact, he wasn't sure of anything anymore.

MAGGIE PULLED INTO the airport cell phone lot and found a parking space far away from anyone else. She couldn't drive with emotion clogging her chest and neck so heavily she could hardly breathe. She'd held it in all morning, but the pressure had grown unbearable during that last kiss. If she intended to make it home safely, she had to let it out.

She'd barely gotten the car into Park before tears started flowing, waves of sobs flooding out of her. The release felt good—nothing like the last time he'd left. These were tears of sadness, yes…but they were mixed with tears of joy, too, and a mysterious something she couldn't put a name to. Her heart brimmed over with thankfulness that they'd had this time together…that they'd made their peace.

"'Tis better to have loved and lost / Than never to have loved at all."

The words from a poem she'd read in high school drifted back to her as the tears washed the cobwebs from her brain. She'd just broken up with Sol Beecher at the time, and she'd thought those words were some of the stupidest she'd ever heard. Losing at love just plain sucked in those days.

But she understood now. Jeff had brought an undeniable richness to her life. She could feel it growing inside her, expanding her heart to hold more love.

And she hadn't really *lost* him. Her high school ring was *lost*—slipped off her finger while she skied one day on Kentucky Lake. Jeff was more like the locket her granny gave her when she was seven, a hidden treasure tucked away in the back of her jewelry box where she kept special memories. Looking at it hurt…God, it hurt. But having it was so much better than *not* having it.

The sobs ebbed away, and her tears dried.

She put the car back into Drive and started home, no longer dreading the empty house quite so much. Russ was happy. Her dad was healing. The salon was thriving. Mom was angry, but she'd get over it…as long as Maggie didn't slip into the darkness again.

And she wouldn't this time.

She had a firm grip on the steering wheel and was determined to accept this new life…starting today.

CHAPTER FOURTEEN

"But maybe she's not still mad at you. Maybe it's more like the world she's mad at."

Emmy tugged one last strand of hair through the small hole in the cap. Maggie knew she was trying to be gentle, but it still hurt. "Ow," she whined, glad the torture was almost over.

"Sorry." Emmy grimaced and caught the strand between two fingers. "Last one." Holding it at the scalp, she continued coaxing it out while keeping the pain to a minimum.

"I know she's frustrated with Dad." Maggie picked up the conversation. "Here it is, only two weeks after major heart surgery, and he's already contemplating ignoring the doctor's orders, chomping at the bit to get back to work. She's afraid to let him go down to the shop by himself…afraid he'll lift something and break one of those wires in his sternum before everything's healed. So she follows him around all day, which in turn aggravates him. He tells her to leave him alone, that he's not a child. She tells him to quit acting like one. And on and on and on."

"Like I said, mad at the world." Emmy reached for the color solution and began dabbing it on the protruding strands with a paintbrush.

Maggie did her best to ignore the stench of the ammonia and how it burned her nostrils. She studied her reflection, once again trying to imagine the occasional streak of red Emmy had almost talked her into. "I guess you're right, and she doesn't hide her anger well."

"Must be tough to see a man as active as your dad reduced to piddlin'."

"Only for four more weeks, hopefully."

"If he doesn't do anything stupid in the meantime…like murder your mom. How's Jeff's eye, by the way?"

Maggie cast a pointed look at her friend in the mirror. "Interesting how you segued from murder to Jeff's eye."

"Interesting how you talk to him a couple of times a week…" Emmy's head tilted, eyes narrowing. "Yet *I* have to be the one to bring him up in conversation."

Maggie couldn't deny that when it came to Jeff, her emotions were still like a game of chance—spin the wheel at any given time and see what the marker landed on. Conversations with him were fun, but the more fun they were, the more cautious she became. She was thrilled they'd had the recent time together and loved the memories, but sometimes her imagination wanted to lead her heart into dangerous territory.

"His eye's okay now, but, other than that, there's nothing to report. Nothing's changed."

"You're wrong there. *You've* changed."

Maggie snorted. "Joining the Ladies' Golf League isn't that big a deal. And I've always wanted to join the gym."

"But you've never done either before."

"I never had time before with all of Russ's activities. I've got empty hours now, and I don't want to spend every one of them here." She waved her hand at the salon, which resembled a beehive at the moment, and felt the tingle of pride.

"So you're telling me Jeff Wells has nothing to do with this sudden urge to stay fit? You're not entertaining the idea of taking him up on his offer to visit California, and you're not exercising because you have it in the back of your mind you have to compete with those sun-bronzed beach babes who are always within arm's reach of him?"

The chair next to her was empty, but Maggie still lowered her voice, unwilling to share the intimate details of her personal life with anyone other than Emmy. "I'm working out because I have time to work out. And, yeah, Jeff had something to do with it, but not the way you're thinking. It was like being with him woke me up from a long sleep. I feel good, and I want to be active. That's all."

Emmy covered Maggie's head with a plastic

shower cap. "Gives new meaning to 'turning you on,' huh?"

Grabbing the front of Emmy's smock, she pulled her friend's ear down to her mouth. "And 'plugged in,'" she whispered.

They giggled like middle-schoolers at the lame joke.

"You should join my kickboxing class." Emmy set the timer for thirty minutes. "Now that your hooha has woken up from its long winter's nap, some of those hubba-hubba guys would be willing to keep it from snoozing."

Maggie paused, thinking about that prospect. Sex with anybody besides Jeff didn't interest her at the moment. In fact, her stomach rolled at the idea. She would have to work on that eventually, but for right now, she was good. "I'm nowhere near ready for kickboxing," she answered, ignoring the rest of Emmy's suggestion. "I'm starting with some spinning and some Zumba. Things I can do at my own pace. Maybe I'll add other things when the weather starts turning cold."

"'Other things' like hot guys?" Emmy bent down to look her directly in the eye, letting Maggie know she couldn't be deterred that easily.

Maggie shrugged one shoulder. "Depends on how cold it gets."

"Doesn't ever get too cold where Jeff lives, does it?" The question sounded innocent enough, but Maggie knew exactly where Emmy's head was.

Sure enough, she continued. *"That's* where I'd be thinking about heading when it gets cold here."

"Well, I'm not," Maggie assured her. "Going to visit him isn't on my long list of things to do."

"'Cause it's at the top of your short list." Her friend gave her a smirk before she walked away. "You just haven't admitted it yet," she threw back over her shoulder.

THE TIME HAD come to tell Eli.

No one from town had mentioned Jeff Wells's name yet, but it could happen anytime, and Rosemary wanted it to come from her—not Maggie or anybody else. She was the only one who could do it right without upsetting him too much.

She set the plate of grilled chicken breasts on the table and went to fetch the pitcher of iced tea from the refrigerator. She heard the bathroom door open down the hall, and Eli's heavy tread came toward the kitchen. She also heard the water still running in the lavatory. Could he honestly not hear that?

"You left the water running," she called, hoping to save him a few steps, but he was already standing in the doorway by then.

"What did you say?" He took off his cap and scratched his head, then tossed the cap on the nearest chair.

"I said you left the water running…again."

He shuffled back down the hallway to turn off the water.

Her hand trembled as she poured the tea. Reminding him prickled her as if she were doing something mean, but maybe if she did it enough he would start double-checking before he left the bathroom. This was the third time it'd happened today, and she was at a loss as to what else she could do about it. The doctor had warned them of the "brain fog"—an aftereffect of prolonged anesthesia—that many patients suffered from, but she hadn't realized it would be this bad.

She was beginning to feel like a prisoner in her own home, afraid to go anywhere else and leave him alone. Just that morning, she'd been out weeding the vegetable garden, had come in all hot and sweaty and needing a shower, only to find the shower running full blast, all the hot water gone, and Eli sitting at the table drinking coffee and reading the newspaper.

He'd left it running for over an hour.

Maggie had offered to stay with him some, and there were plenty of retired men in Taylor's Grove who'd be willing to keep an eye on him. But the idea of having to get what was essentially a babysitter for her husband squeezed the breath out of her.

He came back and took a seat while she dished up the vegetables.

"There's something I've been needing to tell you," she began, trying for nonchalance. She sat down and unfolded her napkin across her lap. "Jeff

Wells was at the hospital the day of your surgery… and the day after."

He paused with the spoon of candied sweet potatoes halfway to his plate. "The son of a bitch was at the hospital?"

She grasped an ear of corn with the tongs, putting one on his plate, then one on her own. "Russ called him, upset and wanting to come home for your surgery. Jeff was in Wisconsin, so he told Russ he'd come down and be here in his place."

"Glad I slept through that." He grunted, and picked up the salt shaker she'd filled with salt substitute. Grimacing, he set it back down. "How'd Maggie do around him?"

The plate of tomato slices she held out to him became suddenly heavy, and she steadied it with her other hand. "She did great. They got along real well. In fact, he stayed at her place while he was here."

Eli's fork clanged against the plate, where he dropped it. "Maggie slept with him?" His face screwed into a look that reminded her of someone on TV who'd just drunk poison.

"Well, I don't know that she *slept* with him. But she let him stay at her house. They even came to the park one night so everyone would hear it from them and not from hearsay."

Eli pushed his plate away. Bracing his elbows on the table, he rested his head in his hands.

"Now, Eli. Don't go getting mad." She braced for the eruption of anger sure to come. Letting it out would be better for him than holding it in, she reasoned, and went on. "I told Maggie she'd lost her mind, but by then it was over and done and there wasn't anything I could do about it, and there's nothing you can do about it, so just go on and eat your supper."

"She seems okay. Or is she just putting on a show for my benefit?" His voice was quiet.

Too quiet. A tiny shiver of apprehension slithered up Rosemary's spine. "She seems okay to me, too," she answered cautiously, suddenly on unsteady ground. "If it's an act, she's putting on a good one, but I told her not to come running to us for sympathy. She's a big girl now. We have enough to deal with."

The eruption came then, but not as she'd expected. A great sob heaved from his chest, followed by...tears? In all their years together, she'd never seen Eli cry—not even when his mama died.

The doctor had told them to expect weepiness, said it was normal for open-heart surgery patients especially. Maybe something to do with coming to grips with their own mortality.

But she'd never expected it—not from her rock-solid husband.

"Eli?" She opened her mouth, but where were the words? This was so far out of her experience she didn't know how to react.

"I feel so ashamed." He wiped his eyes with his napkin, but the tears continued to flow. "I've talked bad about the boy all these years, but he was man enough to be here for Russ despite knowing how we feel about him."

His words shocked Rosemary into silence. What in the world was he saying?

"And Maggie was big enough to forgive him and welcome him into her home. My little girl…" He shook his head as another sob racked his breathing. "Showing kindness, modeling the way I should act, when it ought to be the other way around."

Rosemary covered her heart with her hand, trying to slow its runaway beat. The whole world had gone mad. The two people she used to know better than anyone had become complete strangers to her.

How could she take care of this man if she didn't know him anymore, avoid his trigger points if she had no inkling in what direction they lay?

Fear welled up inside her, and she broke down and wept then, too.

Eli reached out and took her hand, obviously thinking she was in agreement with him.

So…apparently she'd become a stranger to him as well.

"ARE YOU TIRED?" Jeff backed his sister's wheelchair into the family room through the sliding glass door at the back of his parents' house.

"Nah." Chloe's head waggled. "You?"

He laughed. They seldom used the push wheel-chair, but he'd insisted on it tonight, thinking it would be a good workout for him. The hills in the neighborhood hadn't seemed nearly so steep when they first started out, but the last block had left him puffing. "Yeah, but it's okay. You just sit there and relax, and let me do all the work."

Chloe's only answer was a soft chuckle.

He bent down in front of her and waited until her arms settled around his neck—a task that took a while but one he let her do on her own—and then he raised and shifted her to her battery-operated chair. "Oof!" He faked a groan. "Where are you hiding that fifty pounds you've put on since the last time we did this?"

"Weakling," she taunted, eyes crinkling in the grin her mouth could no longer form so quickly.

"Keep it up, wise ass, and I'll only make one milk shake and slurp it up right in front of you."

"I tell on you." How was it she could no longer write her name with any legibility, yet she could still arch an eyebrow so precisely?

He shrugged. "Tell all you want. Mom always liked me best."

Chloe let out the same squeal that comment always rendered. In the past, she would've landed a fist to his arm, but that was before her severe form of MS left her limbs too weak for any extraneous movement. He still jumped away, though, pretending to avoid the blow.

"Get the strawberries and the ice cream," he instructed as she followed him into the kitchen, and he watched her feigned exasperation.

"I alway haf to do everthin'."

He chuckled at their standing joke as he got the blender and the glasses out and set them on the counter. It was so *not* true. His parents—Mom, especially—insisted on doing almost everything for Chloe. But every couple of weeks, his parents had a night out, and Jeff came over to keep his sister company. During their time alone, he required her to do anything she was able to on her own, even if it meant a bit of a struggle—often for them both.

Like right then.

The tub of ice cream was in the lower freezer, and she had managed to work the door open. But raising the tub and placing it on her lap took all her strength.

"Need help?" he offered.

"No."

He pretended to keep busy looking for straws and long spoons while she finished the task and was rewarded with a huge smile when she finally glided over to him with both containers on her lap. He took them, then tweaked her nose. "And we need milk."

She aimed a glare at him as she put the chair in Reverse and backed up to open the fridge and retrieve the milk from the shelf on the door. But he read the satisfaction in her eyes when she returned to him with the carton.

He blended the concoction, adding the dash of

Tabasco just like Dad did, until he was sure the strawberry chunks were pulverized and wouldn't cause problems. Chloe's ability to swallow wasn't the best.

"Family room and movie, or patio and talk?" He knew the answer before he asked the question, but he asked, anyway. This was their first time alone since his trip east, and he knew his sister was dying to ask him all the things she couldn't in front of their parents.

"Patio and talk."

He carried the milk shakes, elbowing the door open and closed behind them. The sun was setting and a vivid red sky met them. Chloe scanned the horizon and let out an "Ooh" as he settled the glass into her drink holder, making sure the extralong straw was on the correct side.

Simultaneously they sucked on their straws and tapped their fingers in their modified form of fist bump before opening their mouths and releasing their traditional expression of appreciation.

"Aahhh."

Formalities over, Chloe immediately got to the business at hand. "So, wha' really happ'n with your eye?"

The question caught him off guard. He'd expected her to launch into the subject of Mags, and he'd been positive his story of getting hit with the golf club had been accepted as the truth. He may have fooled his mom and dad, but apparently Chloe knew him too well.

Where to start?

If he started with EmmyLou, he'd have to explain why he was at Maggie's house…in the safe room… while Mags wasn't home. He took another sip of his shake and grimaced as a brain freeze caused an excruciating ache at the back of his head.

Chloe watched him closely. "Qui' stal'n, buster. Spill."

"Shall I start at the very beginning?"

His sister's eyes infused with delight. "Everthin'."

He didn't have to go into details about how great Mags looked, and their first dinner together. He'd gone through all of that with everyone when he first returned home. So he started with the night they left Russ, glossing over the most intimate details but including enough to let his sister know that he and Mags had stayed together for several nights.

She hung on his every word, enraptured by the story, gasping and squealing as if she were twelve again.

As a preteen with a young and beautiful new sister-in-law, she'd idolized Mags during the short time he and his wife had been together—copying her hairstyle, mimicking the Southern accent. And after he and Mags split, all that affection had shifted to Russ, whom she adored. It had always been Chloe who would ask Russ questions about his mom during his visits. Everyone else avoided the subject.

What little Jeff knew about his ex's life through those years was mostly thanks to his inquisitive sister.

"You call her?" she asked when he finished his rather long tale.

"Four times in two weeks," he answered.

"She come here?"

He shook his head and set his empty glass on the table. "I've tried to talk her into it, but she won't do it."

Chloe dropped her head back and gazed up at the sky for a long moment, then she brought her eyes back to his. "You still love her."

He must've used more Tabasco than he realized because suddenly he felt a burning deep in his gut. "I…uh…yeah, in a way, I guess. I mean, the attraction's still strong, and we'll always have Russ, who gives us a special bond. I still *care* for her. That's a better term for what I feel, I think." The burning eased off, so he must've hit on something. He wasn't going to spend the rest of his life yearning for something he knew was never going to happen. But *caring* was expected, or at least understandable and acceptable. Loving? After all these years? Not so much.

"Thin' you'll ge' back togeth'r?"

"Naw." He shook his head and avoided eye contact by shifting his gaze toward the sky.

No stars were visible, faded out by the lights of the city. No fireflies. No shooting stars, either.

Nothing to wish on.

"Not a chance," he said.

The burning in the pit of his stomach flared to life again.

CHAPTER FIFTEEN

ELI'S HAND LEFT the steering wheel of his truck long enough to tickle the inside of Rosemary's thigh, just above the knee, teasing her dress up slightly. "Resume normal activities, Rosie—doctor's orders. *All* normal activities. You know what that means?" He leered at her and winked.

She slapped his hand...but not too hard, glad to have his playfulness back. Now, if she could only find her own.

"Don't try all that woman stuff—playacting like you don't like it. You missed it as much as I did. Six weeks is too long to go without."

He tickled her earlobe, but she leaned away from him, toward the window. "Keep your mind on your driving, you old coot. Sometimes you have a one-track mind."

"And that one track is leading my engine straight toward your tunnel." He laughed aloud at his joke. She rolled her eyes.

Just because the cardiologist told Eli he was healed and better than before didn't make it so. The doctor had never been in bed with them, didn't know how hard her husband worked when he made love. How could it not be a strain on his heart?

Fact was, *everything* could be a strain on his heart, by her way of thinking. Since the night they'd gone to the hospital after their walk, she'd lived in a constant state of terror he might keel over any minute. She waited on him hand and foot. Avoided arguing. Let him have his way about almost everything.

But he wouldn't get his way about this. She'd already made up her mind.

"Want to go by the mall?" he asked.

Eli offering to go to the mall?

Just more evidence this was a changed man from the one she knew before—the one who complained that his feet hurt as soon as he stepped out of the car at *any* mall parking lot.

"No," she answered. "I'm getting a headache. Let's just go on home."

"Let's run by the salon, first. Tell Maggie the news."

"If you want." She would leave that choice up to him. It had been six weeks since Maggie had her fling with Jeff, and she seemed fine—great even—but how could Rosemary really tell when her daughter remained so secretive about everything, including her feelings? Besides, she was still miffed that Maggie would take such a risk. Condoning a tryst with Jeff would be like telling a recovering alcoholic it's okay to have a drink.

The salon lot was full, but a woman came out the

door just as they pulled in. She motioned to her car a couple of rows over, and they were able to take the space she vacated.

When they entered the salon, they were met by a yell.

"Whoo-wee! Ladies, look at this! Brad Pitt has graced us with his presence!"

EmmyLou tossed her tools aside, left her customer sitting in the chair and came over to leave a big red lipstick print on Eli's cheek.

"Angela's gonna be jealous." He shook a warning finger in the young woman's face.

"Angelina," she corrected as she hugged Rosemary.

Eli nodded. "Her, too."

"How you feelin'?" Emmy's glance darted between the two of them, suggesting it was a collective question.

"Fit as a fiddle," Eli answered.

Emmy's eyes came to rest on Rosemary, and her head tilted in question. Rosemary nodded her agreement.

"Gonna give Rosie a private concert later, in fact," Eli added, eliciting a snort from Emmy.

Rosemary just rolled her eyes. "Is Maggie here?" The office was dark—odd for this time of day— and a prickle of apprehension caught between her shoulder blades.

"No, she had an eye doctor appointment." Emmy moved back to her workstation, and Rosemary followed. Eli stayed where he was, basking in the attention from the other stylists, who stopped their work to give him hugs and ask how he was faring.

"Is she having trouble with her eyesight?" Something else to worry about, Rosemary fretted silently. "She hasn't said anything."

"Just some redness and watering, apparently. Probably allergies. September. Fall coming on." Emmy circled her comb in the air. "Lots of gunk in the air right now."

"Yeah, I suppose."

"We may have to tie an anvil on her butt to settle her down now that Russ is gone." Emmy grabbed a fast-food cup from her station and sipped through the straw. "This morning, she tells me she's thinking about going to Vegas to a trade show next week."

"But, she just went to that one in Orlando back in June."

Maggie had always planned her trade shows around Russ's time in California with his dad, so she'd only gone to the ones that happened during the summer. This was odd behavior. But, then, Rosemary was coming to expect that from her family.

Emmy shrugged. "She's lonely. Keeping busy's good for her."

Guilt tightened the muscles in Rosemary's neck. She should be doing more with Maggie, but taking care of Eli had become a full-time job. And with his new friskiness, that would probably get worse before it got better. So much to do, so little time. All this worry was keeping her from sleeping well, and exhaustion groaned deep in her bones.

As if she'd read her mind, Emmy nodded in Eli's direction. "You keep an eye on that one, and leave Miss Maggie to me. Deal?"

If only it were that easy.

"I'm sure my daughter enjoys your company more than mine, anyway," Rosemary answered in reluctant agreement. "Maybe you could fix her up with somebody."

"Working on it. There's a guy at my gym…" Emmy gave her a conspiratorial wink and flipped on the blow dryer.

Not wanting to have to shout to be heard, Rosemary waved her goodbye and went to collect Eli from his group of adoring fans.

The accumulation of vapors in the air had started to get to her, and she pressed her fingers along the sore ridge on her forehead. She may have lied to Eli before, but now she really had developed a headache.

The fact she was relieved about it, though, filled her with guilt.

Maggie dabbed her eyes with the tissue again and took a sip of her iced tea.

It was times like this, she supposed, when she should be happy to live alone. No one to answer to but herself. Time to wrap her head around this and get her feelings straightened out before she had to explain it to anyone else.

She picked at the thread of her emotions, trying to untangle the tight knot, but it held fast.

Pregnant.

The word itself made her nauseous, and she sipped again, letting the sweet tea trickle down her throat.

How could this have happened? How in the hell could she have let this happen *again*? Weren't the odds of getting pregnant twice while using condoms—and with the same partner—about the same as getting struck by lightning?

Why hadn't she stayed on the Pill after Zeke died? She still would've insisted on condoms, but maybe between the two contraceptives, one of them would've captured the damn renegade sperm.

Her breath shuddered as she sighed, grief giving way to wonder with the mercurial swiftness of the mood swings she'd grown accustomed to over the past four hours since hearing Dr. Donovan's words.

She was going to have another child!

Time was when she'd longed for this. Had held out hope until Russ entered high school and she'd realized the age difference had become too great for the kids to have any kind of relationship.

The laugh that crept out of her held no mirth.

How would she ever find the courage to explain to Russ that his mom had been so lax when all his life she'd been so careful about everything related to him?

Everything except his conception. Her dad had made that joke a couple of times through the years when she'd been overly protective.

Mom and Dad. Images of the first time she'd had to spring this news on them filtered through her mind. Now she would have to put them through it *again.*

"Again." She spoke the word aloud, letting the night breeze pick it up and carry it away. Spoken alone, it sounded so innocuous. A favorite word of her piano teacher, the choral director in high school, her golf instructor. Encouragement to practice until perfection had been attained. Two syllables she'd murmured as a question when Jeff woke her with his tender touch in the middle of the night. No practice needed there—it had been pure perfection.

And she carried that perfection inside her now.

Her hand rested comfortingly on her stomach. Six weeks, Dr. Donovan had figured. No physical changes anyone else would notice for a while.

Jeff had to be told first.

Just like last time.

Last time bloomed large in her memory. His shock. Her tears. His arms around her, trying to be supportive, trembling with the burden she'd laid there. His tremulous smile as he held her face and kissed her eyes and promised everything would be okay.

And everything *had* been okay. They'd done it once…they could do it again.

"Don't worry little one." She directed her voice toward her belly. "We'll be all right."

She picked up her phone for the umpteenth time to make the call. Laid it back down, not quite ready.

Before the doctor's appointment—when she'd only had the home pregnancy test to rely on—she'd determined it best to tell Jeff in person. She'd even laid the groundwork of the trip to Vegas as cover. But Dr. Alexis Donovan's confirmation had thrown her off balance. She felt as if she had stepped into one of those crazy houses at the fair where gravity was out of whack and balls rolled uphill. She just wanted to tell him and get out of there with a quick disconnection of the phone, avoiding the shock and the pain and the accusatory looks sure to follow.

But they would *never* be disconnected.

This was a child. The miracle of a living human being growing inside her, not a breaking news report.

Jeff's child.

She picked up the phone again and cleared her throat as she touched his name in her list of contacts. Her thumb hovered for a fraction of a second before it tapped his number.

She held her breath but not for long.

He answered on the second ring.

"Hey, Mags!"

It was only a few minutes past closing time of the

dealership, but Jeff had gotten up from his chair, glad to be heading home after an exhausting day. He closed the door and sat back down.

"This is a pleasant surprise," he continued. "Unless something's happened to Russ...or Eli's taken a turn for the worse."

"Russ is fine, and Dad's doing great," she assured him.

"Well, then, hey, Mags! This *is* a pleasant surprise. A surprise because I've called you consistently since our time together, but this is the first time you've called me. And pleasant simply because it's you."

Her soft laugh brought a smile to his face—one of only a few that day. "I guess it was my turn. Huh?"

She sounded hesitant, almost shy, and he groped for something to say that would encourage her to call him again. "I'm glad you decided to take a turn." He tried to ignore the way his heartbeat had increased at the sound of her voice and was still zooming despite the fact he was sitting down and at rest.

"Yeah, well, I wanted to see how you're doing."

She was stalling, he could tell, which meant she wanted to tell him something and hadn't yet worked up the courage to come out with it. He could wait. Getting to the point would only shorten the duration of the call, and he didn't want that, so he went on. "I'm fine, but it's been a hellacious day here at work. We had a minor hailstorm yesterday. Nothing big. Mostly just dime-size stuff. But enough that a bunch of cars got pinged, so I've been with insurance adjusters all day."

"Jeez, I'm sorry to hear that."

He leaned back and propped his feet on his desk, trying to relax. "You're in business. You know how it is. There's always something…"

"You got that right."

Was that a snort or a sigh? He couldn't tell, and it made him wish he could see her face. "You should've got me on FaceTime," he chided, but gently.

"I'm sitting outside, and it's too dark. It's after eight here in Kentucky, remember? The days have gotten so much shorter since you were here."

The mention of when he was there, coupled with picturing her alone in the dark with that big old empty house behind her, threatened to bring a melancholy mood to the conversation. He sought to brighten it a little. "Wish I were there now." His ploy didn't work. Verbalizing it made him wish it even harder.

"Well, that's sort of why I called."

Did she want him to come back? That would be tough if not impossible right now.

He sat up quickly and planted both feet on the ground.

"I was wondering if that offer to come visit you is still open?"

Wait! She wanted to come there? "Yes! Yes, of course it's still open. I'd love to have you!" Man, was he sounding desperate? Having his ex come for a visit should *not* excite him this much. He cleared his throat and lowered his voice to *interested* but not giddy. "When were you thinking?"

"Next week. Tuesday, maybe? Come home Thursday? But if that isn't a good time for y—"

"No! It's a good time. A…a perfect time. But that's not very long. Can't you stay through the weekend?"

"I don't want to wear out my welcome."

"You won't be wearing out your welcome. It's going to be hard for me to take any days off right now, so we'll only have two nights together if you don't stay longer."

That *was* why she was coming, wasn't it? For the nights together?

"It'll be enough, I think."

Just a quick Jeff fix, huh? He thought it but he didn't say it—and he wasn't sure if he was flattered or frustrated by the prospect of her needing it.

"Well, okay," he said. "But maybe you'll change your mind when you get here."

Definitely a snort this time. "Or maybe you will."

"Not likely," he answered.

"Yeah, well, we'll see…" Her voice cracked and faded, then came back with an odd quality he couldn't identify. "I, uh, I have to go now…to, um, try and buy the tickets."

"You sure you have to go?" He fought to keep her on the line. "It's nice talking to you."

"Yes, I'm sure." Her voice firmed up more than it had during the entire conversation. "I'll email my flight itinerary when I get it, okay?"

"Okay. Sounds good." There was a meaningful pause, though he didn't know what it meant on her end. On his end, it was a chance for his heart to do that cartwheel it had been holding back. "I'm glad I'll be seeing you again so soon."

"We'll talk again to firm up the plans. See ya."

Firm up the plans? He gave a chuckle, noting the heaviness in his groin.

"My plans are already quite firm, thank you," he said…but she was already gone.

CHAPTER SIXTEEN

"I'M SICK AND tired of this, Rosie."

Eli's grip on Rosemary's arm tightened as he sat down on the edge of the bed and pulled her between his knees. She turned away to break the grip, but he grabbed her other arm, too, and held her fast. Escape was impossible, which caused her heart to hammer.

"I've just got a lot on my mind." The words fell glibly off her tongue with none of the emotion she felt.

He glared, the anger and pain in his eyes holding her more firmly now than his fingers. "Friday, you had a headache. Saturday, you were too tired. Sunday, you were too busy and stayed up until you knew I was asleep. Tonight, you've got a lot on your mind."

"You know how I always worry when Maggie travels. Gallivanting off to Vegas all by herself."

He dropped his grip from her arms and moved it to her hands. "Maggie's a grown woman. You got to let her live her own life…and we got to live ours." He studied her face. "Besides, she's traveled before, and I don't recollect it ever hindering our love life.

Now, tell me what it is that's really eating at you? It's me, isn't it? The operation?"

She nodded and eased down to sit on his leg. "I'm terrified, Eli. What if your heart gives out on you right in the middle?"

"You worried I'll die before you finish?"

His chuckle sent a flash of irritation through her, and she jerked her hands free. "Always the jokes. Well, this isn't a joke." Her teeth ground together in an effort to keep her chin from quivering. "I'm scared, and I'd rather give up sex than give up you."

"We're not giving up sex, so you best just get that out of your head. The doctor says I'm fine." He clasped his arms around her and lay back, quickly shifting her to the side, making her immediately wonder if her shoulder had hit his chest and hurt him.

Before she could ask, his mouth swooped down to capture hers.

His passionate kiss should've left her breathless, but it didn't...not in that way. Her breath stuttered because she realized her excuses weren't going to stop him from trying to convince her.

And maybe that's what she needed to do. Abandon all thought. Give in to the moment.

She took a deep breath, closing her eyes and willing her body to respond. His lips touched her cheek, making a wet path to her ear and below it, down her neck. His hand wandered to the hem of her gown, pulling it up and coaxing her out of it with sweet words and gentle touches. Her body slowly relaxed, and she touched him in return, ridding him of his boxers.

For long minutes, they explored the familiar territory, communicating only through their caresses. It *did* feel good. She'd missed this special closeness.

And then he rolled on top of her.

Her heart flew into her throat, wrenching her eyes open wide. She would miss this special closeness even more if she lost him forever.

"No, Eli!"

"Relax, Rosie." His eyes searched hers imploringly. "It's going to be okay."

She opened her mouth and tried to breathe through the panic as he entered her slowly, realizing too late that it sounded as though she were panting from passion. Encouraged, he threw himself into the task.

Her body went rigid with terror, all thoughts of relaxation gone as his thrusts quickened.

Please, don't die. Please, don't die...the mantra in her head kept time to his rhythm.

Exertion drenched his body with sweat. *Oh, Lord, was he getting clammy?*

She had to do something to end this insanity.

She raised her hips, meeting his thrusts, panting loudly, throwing in moans she hoped sounded normal. "Almost there," she lied, pulling him closer. "Now. Yes!" She sought to put enough frenzy in her motion to make him believe—anything to get this over with as quickly as possible.

Please, don't die. Please, don't die.

He let out a groan of surrender as his passion exploded. A few seconds later, he slumped on top of her, breathing heavy. She could feel his heart knocking against his chest wall and hers, as well. She continued her performance, breathing heavily also, as if the quakes were still rumbling through her.

He rolled off and stared up at the ceiling, not saying anything, his only movement the rise and fall of his chest.

Fear caught her in its throes again, this time convincing her he'd had a stroke. She laid a hand on his stomach, patted him softly. "You okay?"

"Yeah," he whispered, not very convincingly. "I didn't die."

"No, you didn't die."

"And you didn't come." He turned his head toward her, his face a mass of emotions. Fear, hurt, anger…they were all there in the grimace of his mouth and the tears in his eyes. "First time in forty years I couldn't satisfy my wife."

"No," she protested. "It's not you. I told you, I'm just scared and worried and tired. I'm exhausted. I don't sleep well. I just…I just don't know. It's like I don't recognize my life anymore."

He sat up, and she reached to pull him back, but he eluded her grasp. Standing at the edge of the bed, he pulled his boxers back on. "Sorry I've become such a burden." He stomped off to the bathroom, and she heard the *snick* of the lock on the door.

Rosemary threw an arm over her face in a vain attempt to block out the world around her if only for a couple of minutes—the world where she'd somehow become public enemy number one to the people she loved. She was sick at heart, tired to the bone… feeling as if old age had crept up silently and laid a sledgehammer to her back.

Besides being overly temperamental, Eli might be collapsing on the bathroom floor at that very minute, and she was powerless to do anything about it. He'd locked her out…in more ways than one.

She got up slowly, put her gown back on and went to the living room to read. When sleep did finally come, she pulled the afghan over her and stayed there on the couch for the rest of the night…another first in their forty years together.

"WELL, THAT WAS AWKWARD." Jeff's hand swiped his face, and then he turned back to her, eyes tightening with concern as they scanned her face. "Are you okay?"

"Just a little shaken."

A little shaken? Her stomach was rolling enough that Maggie had to focus on a nearby chair to make sure she wasn't at the epicenter of one of California's iconic earthquakes.

She spotted a ginger ale in the refrigerator where

Jeff kept soft drinks and water for customers. "I think I'll take you up on that drink now, though."

Without waiting for permission, she jerked open the door and snatched the can. Wasting no time, she flipped the tab and took a swig. What a hell of a time for morning sickness to grip her. It was nearly five in the afternoon there in California, which translated to almost seven at home, *and* she'd just had an impromptu visit with her former in-laws for the first time in over a decade.

The cold drink hit her stomach and eased the lurching for the moment. She breathed a silent prayer that the ginger would soothe the nausea... or at least stave it off until they could make the drive from the dealership to Jeff's place.

"I had no idea my parents were going to show up." He still eyed her warily. "I hope you believe that."

She took another sip and rewound her thoughts to twenty minutes ago when Milt and Ramona had pushed Chloe's wheelchair through the door of the dealership only ten minutes after Maggie herself had arrived. Her luggage sat conspicuously just inside the door of Jeff's office, and it had taken Ramona all of maybe ten seconds to spot it and shoot a questioning look that dissolved into a knowing smirk in Maggie's direction. "Oh, I believe it. Their shock was evident."

Jeff rubbed his hands along her arms and leaned his forehead to hers. "I didn't tell them you were coming, which was probably a mistake. Not that I was embarrassed by it or anything." He leaned back, eyes wide with apology. "I just didn't think it was anybody's business."

Another round of nausea punched her gut, and she realized the tempest had started brewing not with Jeff's family's arrival but with Jeff's amorous greeting when she'd first walked through the door. "You don't have to apologize." Another quick sip. "I didn't tell anyone, either."

"Not even Emmy?"

"Not even Emmy." She drew a quick cross over her heart. "Not yet, anyway."

His hands left her and settled on his hips. "Well, is there anything else you want to see?"

She looked around. His quick tour of the dealership after she'd arrived had been thorough. And, wow, had it changed. Doubled in size, or maybe more.

The force of a semi plowed through her insides, convincing her she'd never make it through the drive to Jeff's without puking—no matter how close it was.

"Just the restroom," she said, and made a dash for the private one inside his office rather than the public one down the hall.

She hoped he hadn't followed her into his office as she locked the door and threw up the lid of the stool just in time to empty the contents of her stomach as quietly as possible. Relief was instant—as it had been when she was pregnant with Russ.

After washing her hands, a quick snoop in the cabinet holding Jeff's private stash afforded her everything she needed. A dab of toothpaste on her finger allowed her to "brush" her teeth, and the mouthwash left her feeling her secret would be secure until they could make the drive to his place.

And then…

She couldn't think about that right now lest it cause the nausea to return.

Jeff was still standing where she'd left him, checking his phone. When he heard her approach, he looked up, and the smile he gave her was so genuine and tender and sweet she felt tears sting the backs of her eyes. That might be the last time in her life she saw that look. How she wished her phone was in her hand, too, so she could snap a picture and keep it forever.

"Ready?"

She took a deep breath and nodded. "Ready."

Jeff actually lived in Carlsbad, only a few miles from the dealership, but the heavy traffic made the drive over forty-five minutes.

Maggie was even more thankful she'd gone ahead and done her thing back at the office. No way could she have made it that long without heaving on the side of the road. As it was, they were able to have a thorough discussion about Chloe, whose changes had been the most disturbing discovery of Maggie's afternoon. If she'd thought Russ's pictures of his aunt had prepared her, she'd been horribly wrong.

But Chloe's unadulterated delight at seeing her warmed Maggie's heart.

"She wouldn't want you crying about her, Mags."

Maggie ran her fingertips beneath both eyes, swiping away the tears that had started without warning. "I'm not crying as much about *her* as I am about the fact I wasn't with her through any of this. We were so close. She was the little sister I never had." She paused, catching his eye as the traffic came to another complete stop. "How do you stand it?"

"I always remind myself that she's still the same person. Her thoughts, her feelings, her personality— they're all still Chloe. The physical changes aren't robbing her of those. They're only robbing her of the ability to show those things as quickly as she used to. I can understand what she says because I know her mind. Who she is hasn't changed."

The ache in Maggie's heart eased some at his words.

"You ought to see her and Russ together." Jeff's grin lifted her spirits even more. "They adore each other. Their wit was cast from the same mold, and neither of them lets the other get away with anything." He laughed and shook his head, and Maggie's ache returned as quickly as it had gone.

Jeff Wells was an extraordinary person. When life knocked him down, he got up and brushed himself off. She'd seen that trait in Russ and had thought it came from her.

Now she wasn't so sure.

Jeff had been through a lot, too.

And she was about to put him through even more.

"RUSS'S PHOTOS DON'T do this place justice. It's beautiful." Maggie shaded her eyes and scanned the fairway below the second-floor pool lanai.

"I knew you'd like it." Jeff smiled. He *had* known instinctively Mags would like his condo because the La Costa area of Carlsbad was exactly the type of place she'd always described them living in if they ever decided to move to California.

Things might've been different if they had.

But now wasn't the time to lament the past. The fact that Mags had accepted his offer and was actually here pointed to the possibility that this exes-with-benefits thing might work for the two of them.

He planned to show her a good time...a *really* good time. From there? They'd just have to wait and see.

He rubbed her back and felt her muscles tighten at his touch. She was nervous. Having second thoughts maybe about coming. The wariness in her eyes when he'd kissed her hello upon her arrival had been unmistakable. Oh, she'd responded, but her mouth had been hesitant, almost reluctant.

Then again, other people had been present, so

perhaps it was simply embarrassment at his public display of affection.

He slid his hand into her hair and turned her head toward him, capturing her mouth in a soft kiss. Sure enough, her lips trembled beneath his.

She needed time to unwind.

He pointed to the pool. "Want to go for a dip? We have a while before dinner." He'd splurged on a sumptuous French cuisine delivery service, which prepared the best beef bourguignon he'd ever eaten. Its scheduled arrival time was eight o'clock sharp.

To his surprise, Maggie declined. "I'd really rather just go back to your place. Somewhere we can be alone."

Though technically they were alone, the pool lanai was a common area, so anyone could walk up on them at anytime.

Maybe she wasn't as *reluctant* as he'd thought. "Alone it is," he agreed, and with a hand at the small of her back, he guided her back to his place. "We'll want red for later, but I have a nice pinot grigio chilled. Ready for a glass?"

She shook her head as she settled on his couch. "I'll just have water right now. But you go ahead."

He opened his mouth to insist that a drink would relax her—and the way she gripped her hands so tightly in her lap said she needed to unwind—but he decided not to push the issue. "I have sparkling water or flat." He held up both bottles from the bar.

"Sparkling would be great."

He prepared the drinks and came back to sit beside her, not right next to her but within a comfortable arm's reach. She thanked him and set her drink on the table after only a small sip, returning her hands to their clasped position and squaring her shoulders as if she were facing a firing squad.

He realized then that her behavior went beyond nervousness. She was upset, and his mind whirred to figure out what he had done.

Had she come all the way out here to tell him their time together had been a mistake? His heart hammered at the thought, but his mind rejected the idea as overreaction. Was something wrong with Russ? No, he'd talked to his son that morning. Everything was great.

Was something wrong with Mags?

He set his drink on the table, prepared to take her hands and coax her into talking, but something about the somber way her eyes held his, the way her mouth went from a grim straight line to a twitch of a smile and back, sounded an alarm buried deep in his memory. Before he could excavate the source, her words hit his eardrums with stunning force.

"Jeff, I'm pregnant. With your baby. Again."

The sounds didn't bounce off the membrane but bored through it as if secured to the bit of a hand drill. Round and round, they ground through bone and fluid and gray matter, reaching the very center of his thinking process. Logic and emotions caught together and whirled into a conglomerated mass that congealed at the back of his tongue and rendered him unable to produce intelligible speech.

He took a large gulp from his glass, his eyes never leaving hers, giving her time to laugh…and tell him she was only joking. He watched her hand reach for her water.

No wine. Water.

This was no joke.

The drink unlocked his tongue to some degree. "Pregnant."

She nodded. "With your baby."

"Again." He set the drink down, not trusting his hold.

"I'm sorry," she whispered, and her chin quivered, strangely juxtaposed against the steady directness of her gaze.

"Don't be. Sorry, I mean. Not 'Don't be pregnant.'" He scooted toward her and took her hands. They were cold and sweaty. Trembling. Or was that his? "Oh, my God, Mags. Oh. My. God." He breathed in but couldn't seem to force air past the area around his collarbone. He reached to loosen his tie, then realized he wasn't wearing one. "I can't believe this." The next breath seeped deeper into his chest, to the crawl space around his heart. "We're going to be parents again."

"You're not angry?"

"No." He shook his head and scattered his emotions into manageable piles. "Shocked. Worried. Mystified." He felt the tremulous smile playing at the edges of his mouth, waiting for permission to show itself. "Thrilled. Determined. Blessed. Not angry." He watched her shoulders slump and realized how high with tension she'd been carrying them since she arrived. "How long have you known?"

"The day I called you, I'd been to the doctor and found out for sure. But I'd known for about a week before that. I skipped my period, which is rare for me. And I'd done a home pregnancy test."

He held his arms out to her, and she leaned into him willingly, sighing deeply as he enfolded her. Another sigh shuddered against him and morphed into a soft sob.

He tightened his hold. "Don't cry." She shook against him harder. "Shh. This isn't something to cr—" Panic stabbed his heart. He grasped her arms and pushed her away to an arm's length, maintaining his hold. "How do you feel about it? You're not thinking about..." He swallowed, unable to say the word.

She gave a long blink as she shook her head. "No. I want the baby. I've just been so worried about what your reaction would be."

The panic left him with a *whoosh*, and a new emotion rushed in to fill the vacant gap. He sprang to his feet, pacing, unable to remain still. "I'm going to be a father again! Oh, my God." His fisted hands flew into the air in a gesture of triumph that felt better than a hundred holes in one. Memories of

Russ flooded his brain, sweeping him back across the years on a wave of joy. Another boy? Or maybe a girl this time? He pressed his thumb and finger against his eyes to squeeze away the threatening tears.

Another wave brought another emotion that threw him onto the opposite shore, and he saw himself sitting in Russ's bedroom looking through a photo album in which he was conspicuously absent.

The image twisted his insides like they'd gotten caught in a wringer.

He brought his pacing to an abrupt halt and stooped beside Maggie. Resting his elbows on his knees, he took one of her hands in both of his. "I don't want to be an absentee father, Mags. Not this time. I want my child with me here—all the time." He gave her the most imploring look he could muster. "Move out here. We'll raise this one together."

CHAPTER SEVENTEEN

MAGGIE'S HEAD SPUN at Jeff's suggestion.

"Me? Move out here?"

He nodded, his beseeching eyes pinning her with his unrelenting gaze. "It would be perfect. We could get you a place right here—in this building. I know of several that are empty."

"No." Her mind wouldn't even allow her to address the idea. "I've got the salon. The house."

"Sell them." He stood and started pacing again, running his hands through his hair and behind his neck. "Use the money to buy into a salon out here. I'll be able to help you out financially—and I can take care of all the baby's expens—"

"No!" Maggie surged to her feet. He would not take over and plan her life. "It's not just a house and salon back there, Jeff. It's my life. It's everything."

He came to her. Bracing his hands on her shoulders, he leaned down and looked at her. "But you could start a new life here. It would be good for you. I mean, Taylor's Grove is a nice town, but there's a whole world out there, Mags. You always loved when we visited here…"

His look and his touch sent a warm sensation spiraling through her and caused her heart to skip a beat. She fought to think clearly. "But those were *visits*. I *love* Kentucky. It's home. It has seasons."

"But you love summer. And it's always summer here—in some form." He grinned, obviously thinking he was winning her over.

She pulled out of his grasp and turned her back on him, suddenly frightened by the powerful hold this man had on her. His arms came around her from behind, his mouth close to her ear. "We've joked about being exes with benefits. It would be so great to be able to have you close. We could continue to explore this…this renewed attraction. We care for each other, Mags. If we lived closer and had more time together…"

My heart would be putty in your hands in no time flat.

"…maybe we could give ourselves another chance t—"

"To fail?" She broke from his embrace and spun to face him, arms firmly locked across her chest.

His hands settled on his hips. "We might not fail."

"I'm not into taking chances anymore, Jeff. Not with a baby to think about." She raised an eyebrow. "But if you want to have more time in this child's life, you could move to Taylor's Grove…or Paducah. Of course, that would've been an option the first time around, too."

The flash of pain in his eyes told her the remark

landed well. For the second time in her memory, she saw defeat shadow his face. The first had been the night they'd decided divorce was the only option.

"I can't leave the dealership, Mags. Too many people depend on me. Mom and Dad. Chloe."

Having seen Chloe that afternoon, she knew he was telling the truth. His family needed him. On the other hand, she could do fine by herself... Her arms dropped limply to her sides as the smugness and anger drained from her. They were at an impasse. With a nod of understanding, she crossed to him and took his hands. "Yes, you have your hands full here. I didn't realize how much until this afternoon."

He shrugged and for the better part of a minute they stood in amiable silence.

His chest rose and fell as prelude to his comment. "We'll figure something out." He drew her into a hug.

She nodded, unable to speak around the emotion clogging her throat as she imagined once again going through the agony of waving goodbye to her child at the airport as he or she left for the holidays or the summer...all those lonely times ahead when he or she would be away.

"Russ turned out fine. We can do it again," she whispered at last, and heard him sigh deeply in response.

He leaned back to look at her. "Does he know?" She shook her head. "I haven't told him yet.

Haven't told anyone. I thought you deserved to be the first to know."

He tucked a loose strand of hair behind her ear and gave her a little smile. "I appreciate that. When do you think we should tell him?"

We?

Her heart skipped at the thought that he wanted to be part of the announcement.

"I'd planned to tell him when he comes home at Thanksgiving. I want to do it in person. This news just doesn't jibe with a phone call." She laid out the plan she'd already made. "I'll probably just barely be showing by then, so I'm hoping with the right clothes, I can keep it a secret that long. If anybody notices the weight gain…well, nobody but Mom would say anything. We can tell Russ—and then everybody else?"

"That would be great." The warmth in his smile made her a little giddy. "I'll get online after we eat and buy my tickets."

The intercom on his door buzzed. "I hope you're hungry," he said as he moved to answer it.

Nerves had kept her from eating much all day, and nausea had taken care of what little she'd consumed. "I'm starved," she admitted.

"Good." He clapped his hands together. "Because we're about to have a meal that will start Junior craving the finer things in life."

No, the finer things in life would be a mom and dad living together in a loving relationship.

The thought pinched her heart...and she pinched her mouth shut.

Some circumstances in life couldn't be helped. You just had to make the best of it.

And a long-distance relationship was the best either of them had to offer.

JEFF SLIPPED SILENTLY from the bed, leaving Mags sleeping, peaceful and sound.

The beef bourguignon had been delicious, but it wasn't sitting well in his stomach. *Nothing* was sitting well, as a matter of fact. Not dinner. Not wine. Certainly not the plans he and Mags had discussed.

He slid the door open and stepped out onto the balcony. The lights of the city drowned out all except the brightest stars, but a half-moon was shining, and it gave him something to focus on while his mind searched for an answer to this dilemma.

He was being given a second chance at fatherhood. His heart swelled with happiness. The one bright star in his life was Russ, and now he would have another. Did two constitute a constellation? He smiled to himself and took a seat to bask in that for a moment, stretching out in the chaise Jennifer had used for nude sunbathing. He hadn't sat in it for quite a while, and the faintest scent of her perfume mixed with coconut oil still wafted up from the cushion. His jaws tightened involuntarily.

A few years ago, he'd been so sure Jennifer was The One. She'd seemed to enjoy Russ's Christmas visit, lavishing him with attention and gifts for the two weeks he was with them. But then summer had come and when Russ's two weeks stretched into two months, she'd become a different person. Not The One by any stretch of the imagination.

The One would be someone who would love his children—the plural form of the word warmed him all over—as if they were her own. But a woman like that was hard to find. And apparently *thinking* he'd found her didn't necessarily mean he'd actually accomplished the feat. Sometimes it took years to know for sure.

He was thirty-eight, for God's sake…had already wasted precious years.

While other guys his age were settled and living the life he wanted, being a part of the game—wife, kids, stability—he sat on the bench, waiting to be called into action.

And now, the cycle was starting all over.

He closed his eyes, imagining how it would be this time around—and the images churned the beef bourguignon like a wind over the ocean. He was headed for tumultuous seas if he didn't handle things differently this time.

Being an absentee father? Having only two-and-a-half months of his child's life each year? And that wouldn't start until the child was old enough to travel alone. The first few years—the formative time when he needed to establish his relationship—there would be even less time than he'd had with Russ.

That was unacceptable.

The whole damn, freaking situation was unacceptable!

He pushed from the chair and leaned over the balcony railing, taking deep breaths until his nostrils were totally cleansed of the scent of the wrong woman.

Head cleared, he turned and gazed through the door at Mags—the mother of his children. *Both* of them. Getting the same woman pregnant twice—surely the universe was trying to tell him something. And, if not the universe, surely the pounding of his heart was making him acknowledge what he already knew.

Mags was the right woman. The One. The person who would love and care for his children like no other could. The one who would put them first in her life until the day she died.

He cared for her deeply. Loved her. And she loved him, too. He felt it in his heart, read it in her eyes. They were getting along really well—if eight days together was any indication.

They needed to be together, needed to raise this child together. They deserved this, and the child deserved this. But the daunting task before him was convincing Mags he was right.

He slipped quietly into the bedroom and back into bed.

She turned to him in her sleep, snuggling against him as he slid one arm under her neck and the other across her hip.

He nestled his nose into her hair and breathed in the light, fresh scent of her cologne, letting it fill his head and heart.

Like a magic potion, the scent seeped into his soul, lightening his mood with the hope that tomorrow he would find a way to make his vision of their future together a reality.

MAGGIE COULDN'T HOLD back the laugh as she took the bouquet from the delivery guy, and he answered with a grin of his own.

"Not that it's any of my business," he said. "But from the looks of things, I'm thinking congratulations might be in order?"

"Yes, they are. Thank you." The clear vase held a dozen roses—six pink scattered among six blue, with a large, double-colored bow adorning the front.

"Well, take care."

"I will, thanks."

As he moved away, she closed the door and set the bouquet on the dining table, admiring the gorgeousness and sniffing carefully. With Russ, smells had often triggered her morning sickness.

Two tiny clothespins—one pink, one blue—fastened a card to the ribbon. She unclipped it and moved into the living room space, gaining some distance from the flowers just in case the scent got to her.

The message on the card was simple. *Mags— thank you.*

She blinked back the tears. Since calling Jeff last week, she'd been over the scenario of telling him the news so many times, it had bordered on obsession. But never had she imagined the totally positive and supportive behavior he'd exhibited. Coming here to tell him had been the right decision—even though she'd had to do it on the sly. And waiting to tell Russ together was the right thing, too. They needed to make this as much a family deal as they could, considering they weren't really family in the normal sense of the word.

Her stomach tightened ever so slightly so she moved onto the shady balcony off the living room— away from the aromatic bouquet—and stretched out on the chaise.

Before leaving for work that morning, Jeff had insisted on throwing away the cushion from the chaise on his bedroom balcony. She didn't know what that was about. It looked fine to her, but he'd said it was worn-out and had offered to switch this cushion to that chair. She was glad she'd told him not to bother. Part of her time had been spent at the pool in the sun earlier in the day, and now she had a couple of hours to relax in the shade, feeling much more at ease than she deserved to, considering her circumstances.

She closed her eyes and imagined Russ's many possible reactions when they told him.

A buzzer sounded, and she jerked to a sitting position. Oh, good Lord, she'd fallen asleep! She was meeting Jeff at the restaurant when he got off work in a little over an hour—and she still needed to shower and wash her hair.

She hurried to the intercom. "Yes?"

"Delivery for Maggie Wells."

Her breath caught at the name. "Y-yes. Bring it up." Although she'd kept the Wells name until she'd married Zeke, after his death she'd gone back to Russell. Maggie Wells was someone from a different life altogether. Hardly a resemblance remained to connect her with who she'd been then.

This delivery person, a young woman, gave her a cheerful greeting when she opened the door, handed her a gaily colored gift box in lime green with a festive lemon-yellow ribbon and bow, bade her adieu and hurried away.

A shifting of the weight indicated more than one item inside as she carried the box back to the master bedroom. No card on the outside this time.

But only one person would've called her Maggie Wells.

An odd sensation passed through her, and she plopped down on the bed, suddenly not trusting her legs. She eyed the box sitting on her lap with its pretty wrappings. There was nothing sinister about it, so why were her fingers trembling as they grasped the ribbon? Why the hesitation to open it?

She set it to the side and walked over to the balcony, stepping out into the sunshine and fresh air. A few deep breaths cleared away the misgivings and convinced her the rise in her hormone level was intensifying everything.

Making her a little crazy.

She grinned and shook her head. She'd been through this before, but now she was forewarned and could keep it under control.

She went back to the box and gave the ribbon an unceremonious yank. It slid smoothly away, and she lifted the lid and cautiously peered inside. Sure enough, there were several layers separated by orange tissue paper. She took the box that lay on top and slid it out of its velvet enclosure. The box was long and narrow. Jewelry maybe? A bracelet? A surprised gasp exploded from her lips.

Nestled inside was a cartridge writing pen, heavy and ornate. The top was black encrusted with silver filigree. The bottom was solid black except for one word—*Mags*—engraved delicately in silver. Three cartridges lay inside the box—black, steel gray and gold. She replaced the pen in its box and set it on her lap.

Tossing away the next layer of tissue paper uncovered three CDs—well, actually four since one was a boxed set—bound together with a green ribbon that matched the box and a yellow card that matched the ribbon from the outside of the box. She read the card first. "Let's brainwash this one early on as to what good music really is." That brought a soft laugh as she recalled Russ telling her how his dad always complained about his choice in music.

She smiled, scanning the three titles: Miles Davis—*Kind of Blue*, The Beatles—*Sgt. Pepper's Lonely Hearts Club Band*, and Sting—*Sting Live in Berlin*.

She placed the CDs behind her and uncovered the bottom layer. Tied together were…two leather journals? She pulled them out of the box and looked closer. Not journals. Calendars. One for this year and the other for next. A card dangled from their ribbon also.

"Bring these tonight. We'll begin making plans for the future."

What did that mean…*plans for the future?*

Her insides gripped with apprehension, and she had the fiercest, most unnerving impulse to throw her toiletries back into the suitcase and hightail it to a hotel.

"Stop it, Maggie. You're overreacting. Reading way more into this than it calls for." She talked herself off the ledge and eventually into the bathroom to get ready for dinner.

But she couldn't shake the feeling that tonight was going to be memorable…though not in a good way.

CHAPTER EIGHTEEN

MOST NIGHTS WERE pleasant in Carlsbad, but this one rated somewhere between spectacular and perfect. Dinner—both food and service—had been outstanding. A light, balmy breeze stirred the flowers in the pots beside their table—their very private table, with no one near them, on the restaurant's patio. Despite the warmth, the waiter had insisted on lighting the small fire pit in the center of their table just for ambience. And Jeff couldn't remember a time when Mags had looked more beautiful. The fire brought a glow to her fair complexion and sparkled in her eyes when she looked at him.

The effect was enchanting.

She'd been uptight when she'd gotten out of the cab but had visibly relaxed over the course of dinner. Now she stopped perusing the dessert menu long enough to catch him staring at her...again. She shook her head, but her lips curved up at the edges. "Would you stop?"

"Don't think I can," he admitted. "I'm having a hard time keeping my eyes off you."

"You mean my cleavage." She hid the round neckline behind the menu.

It was the same dress she'd worn in Chicago, and she'd been almost apologetic about wearing it, explaining how it was getting too cool at home to wear it—and she was afraid after this pregnancy, she might not be able to fit into it again.

He didn't care why she wore it—only that she looked amazing in it.

"Well, there is that," he agreed. "But it's the face I'm most interested in. If this one's a girl, I hope she's a miniature version of you."

Maggie squinted an eye his direction before returning her attention to the sweets on the menu. "That would be only fair since our son is you made over. I have him ten months of the year, but he looks, walks, sounds and acts like your clone."

Jeff winced. Russ had been on his mind all day. He loved that boy to a magnitude he didn't even know existed eighteen years ago. But this time, he knew what he was in for. He'd only learned of this other child twenty-four hours ago, yet the bond was already there.

The thought of Mags leaving tomorrow created an overwhelming feeling of emptiness.

"Taking this long to decide probably means I don't need dessert." She set the menu to the side and leaned over the arm of her chair to retrieve something from her purse. She came up with the new pen and both of the calendars he'd sent her. "I promised you planning after the meal, so let's plan." The edge had returned to her voice. She flipped the first calendar to November and held her pen poised. "Russ gets the entire week off, so what day do you think you'll come in?"

Her sudden strictly business attitude made Jeff shift uncomfortably in his seat. "What day do you *want* me to come in? I'm assuming I'll be staying with you, so do you want some time alone with Russ first, or do you want me to be there when he arrives? Maybe I can come in a day or two early?"

"I think the day of is fine. That'll be Saturday. Try to get there early enough that you'll be at the house when he gets home. We may as well tell him first thing." She made a notation in the blank for the third Saturday in November and breathed in a deep breath. "What else?"

"I hope to be able to attend some of your doctor appointments. I'd like to be there for the first heart-beat and the first ultrasound."

Maggie's lips compressed. "That's a lot of traveling."

"Yeah, but it'll be worth it."

It *was* a lot of traveling, and he wasn't sure how he was going to swing the cost and the time away from work—hadn't planned that far yet—but he'd figure it out. Too many other things had occupied his mind today, and he pressed on to those. "I was hoping maybe this year we could do Christmas together, too."

He watched her swallow hard as she laid down

the pen, and he had the distinct feeling their perfect night was about to slip down a few ranks.

"We need to get something straight." She eyed him levelly, and the grim set of her mouth told him he wasn't going to like what she was about to say. "I appreciate how supportive you've been. Your reaction to the news has been everything I could have hoped for and more. But making plans for the future as if we're a couple is a little silly, don't you think?" Before he could respond she went on. "I mean, yes, I'd love for you to be at the birth. I want that. But we can't pretend things are going to be much different than they were after we divorced and you moved back here. Fifteen hundred miles separate us. Trips back and forth are expensive, and neither of us will allow the child to travel alone for years. A lot can happen…in years."

The quiver of her chin coiled his stomach into a knot. He laid his hand on top of the one she rested on the table. "Like what? What are you trying to say?"

"My heart can't take this, Jeff." She shook her head slightly and dropped her eyes to the book on the table. "It's not good for me to be around you this much." She pulled her hand from beneath his and laid it in her lap. Lifting her gaze back to his, she gave a long blink.

He leaned close, his heart beating a staccato rhythm against his chest wall. "You're afraid you'll fall back in love with me."

"Yes…no…I *won't* allow myself to fall back in love with you. We've talked about this before, but being with you—off and on and off and on— will only keep me in a constant state of upheaval. I can't—*won't*—allow myself to become dependent on you again…in *any* way. Not physically. Not financially. Most certainly, not emotionally." She reached up and closed the calendar. "I don't want to make plans for the future with you. We'll just have to play it by ear."

That she still loved him was evident in the tears she held back…*but* she held them back. What could he do to make her let go and open up to him…give them the chance they deserved?

His heart leaped into his mouth as he scooted his chair over until he could take both of her hands. "We still love each other, Mags. We both know that. Let's give it another try." She tugged at her hands but he held them firmly, determined to make her hear him out. "Get married. Live together. Raise this child together. We can make it work this time."

"No." Her head wobbled, but her voice held firm. "I won't do that to you again."

"That…?"

"Force you into a marriage."

"Do I sound like I'm being forced? I *want* this."

"You *think* you want it…*now*…smitten by the idea of a do-over. But ten seconds ago, you said 'Let's give it another *try*.'" A tear broke free and slid down her cheek, and he reluctantly let go of one of her hands so she could dab it with her napkin. "I can't *try* anymore, Jeff. I've failed twice. If I ever get married again, it has to be a sure thing. I can't open my heart again for anything less."

"It was just a figure of speech," he protested, and the sinking feeling in his stomach told him he was losing ground. "Nothing in life is a sure thing. Life's a gamble. 'You pays your money, you makes your choice.'"

Her free hand covered her belly protectively. "I won't gamble when the happiness of my child is the stakes."

God, she could be infuriating! "You're twisting my words."

"Love. Marriage vows. Promises. They're all just words." Her tears began to flow in a steady stream, coming faster than she could dab at them. He finally freed her other hand and leaned back in his chair. "You may have forgotten what it was like, but I haven't," she whispered through clenched jaws. "You've been a wonderful father, but you were a terrible husband."

Damn! Her words hit with the force of a semi.

Out of the corner of his eye, he saw the waiter approach and do an about-face. Then Jeff realized the three elderly women at a table near the front of the patio were eyeing them and whispering. He didn't want Maggie's distress to become a spectacle…and this was not the place to analyze his own.

The joyride he'd been on for the past six weeks

came to a screeching halt, and he felt himself being hurled through the air.

He braced, knowing with absolute certainty the impact would hurt like hell.

"You want to finish this at home?" Jeff asked, and Maggie wondered that he could keep his voice so gentle while the aura around him pulsed with pain and frustration.

She nodded in lieu of speaking, aware she'd already said way too much but maybe not nearly enough. She hadn't realized her intentions were to hurt him until the words slipped out, but the bitterness was undeniable, the emotions behind it real.

He signaled the waiter for the check and paid it while the silence between them grew heavier with each passing minute. They were both aware the defensive wall they'd built between the past and the present had finally cracked, and the vast ocean of who they used to be would crash through any second now.

Walking to the car, Jeff took her elbow as she stepped off the curb and kept a hand at the small of her back. The heat, which before had been a pleasant sensation, now felt like a branding iron of guilt.

She'd let this go too far despite her better judgment. She'd known from the first moment she'd seen him again—at the airport in Chicago—that she needed to keep her distance. Had reminded herself of it daily since then. Her mom had tried to warn

her, as had her dad, Emmy and Faith. But no...
she had to prove to them all she was a changed
woman...had to prove it to herself.

This is what it had come to.

The anger and frustration charging the atmosphere in the car peeled the years away like layers of
cheap shellac. By the time they reached Jeff's place,
most of her exposed area lay between the ages of
twenty-one and twenty-seven. The dark and lonely
years when the only thing that spurred her to get
out of bed in the morning—or even to take the next
breath—was her son. The years when she blamed
Jeff Wells for every misery life threw her way.

They stalked from the parking garage, hardly
glancing each other's way, and when they reached
his front door, he pushed it open and motioned her
in first. He followed her and she jumped at the
sound of his keys hitting the table with force, then
sliding off the other side to land on the floor.

She immediately made for the bathroom.

"Do *not* walk away from me now," Jeff growled
behind her. "We're having this out once and for all."

She refused to acknowledge his order by turning
around. "I'll be back," she snarled over her shoulder.

She took her time in the bathroom, knowing she
had to pull herself together, refusing to face him as
the red-as-a-beet apoplectic crybaby she saw in the
mirror. She applied a cool washcloth to her over-
heated face, then reapplied a dusting of her pow-

der foundation. The few minutes of respite put her somewhat back in control of her emotional state.

Oh, yeah, her blood still simmered, and she *would* have her say, but she would do it with the grace of the more experienced woman she recognized in her reflection, *not* the younger version of herself.

She'd fought hard, damn it, for those ten years. She refused to lose them now.

With a purposeful stride, she walked back to the living room, where she found Jeff leaning against the wet bar, legs crossed leisurely. His coolness might have irritated her if she hadn't noticed the muscle twitching in his jaw, which gave away his true state.

"Go ahead, Mags. Let me have it." His chin jutted forward. "Tell me why I was such a terrible husband."

She crossed her arms, then forced herself to uncross them. But she allowed her fingers to curl into tight fists as her arms fell to her sides. "Well, for starters…despite being gone sixteen hours a day, you tried every way in the world to control me, calling constantly, asking where I was, what I was doing."

"I was worried about you."

"You weren't checking on me, you were checking *up* on me—trying to dictate what I could and couldn't do, where I could go…with whom."

His eyes bored into hers. "You were nineteen and acted fifteen, so *I* had to act forty. You were out of control, and one of us had to be the adult in the relationship."

"I didn't need to be controlled," she snapped. "I was fighting to become my own person. I'd gone from living with my parents to living with you with barely even a year of freedom to my name."

"But somebody had to watch out for you, Mags. You were reckless and pregnant with *my* child. You acted impetuously…like the time you dove off Sol's boat when you had no idea how deep the lake was at that spot."

She'd forgotten about the incident, and yeah, it might've been stupid, but it was only once. "I had to account for every dime I spent—" She ignored his comment and went on. "You kept the checkbook, which meant I couldn't even buy you a birthday present without your knowing exactly how much it cost and where it came from."

"You paid no attention to the cost of anything." His hands shoved into his front pockets, one of them coming out with a couple of coins, which he shuffled back and forth. "Eli and Rosemary had always lavished you with anything you wanted. You were spoiled rotten, and I couldn't give you the lifestyle you were used to. I was busting my ass, working two jobs, and you were spending all our money—"

"It was never *our* money. It was *your* money—" her finger punched the air in his direction "—that you allowed me to use occasionally."

"You were spending *our money*—" he ground the words out "—on frivolous shit."

The nineteen-dollar palazzo pant outfit sprang to mind, making her feel silly for even having this conversation. But she shoved the awkwardness aside. There was something cathartic about this. It was moving her *toward* something, though she had no idea what. "You suffocated me!" Her fingernails dug into her sweaty palms. "You made me feel like I was living in a bubble and the oxygen was running out."

"We *did* live in a bubble. But it was you who insisted on staying in Taylor's Grove in the house right next to your parents. You ran to them with every little thing, blaming me for everything that went wrong. It was never just me against you like a normal couple. Your parents always took your side and made it three against one, and at twenty-one, that felt like me against the whole damn world! *Your* world. *Your* town." His nostrils flared.

There it was. *Finally!* A strange sense of satisfaction rolled through her.

"I had a wife and a baby to take care of," he continued. "I was trying to make a living, go to school, keep the scholarship that I eventually ended up losing, be a husband and father, and things were turning out totally different from the way I thought they'd be when I moved to Kentucky from California. Everything felt out of control."

He scratched his head roughly, his telltale sign of

frustration, but his honesty dredged up what lay at the bottom of Maggie's resentment—the truth she'd never been able to put into words, even while she'd been in counseling. It was like she'd stepped out of her body and was viewing herself with a new perspective...because, of course, she was.

She wasn't *that person* anymore. Would never allow herself to be *that person* again.

"And the more you controlled me...the more I *let* you control me—" her voice suddenly went very quiet, all the anger that had infused it gone "—the more I felt you didn't love the real me. You tried to make me into someone I wasn't, as if you were afraid that, if you let me be my own person, I was going to turn into someone you didn't like...and certainly couldn't love."

Jeff's chin lifted as if she'd connected with an upper cut. His mouth opened and closed, and he ran his hand down his face.

She took the quiet moment to sink into the chair, drained and exhausted by the past six weeks—the past eighteen years.

"And that's why I can't think about marriage to you again, Jeff. You still control me. You talk me into dinner in Chicago, accompanying you to Lake Geneva, letting you stay at my house..." She pointed to the calendars protruding from her purse. "And making plans for the future." She shrugged and took a long breath. "I lose myself in you. Forget who I am. Even after all this time."

A shadow of sadness and acceptance settled on his face—she recognized it because she felt it, too.

"I…I don't know what to say, Mags," he said at last. "I never meant to make you feel that way. I'm sor—"

She held her hand out to stop him and shook her head. "Don't say you're sorry. Please. Haven't you been listening? Neither of us should *ever* have to apologize for being who we are. We just don't work together—at least, not for the long-term…and not for the right reasons."

He studied her and then swiped his hand around the back of his neck, letting out a long breath. "Want to sit outside for a little while?"

"No." She stood up. "I'm tired. I think I'll go to bed. Long day tomorrow." She started in that direction, stopping long enough to take his hand. "Are you coming?"

"You go on." He motioned toward the hallway. "I'll be there shortly."

Shortly must be a relative term, she decided, when his weight shifting onto the bed woke her… four hours later.

CHAPTER NINETEEN

"YOU CAN BE pissed at me all you want, Chlo, but it won't change anything." Jeff held his sister's hands firmly as she struggled to lower herself onto the chaise. "I didn't tell anybody she was coming. It wasn't anybody's business—yours included." When her butt settled into place, he lifted her legs and swung them onto the chair so she could face the pool.

"Humph." She snorted her displeasure again—her standard response since his mom and dad dropped her off a half hour ago.

"Do you want a towel?" He held one out. She didn't respond—choosing instead to focus her attention somewhere to the left of him as if he didn't exist—so he tossed it onto her lap.

She swiped it onto the concrete with her forearm.

Water dripped from her bangs and ran down her face in little streams that had to be annoying, but if she wanted to continue being obstinate, by God, he'd let her.

He stalked away to the diving board and dove in, determined to rid himself of the soreness that had plagued his back and shoulders since his discussion with Mags on Wednesday night. He did a few laps, then flipped onto his back and added a few more using the backstroke. On his way past Chloe, he glanced her way. She was squinting against the sun, and he chided himself for leaving her sunglasses in the bag beside the chair.

He exited the pool at the shallow end, leaving a dripping trail to where she sat, and fished around in the beach bag until he found her glasses. Standing over her, he shook his head like a wet dog, spraying her with cold droplets.

She grunted and closed her eyes sullenly, obviously not wanting to give him the pleasure of knowing he was aggravating her.

He chuckled, just to annoy her more, and slid her sunglasses into place before toweling off in her direction and then taking the seat beside her.

They sat in silence, the only people at the pool this gorgeous Sunday afternoon. The swim had loosened his muscles some, and the warm sun helped, also. He closed his eyes and tried to relax—tried to ignore the image of Mags walking away from him at the airport that popped up anytime his mind wasn't occupied by work.

"Din't go well, huh?" Chloe said at last.

It was his turn to grunt disapprovingly. "Nope. Not at the end, anyway, which pretty much colored the whole visit."

"Wan' talk 'bout it?"

"No."

"Why?"

"It's none of your business."

Another couple of minutes of silence passed.

"Shoul' talk 'bout i'. Helps."

"There's nothing to talk about. She says she loses herself in me, like my personality overpowers hers. She made me sound…overbearing." The word that had niggled at the back of his brain since Wednesday night surfaced. He stretched his shoulder blades apart and raised the arms of his chair to let the back down into a more reclining and, hopefully, more comfortable position.

"You can be."

"No, I'm not." His fingers cramped, and he loosened his grip on the chair arms.

"Yeah, ya are. You an' Russ. Stron' pers'nalty… overbear'n. Flip sides, same coin."

Irritation brought Jeff to an upright position. "How can you say that? You're crazy about Russ, and you know there's never been a kinder, more loving kid."

"Jus' like you. Crazy 'bout you, too." She turned her face toward him and gave him a satisfied grin—the first one he'd received from her today.

He swung his legs around to rest his feet on the concrete between their chairs and leaned toward her on his elbows. "Do you really think I'm overbearing?"

Chloe nodded. "Abs'luly. Take charge. Follah me. That's you."

He grabbed a towel and threw it over his head, shaking out some more of his frustration along with the pool water. "Well, somebody has to step up to the plate and make decisions. Nothing gets done if everybody sits around with their heads up their asses. I get things done."

"An' 'cause you do, others don't hafta...or don't get to, eve' if they want to."

She made a good point. Jeff wadded the towel into a ball and slammed it down beside his chair. "Damn. I do that a lot with you, don't I?"

"Yeah." She sighed, and he recognized the echo of frustration.

How often had he made decisions for Chloe and about her without ever asking what she wanted or needed, as if the disease had robbed her of the ability to think for herself? Like the sunglasses. He'd put them on her like she was three. And sitting here. *He'd* made the decision to swim today, never asking her preference, just assuming if he wanted to swim, she did, too.

"Was there something else you wanted to do today, Chlo?" Guilt tinged his voice.

"No, wanna swim. Bu' it woulda been nice to be asked."

"I'll make a point of asking from now on." He settled back into his chair, noting the tension still making his neck muscles tight and sore. He'd been given a bit of insight into how other people viewed him. And while he appreciated that, it didn't change anything. It didn't put him any closer to his goal—to win Maggie over and raise this second child together full-time.

The question was how to make those demands on her without appearing overbearing?

This would take some thought.

"Sooo, you wanna hear whah else I really wan' do this afternoon?"

"Gonna test me already, huh?" He grinned, intertwining his fingers to rest his hands on his belly. "Okay. What else do you really want to do this afternoon, sister dear?"

"I wannna hear 'bout Mag visit."

"Not gonna happen. I told you it's none of your business."

"Humph."

Jeff lowered the chair to a flat position and rolled over on his stomach. Chloe was pissed again, which would give him a good half hour of silence. He intended to fill the time with a nap.

"So, can I call you?"

Bryan Palmer kept his voice low, and Maggie realized he knew the answer to the question before she spoke. She glanced a wary eye toward the driveway where his friend Holden and Emmy were saying their goodbyes—their very *physical* goodbyes. Well, actually, they weren't saying anything. Their mouths were too occupied to make any sounds that didn't belong behind closed doors.

Maggie opened her mouth to reply, then hesitated.

"Yeah, I thought not." He shrugged and shot a glance in the direction of the car. Turning back, he gave Maggie a winsome grin that at one time would have curled her toes.

Not anymore.

"I had a good time tonight. Really. I'm just not in a place to start seeing anyone right now."

So, so, sooo not in a place.

"No problem." He made the three steps off Emmy's porch, then shoved his hands in his pockets and turned back, standing in the middle of the sidewalk. "But if you change your mind…"

Maggie nodded. "I'll see you at the gym."

Bryan was cute, funny, thirty-five, divorced for three years, and drool-worthy, with a body that looked like it was sculpted in stone.

How in the heck would she explain her lack of interest in him to Emmy? The *I'm too busy/I'm too tired/I'm too everything* excuses were beginning to sound thin even to her.

She waved goodbye to Bryan one last time as he got in his car, and then she returned to the kitchen to start cleaning up the mess left from the Sunday-night supper of grilled pizza.

A couple of minutes later, Emmy made her entrance into the kitchen, singing loud, as usual. Maggie cringed at her song choice—Matchbox Twenty's

"She's So Mean"—and wondered if she was making a point.

Emmy clasped her hands over her head and gyrated her hips to swivel in a circle as she sang, using the action to sidle up beside Maggie. The suggestive shimmy started in her shoulders, and it was like, once the movement hit her breasts, there was no way to stop it. The rest of Emmy's body had no option but to follow.

Maggie rolled her eyes and slid the leftover veggie pizza into the plastic container.

Emmy stopped the music midverse. "You a cwazy woman, Maggie Russell Wells Gunther Russell." Her friend thought the names sounded cool strung together like that. "Hot, hot, *hot*—" she shouted the last one. "Bryan was yours for the taking, and you turn him down like a piece of bad sushi."

"I agree, Bryan is indeed hot, but, I dunno— something just didn't click." Maggie put the lid on the plastic container and pressed in the middle until she heard the satisfying pop. She turned her back and headed to the fridge so she wouldn't have to make contact as she lied. "I'll keep him in mind in case, you know… When I start dating again." The plastic box fit perfectly into an open slot on the second shelf.

Maggie moved back to the table as Emmy drew out a long, dramatic sigh. "He's probably already found somebody else." She pulled some of the topping off the leftover pepperoni pizza and leaned her head back to drop it in. "Why, oh, why—" she stopped to chew "—didn't we go to your house and swim? The only thing better than seein' them thar men clothed would be seein' 'em nek-kid. Mmm-mmm. Fine they be."

Maggie chuckled and stacked the dirty plates, pausing with one in her hand. "I would appreciate a little more honesty next time, though. Telling me you're 'having a few people over' when you're actually trying to fix me up isn't best-friend protocol."

"But I did it, didn't I?"

"Yes, you did."

"Then it must be best-friend protocol. Ha!" Emmy picked at the pizza again, locating a mushroom to nibble on. "Who in their right mind *ever* decided mushrooms were good food? I mean, they're rubbery and they got no personality. Just little rubbery sponges that suck up the flavor around them. Like eatin' a leech."

"Ew!" Maggie took the stacked dishes to the sink for rinsing, trying to shoo that image from her mind. She didn't need a bout of nausea right then.

"And speaking of best-friend protocol, if I'd told you the truth, you wouldn't have come, and I promised your mama I'd try harder to fix you up with somebody."

"You what?" Maggie was glad she'd gotten the plates safely to the sink before that came up. She whirled around to Emmy's smug smile. "Y'all have been talking about me? When? When did you tell her that?"

"Week before last. The day you went to the eye doctor. She and your dad came into the salon."

The day of my ob-gyn appointment. The day she confirmed I'm pregnant.

"And don't go gettin' your panties in a wad." Emmy came to the garbage disposal with the last piece of leftover pizza, now plucked clean. "Move. I do this better than you." She waved Maggie away from dishwasher-loading duty. "We're doing this out of love, and you know it. *She's* concerned about the hold Mr. Wells has on you, and *I* figure, now that Mr. Wells got you back in the saddle, might as well keep you riding."

"Oh, good Lord." Her best friend and her mom colluding to find her someone to date. How pitiful was that?

Maggie gathered the beer bottles and transferred them to the counter along with her lemonade glass. Her argument that she'd read alcohol was a cause of belly fat in women had won her a pass on questions about her drink of choice. But when one of the guys—Holden? maybe—remarked that *he* thought the leading cause of belly fat in women was pregnancy, she'd felt her face grow hot, though thankfully no one paid any attention.

"You ever think about the word *rut*?"

Maggie was used to her friend's strange thought

processes, but this one was really out there. "Where'd that come from?"

"I was just thinking how you'd gotten into *a* rut, never doing it with anybody. Then Jeff got you *in* rut—you know, like a buck in rut? Wanting it all the time?" Emmy talked as she rinsed every speck of food from the dishes before loading them. "And now, if we don't keep you in rut, you'll get back into *a* rut." She cackled at her cleverness. "Damn, I am deep!"

Maggie laughed, but all of this talk about Jeff made her want to cry, too. And then, without warning, she was fighting back tears. And Emmy was looking at her. She blinked fast, trying not to let any escape, but her hands were full of silverware and wads of dirty paper napkins.

"I knew it."

Emmy's declaration pushed Maggie's heart into her already tight throat. She couldn't breathe, let alone ask what Emmy knew.

"So what are you gonna do about it?" Emmy took her elbow and guided her to a chair. "Sit, Ubu." She'd picked that phrase up from some TV show years ago, and it had become part of normal Emmy-speak.

Maggie tried to smother the flame of panic. She couldn't tell anyone. Not yet. "What do you mean?"

"You love him, Maggie. You've always loved him. You're always going to love him. There's never going to be room in your heart for another man because Jeff Wells occupies the entire space. What are you going to do about it?"

While half of her felt relief that her secret was still secure, the other half ached at Emmy's question. Maggie bit her lip in an attempt to quell the tears. Sharing part of the truth might be okay and could win her some time—and maybe hold Emmy off on fixing her up with anyone.

"I've already done something about it, Em."

Her friend plopped into the chair next to her, all eyes and ears. "What?"

Maggie took a deep breath. "I didn't go to Vegas last week. I went to San Diego to see him."

Emmy's jaw went slack. "And…?"

"And things went really well the first night, but kind of became hell in a handbasket the second."

"You fought?"

"We got into a heated discussion about all the things that went wrong when we were married." She left out his proposal. Being married to him again had been her standard fantasy for so long, the memory of turning him down still made her reel in disbelief. "I told him about what I resented. I mean, I always thought we were just too young, had our freedom jerked away from us too quickly. But, as I talked, I realized it's me with the problem, not him. I *am* the problem. He has a strong personality, and I just can't hold my own with him."

Emmy's eyes filled with tears, too, and she leaned

closer, directing her gaze straight at Maggie's. "You *do* have a strong personality, Maggie Russell Wells Gunther Russell. In fact, you're the strongest woman I know." Maggie's stomach tightened at the same words Jeff had said to her once. "And you need someone like him. Maybe not him—but someone *like* him."

"There's no one like him." The air in Maggie's lungs shook so hard it made her cough. "I had this dream last night that sums it up…" She blinked hard to rid her eyes of the tears hanging there. "When I'm with him, I feel *so good*…it's like being on a motorcycle riding at top speed. But, in the back of my mind, I know I should be slowing down because I'm approaching a canyon. But he's telling me I can make the jump. And I get to the edge, and I do it. And then, I realize he's not beside me. I'm suspended out there in midair, an—" Her voice cracked. "And I'm all alone." That was the point at which she'd woken up last night, and the same sob had welled up in her chest then as now. In the bed, alone, she'd let it out. Now, she breathed through the pain of keeping it locked down.

"You're never all alone. I'm here. Your mama and daddy are here." Emmy took her hand. "You got lots of friends. Lots of people who love you. A son who adores you."

And a baby on the way.

It was on her tongue to blurt out, but she locked it down, as well, thinking of Russ.

"I know you're right." She wiped her free hand over her face. "I should be counting my blessings, not grieving over the past and something that just isn't meant to be."

"Which takes me back to my question." Emmy squeezed her hand. "If you give him all the space, how you gonna make room for someone else?"

"I will." Maggie gave a resolute nod. "But you understand why I can't do it right now. It's only been a week, and he's still too fresh in my mind. Give me some time?"

Emmy stood and went to what she called her "junk drawer." She opened it, grabbed a red marker and strode to the giant Chippendales calendar hanging on the wall. She lifted the pages, taking time to make a couple of pelvic thrusts in the direction of Mr. November and then proceeded to draw a huge red circle around November 11. She turned back to Maggie with a sly grin.

"Let it be known, y'all—" she held the marker like a microphone and scanned the faces of her imaginary crowd "—that I'm going to provide my best friend with a hot, hot, hot—" she, again, screamed the last word "—military hunk who'll be more than happy to give Maggie Russell Wells Gunther Russell a Veterans Day she won't forget."

Maggie gave Emmy what she hoped was a convincing smile, pretending that date would be fine, all the while feeling guilty for her duplicity.

There was only one thing in her life she wouldn't ever be able to forget—the feel of Jeff Wells's grip on her heart.

CHAPTER TWENTY

"DADGUMMIT." ELI GRABBED his foot and started hopping in pain.

Russ let out a heart-wrenching wail. "You bwoke my twuck, Gwandpa. The twuck my daddy sent me."

Rosemary squatted beside her grandson as Eli landed hard in the chair. "Here, sweetie," she said gently, "let Grandma see." Her heart splintered at the sight of Russ's favorite truck—the one he'd been sleeping with for the past week—lying in pieces on the wood floor. Some of the pieces were crushed, and she gathered them into her hand. "I don't think it can be fixed, precious. But we can find you a new one just like it."

"I don't want a new one!" Russ cried harder, his little face contorted with the agony of the loss. "I want this one. The one fwom my Daddy. Fix it, Gwandma. Pwease?"

Her body shook with the effort of holding back tears. It was unfixable. She placed the pieces on the floor and searched for any two that might go together, desperate to salvage something, but they kept falling apart. Nothing fit.

"Mom?"

Maggie called her, but she didn't look up.

Her hands started to shake so badly she couldn't get the pieces she held to line up. What was she going to do? She couldn't fix it.

"Mom?"

Rosemary opened her eyes partway, squinting against the sunlight coming through the window near her head. Maggie was standing beside her. She sat up quickly—too quickly—and the room spun.

"What time is it?" she asked, waiting for the room to settle before she tried to stand.

"Almost ten." Confusion rang in Maggie's voice.

"Ten?" Was that possible? She hadn't slept past seven in forty years. "Oh, good heavens! Eli?" He was an early riser. If he was still in bed, it could only mean he'd died in his sleep. She sprang from the couch in a panic, her heart slamming against her chest wall, and bolted to the bedroom. There she pulled up short.

The bed was empty and already made. He'd gotten up and left her sleeping on the couch. Relief flooded her and, on its heels, the profound sadness that greeted her every morning these days. She sensed Maggie had followed her into the bedroom, and while she wanted to collapse on the floor right where she stood, she wouldn't give in to the dramatics. Instead, she went to the bed and leaned against it for support, pretending to smooth out some nonexistent wrinkle in the comforter.

"Want to tell me what's going on?" Maggie asked.

Rosemary glanced at Maggie but continued pulling at the bedclothes, getting a grip on her emotions. "I stayed up late reading and I guess I fell asleep on the couch."

"The couch is made up with a sheet and a blanket and your pillow from the bed. You didn't just fall asleep while reading, so let's try this again. What's going on?"

"Nothing."

"Are you and Dad having trouble? Is that why you're sleeping on the couch?" This time, the confusion in her voice went sharp with fear.

"Oh, for heaven's sake, Maggie. Of course not." She forced a chuckle to add authenticity to her lie. "I haven't been sleeping well lately, and your dad needs his rest so his heart can recover. I didn't want my tossing and turning to keep him awake, so I've been sleeping on the couch some."

Ten nights straight counted as some, right?

"What brings you by this morning, dear?" Rosemary changed the touchy subject, shooing her daughter out of the bedroom and down the hall.

"I just thought I'd stop by on my way to work. Maybe beg a cup of coffee."

They both stopped in the kitchen, looking around in surprise at the mess.

"Dad fixed his own breakfast, too?" Maggie's eyes widened.

It looked as though he'd made a half-assed

attempt to clean up after himself. His dirty dishes were in the sink, but the butter and jelly were still on the table, and a half carafe of stone-cold coffee sat on the counter.

"You must've been dead to the world if you didn't hear him." Maggie laughed, her mood lighter now. "But then, you were still sleeping hard when I woke you."

Rosemary shuddered at the vague memory of the dream she'd been absorbed in. "I'm glad you woke me when you did." She didn't add that, as tired as she still felt, she might've slept all day. She needed caffeine. "Here. Let me get some coffee brewing." She poured the leftover into the sink and rinsed the pot, groping for conversation, which didn't come so easily with her daughter anymore...or anyone else for that matter. "You're going in later than usual today, aren't you?"

"Yeah, I've been sleeping later, too." Maggie walked to the window and peered out toward the backyard. "Where's Dad, anyway? The truck's here, but the shop's dark and none of the doors are open."

That's odd.

Rosemary's heart jumped from normal to racing in the span of two beats. "He hasn't collapsed out in the yard, has he?"

She was out the back door in a split second with Maggie at her heels.

The path to the machine shop was a clear shot,

and there wasn't a body sprawled out between here and there.

Maggie had disappeared at a jog around the corner of the house, and Rosemary met her three-quarters of the way around in the side yard. "He's not here. Did he say anything last night? Any plans to go anywhere today?"

"No. If he had plans, he didn't mention them." But then, they hadn't spoken much the past few days, and what he did say was tinged with hurt and resentment. While Rosemary had just been too tired to make conversation.

"Maybe he has the cell with him." Maggie pulled hers out of her pocket and punched a button with her thumb as they moseyed their way to the front yard.

"If he does, it'll be the first time...stubborn old coot. I've asked him to carry it with him, but do you think he'll listen to me? Nooo. Uh-uh. He'd rather have me here, worrying—"

Maggie's hand gripped her arm suddenly. "Oh, my God, Mom. Look."

An instant pall of dread came over Rosemary as her gaze followed her daughter's finger to the end of the driveway.

MAGGIE CLOSED HER MOUTH, unaware at what point it had fallen open. But the sight that was turning into her mom and dad's driveway sent a shock to her system.

A shiny monster-size motor home with her dad

beaming at them from the window of the driver's side was coming toward them.

"The brain fog has taken its toll," her mom whispered, and then louder added, "He's completely lost his mind."

The engine was surprisingly quiet for such a huge vehicle, and it rolled to a smooth stop.

Her dad stood and waved, a smile splitting his face ear to ear. The door opened on the far side, and then he appeared around the front. "Well, what do you think?"

"What do I think?" Her mom's fists were planted squarely on her hips, and Maggie had never seen her face quite that shade of red. "I think when the doctor opened you up, he must've vacuumed out all the parts you used for rational thinking."

Her dad's smile didn't falter. "My rational thinking parts are as good as they ever were—just like everything else." He pointed his finger at her. "I promised you right before I went into surgery I was going to retire, and you and I were gonna travel and see the world. I'm just keeping my word. This time next week, we'll be enjoying the Grand Canyon in our new RV—our home away from home." He gave a loving pat to the side of the vehicle.

"You bought this monstrosity?" All of that rosy flush drained from her mom's face, replaced by sickly white.

"Yep."

Even Maggie's head spun at how much this thing

must've cost. Could they afford it, or had her dad really gone off the deep end as much as her mom had been implying over the past couple of months? "Is it really a new one, Dad?"

"Naw." He ran his hand across the shiny black paint. "It's used. But it's in great condition. Less than fifteen thousand miles on the odometer. Bought it from a guy in Murray. His wife died, and he just doesn't want to travel in it anymore." He motioned. "Come take a look at the inside."

Maggie had seen large motor homes on TV, but she'd never actually set foot inside one. She was stunned when she stepped up into the lovely interior, which sported gleaming walnut cabinetry and two beige leather couches—one on each side of the coach.

Her dad led the way, pointing out the amenities. "Double-sided refrigerator, convection/microwave oven, two gas burners on the cooktop. Nice size sink with hot and cold running water." He clapped his hands together, more excited than Maggie had ever witnessed about something that didn't involve Russ. "You haven't seen the best part."

He moved to the front and pushed a button. A grinding noise sounded beneath the floor where they stood. "Hydraulic jacks," he explained. "To get her level."

Her mom wandered back toward the bedroom area, not saying anything, but when she made the about-face, the firm set of her mouth and the arms folded tightly across her chest told Maggie she was not a happy camper.

A tension like she'd never felt before between her parents filled the space. It was unsettling. Maggie had the sudden urge to skedaddle and let them have the "discussion" her mom was obviously gearing up for.

But her dad was like a kid at a carnival. She couldn't walk out and leave him just yet.

"Okay, now she's level." The sound underneath had stopped and four red lights on the dashboard all turned green. "Now, watch this." He pushed another button. The coach shuddered with a creak and a groan, and then the side she was facing began to move. The entire driver's side of the coach, including the couch, the dinette and the refrigerator, slid outward, adding an additional three feet of floor space to the length of the room. Another button, and the entire passenger-side couch and kitchen area did the same.

"Wow! It's like magic!" Her dad's enthusiasm caught up with her. She turned to see if the magic was having the same effect on her mom and was met with an angry glare. Apparently not.

"Don't encourage this foolishness," her mom hissed.

Dad seemed oblivious to Mom's reaction as he darted past them to the bathroom area of the coach. "Garden shower. Lavatory." He opened and closed a door on his left. "Private room for doin' your business." He pressed a button on the wall and the bedroom area slid out, just like the front had done, making a walkway around the bed. "Queen-size bed and lots of closet and drawer space."

"Humph," her mom replied.

"It's great, Dad." Maggie gave him a hug of approval.

"You always take his side," her mom snapped.

Oh, yeah. Definitely time to leave.

Maggie glanced at her watch and feigned alarm. "Oh, crap! I've gotta go or else I'll miss my first client…"

"You don't want to go for a ride?" The disappointment on her dad's face was genuine.

"Tomorrow," she promised as she gave them each a peck on the cheek.

"Okay." Dad grinned and flipped open one of the cabinets over the bed to peer inside.

Mom's look said there wouldn't be any riding in the vehicle tomorrow. It would be back to its original owner by then.

ROSEMARY HAD BEEN seething at idle, waiting until she heard Maggie's car start before she shifted her anger into forward gear.

"You've gone too far this time, Eli." She thrust a finger in his direction to poke him in the chest but caught the gesture before it made contact and instead detoured it upward, shaking it in his face. "I've been very understanding of all your foolishness since the surgery. But this absolutely takes the cake as the most asinine thing you've ever done. Now, you take this contraption back to where you bought it and get our money back."

"No." Eli's voice was calm. "The day after tomorrow, I'm headed out west to see the Grand Canyon. I've already made reservations at the campground there, and I'm going. You can either come with me, or you can stay here." He reached down and took her hand, and the touch quieted something inside her. She ground her teeth together to get the anger back.

He sat on the bed, putting their eyes on a level plane. "You've been a good wife, Rosie. The best wife a man could ask for. And we've worked hard for the past forty-one years without ever taking any time for the two of us. You never complained, just went along from day to day." He reached up to brush his fingers through the hair at her temple. "But I've seen with my own eyes what my surgery's done to you. You're not yourself. And I'm so afraid if I don't get you away somewhere so you can rest and relax, I'm the one who's going to be left here alone. I couldn't bear that."

His words sapped her of any remaining aggravation. She sat on his knee and put her arm around his shoulder, studying his face. His color was better than she'd seen it in years, as was his energy level. But she couldn't shake the worry. "Won't driving this big thing put a lot of pressure on you?"

"My heart's fine. When are you going to let

yourself believe that? They fixed it. There was no damage from a heart attack. It beats fast when I'm excited and slows when I'm not, just like yours does. It works the way it ought to."

"You didn't answer my question."

He took a breath, and his mouth rose at one end. "I checked with the doc, and he said if it was something I wanted to do, to go for it. You've been walking around in a coma for two weeks, Rosie. You haven't even noticed when I've been gone."

Rosemary thought back to the times when his truck was gone during the day. She'd assumed he'd gone uptown to shoot the breeze. "Where've you been going?" Now he had her curious.

"The guy who owned the coach has been giving me driving lessons. He picked me up this morning right here." He waved his hand toward the house. "I actually bought it the day after you started sleeping on the couch. That was the day I knew I had to do something drastic to get my Rosie back."

"Oh, Eli." She leaned her forehead to his cheek, and his arms closed around her.

"Now, I know it's going to take a while for us to get back to how we used to be. But a couple of weeks of travel and having fun will give us a start."

She pushed back to look at him. "A couple of weeks is a long time for two people who've never been away from home for more than a weekend."

He grinned. "That's what's great about this. We take our home with us." He patted the bed and winked. "We've got our bed, which I've already made up with our own sheets and blankets. We just need to bring our pillows." He shifted her off his lap and stood up, pushing the button to bring in the slide. "And lookee here." He opened what looked like a closet. "A stacked washer and dryer unit, so we can do laundry." He took her hand and led her back to the front room, opening the cabinet over the kitchen sink, which was filled with dishes.

"The guy sold me everything with it. Dishes, silverware." He opened a large, deep drawer filled with cookware. "All kinds of pots and pans, too. Movie DVDs, a coffeemaker, toaster, waffle iron. I'm telling you, Rosie, it's ready to move into. All it's waiting for is groceries and our clothes."

Rosemary's heart fluttered with a good kind of excitement—a feeling she hadn't felt in far too long. The flutter wasn't strong, and it didn't overpower the anxiety she was experiencing, but she couldn't ignore it, either. "Well, if you're determined to go…"

"I am." Eli pushed the button and the kitchen slid back in.

"I would worry myself sick, thinking about you being out on the highway, all by yourself."

He chuckled and brought in the other slide. "You're gonna worry yourself sick either way. You might as well get in some sights while you're at it. Now, come here." He pointed to the passenger seat. "Try it out."

She sat on the soft leather, which had been sat

on enough to be broken in. "It *is* comfortable," she admitted, playing with the buttons on the side to adjust the seat to her preferences while he raised the hydraulic jacks. "But, what about the cost, Eli? I know it was expensive."

"Life's short, and we can't take our money with us. Let's enjoy it and each other, while we can. Okay?"

"Okay." Her throat closed around her answer.

"Now, buckle your seat belt, 'cause we're taking 'er for a ride."

"Well, somebody's getting taken for a ride," she quipped. "But I think it may be me."

"See there." Eli laughed as he eased the big rig out of their driveway. "You're getting back to your old self already, and we haven't even driven out of town."

CHAPTER TWENTY-ONE

"YOU WOULD TELL me if anything was wrong, right?" Jeff tried to convince himself the odd quality to Maggie's voice was simply the underlying tension between them, but he couldn't shake the feeling it was more than that.

"Nothing's wrong." A loud yawn interrupted her part of the conversation. "I'm just tired, and standing most of the day makes my back hurt. But Dr. Donovan tells me that's to be expected when you're pregnant at thirty-seven as opposed to nineteen."

"I suppose that's true." He shuffled some of the papers lying on the desk in front of him, groping for conversation topics to keep her talking a while longer. "Are you still going to the gym? Maybe you should give that a break for a while." Damn! There he went, telling her what she should be doing. He'd been really watching what he said lately, trying to be ultra-supportive and concerned, while not giving in to advice or anything that would come across as overbearing.

"I haven't been going as much as I was, but I'm trying to get in a couple of low-impact aerobics classes a week. And I walk during my breaks at work. I might get a treadmill for home, but I just don't have the energy to shop for one right now. But this exhaustion will pass. I slept through the entire first trimester with Russ, if you remember."

"I do." Jeff smiled at the memory of coming home and finding Mags asleep at the oddest hours of the day. "And when you hit the third trimester, you couldn't sleep at all. The three months in the middle were almost normal, though."

She didn't respond to that, and he sensed she was about to make an excuse to hang up.

"I talked to Russ yesterday," he said.

"Yeah, me, too." Another yawn. "Sounds like calculus is kicking his ass."

"I told him to get a tutor or sign up for a study group." Parenting advice didn't count as being overbearing, did it? Parents were supposed to tell their kids what to do. He held his breath, waiting for her response.

"And I told him he should stay in more and study, and go out less. The thing is, high school was easy for him. He's never had to study, and doesn't even know how to, really. A study group would be good for him."

His breath eased out at her words of agreement, followed by another long pause. "He said Eli and Rosemary made it to the Grand Canyon and are having a great time."

"Yeah. At first, I thought Dad had lost his mind,

but Mom sounds like a different person on the phone. It's been a good thing for both of them, I think."

"All couples can benefit from having time alone, away from everything," he said gently, prodding her to talk about their situation.

She gave a loud sigh. "Oh, Lord, please don't let her come home pregnant."

Jeff chuckled, hoping she was kidding and not making commentary about herself. The thought sobered him. Just because their last time together didn't go well…that wouldn't cause her to…? His heart stalled. "You're still okay with this, aren't you, Mags? This pregnancy?"

"No regrets, if that's what you're asking. But I'm really tired, and I do need to go to bed."

Because ignoring her not-so-subtle hint might be construed as overbearing, he gave up on any more attempts to keep her on the line. "I understand. Get some rest. I'll talk to you soon." Which meant the next time he called her. She hadn't called him since her visit, which was frustrating if he thought about it too much.

"Okay. Bye."

"See you soo—"

He tossed his phone onto the stack of papers and rested his forehead on his thumbs, pressing into the soreness that seemed to be a permanent fixture these days. A month ago, he was so sure he and Mags were headed toward reconciliation. Now they were hurtling backward at a speed so fast it was difficult to keep his bearings.

Just keep focused on the baby. She's the key.

For some reason, he'd started referring to the baby as a girl. Maybe it was intuition and maybe just wishful thinking. But whether the baby was a he or a she, the child gave him and Mags a reason to be together, and he was determined to give all he had to making that time together count.

He ran his fingertips over the word he'd written on his calendar across the third week of November— *Russ.* He'd started to put *and Mags,* but he didn't want his dad asking questions when he came to fill in at the dealership.

Anyway, he didn't have to write her name on his calendar. It was written on his heart.

And if all went well, maybe he wouldn't have to ever write the baby's name on a calendar.

Maybe they could find a way for them all to be together…maybe he could *make* a way.

If all went well.

IF ELI'S HEART can take this, it can take anything, Rosemary decided, because right at that moment hers was so filled with awe and wonder it proved impossible for it to keep a steady rhythm. It had been that way for the past two days, ever since their arrival at the Grand Canyon.

She'd been given a glimpse of a whole new world. The idea that the seemingly innocuous river at the bottom of the canyon had cut through and eroded away the land until a gorge so expansive had been created was almost more than her mind could grasp. Time after time since their arrival, they'd returned to the overlook, drawn by the majestic view.

But it wasn't the canyon alone that had her heart thrumming. It was the helicopter tour through the canyon this morning—a ride so terrifyingly exciting she'd had to breathe into a paper sack to combat hyperventilation. It was the drumbeat of the Native American dancers they'd watched this afternoon still pulsing through her veins. It was the stirring sensations she'd felt this evening while watching the IMAX movie.

Now, it was Eli's easy laugh beside her and the happy gleam in his eyes that shimmered in the campfire light.

"Careful. It's hot." He dangled the straightened clothes hanger over her lap, and she gingerly slid the marshmallow—toasted to a yummy, golden perfection—off the end and popped it into her mouth.

Was there anything more delicious…well, except for the man himself? The old, familiar stirring deep in her belly was even more pleasant than the sweetness that filled her mouth.

"No more for me." She lifted the half-empty bag of marshmallows from the seat beside her.

Eli stuck the end of the wire back into the fire to burn off the last remains. "I'm done, too."

The smell of burnt sugar filled her nostrils and settled on her tongue, reminding her of the caramel pie filling she used to make every Sunday—the one where she caramelized the sugar in a cast-iron skillet. "Think I'll make a pie tomorrow." She stretched out her legs to warm her feet.

Eli shook his head in mock amazement. "I'll swear, Rosie. You've taken to this motorhome living like a duck to water." He paused, then pointed to the large rig parked in the next site over. "Talked to Pete a long time today about full-timing. He said it was a tough decision, but one they've never regretted."

Rosemary thought about the prospect of selling the house and moving into the RV full-time—a daunting idea but one that certainly held some appeal. "I can't believe I'm saying this, but I love this. All of it." She waved toward their coach and then took in the campfire and the rest of their surroundings. "I love the comfort of the coach and the thrill of seeing new places." She reached over and patted his hand. "I love you." Then she took a deep breath, enjoying the fresh, clean scent of the cedar burning in the fire pit. "If it weren't for Maggie, I believe I could sell the house and do this year-round."

"We could sell the house, but not the shop." The uncommonly serious tone to Eli's voice grabbed her full attention. "The shop's insulated and has running water. Make a small living quarters in it, like maybe a living room and a bathroom, but include space big enough to pull the rig in. That way, we could travel most of the year, but go back to Taylor's Grove when we wanted to, like through the holidays. Lots of people our age are doing that now."

"Lots of people our age don't have a daughter living nearby whose husband died and whose son just went away to college, leaving her alone…and lonely."

Eli's bottom lip protruded in thought. "Maybe she'd look harder—put herself out there more—if we weren't such a handy time-filler for her."

The gladness that had filled Rosemary's heart so thoroughly a few minutes before started to seep out along with her deepest fear. "I'm afraid she'd turn to Jeff."

Eli's gaze met hers and held fast. "Maybe she needs to."

His words were like a spark from the campfire that had made its way into her stomach. "How can you say that? You and I witnessed firsthand what she went through after he left. It was worse than withdrawal from a drug."

"So maybe that's when we should've realized he was ingrained in her soul. Maybe *that* was our failure—not encouraging them to try and work it out. We took her side. Blamed him. Made her feel like she had every right to walk away, and maybe we were wrong. Maybe we were too much in her life and maybe we still are. Maybe if we weren't there she'd finally figure out what she really needs...and *who*."

"What's brought on this change of heart, Eli?"

His mouth twitched at her word choice and he gave her his *you know the answer to that* look. But then his face turned somber and reflective. "I was looking death in the face, Rosie, but I was too blind to see it. Got me to thinking about all the other things I was blind to. The love that beams from Russ when he talks about his dad? I've seen that same love reflected in Maggie's eyes every time the man's name comes up. Yeah, it's shadowed by pain. But it's right there plain as day if you're open to seeing it." His voice had become more vehement, more passionate than Rosemary had heard in years. While she didn't agree with his logic, it stirred her just the same. And when he reached out and took her hand and said, "You're ingrained in my soul, Rosie. It's you I really need..." she was a goner.

She stood and tilted her head toward the coach. "Maybe we need to go in and christen that bed good and proper."

He was on his feet in a flash, pulling her into a kiss that caused the burn in her belly to explode into full flame. "You go on," he said when their mouths finally parted. "I'll put out the fire."

"Don't you dare." She gave a low laugh. "This is going to be fast and furious, and I'm probably gonna need a few more marshmallows afterward to get my energy back."

His grin was wary. "You're not afraid of killing me?"

She shrugged in resignation. "Guess if I do, you'll die happy."

"A man can't ask for more than that."

He clapped his hands to her rear end and pulled her to him once again. The campfire heated her backside, and Eli heated her front.

He was toasting her like he had the marshmallows—to hot and yummy perfection.

"AND THEN HE SAID, 'This isn't moonshine. Moonshine's clear. And if you pour some out on the ground and throw a match to it, it burns blue, like your eyes." Emmy was in the middle of one of her many tales—standard fare for Rowdy Friday—the once-a-month get-together with anyone from the salon who wanted to get out and have some fun to kick off the weekend.

Maggie shifted in her seat, trying to stretch her back muscles, which were still aching from standing all day and then sitting in the hard restaurant chair for several hours now. She hoped this story didn't have too funny a punch line. Her stomach was cramping from laughing at all of Emmy's wild stories.

"So, I just smile at him and bat my eyes real flirty," Emmy continued. "And I say, 'Well, this is the way we make moonshine in Kentucky. It's sweet and spicy, just like our women, and no one would dare pour any on the ground because it would be a sin to waste a drop of it. But if it burned, it would burn black and blue, just like *your* eyes are gonna be if you don't get your hand off my ass.'"

The group gave a collective squeal at Emmy's sassiness.

"Did he move it?" Bev asked. "Or did you have to teach him a lesson?"

"Oh, he moved it all right." Emmy glanced coyly about the room. "But I ended up teaching him a few lessons later on, anyway." She grinned around the straw she'd been chewing on. "Course, he taught me a few, too."

"You always get your man, EmmyLou." An eye roll accompanied Janessa's snarl. "Or, at least, in *your* telling of it you do."

Generally, the people who worked at the salon got along well. But Janessa and her boyfriend had broken up last week, and she was still tender, evidenced by the fact she hogged the conversation for forty-five minutes, slamming him and the woman he'd broken up with her for. Everybody had been supportive and let her vent. But Rowdy Friday's were supposed to be fun, not downers. The group had shown a definite upswing in attitude once Emmy took the floor.

"If I don't get him, I didn't want him." Emmy's perfect eyebrow arched to a point as she leaned across the table toward Janessa. "Men are like shoes. Why waste your time on the ones that hurt when you could be out shopping for the ones that fit just right?"

Maggie winced. The advice was solid, but if Janessa started in on another of her monologues, Maggie's rear was going to go completely numb.

Evidently, she wasn't the only one who felt that way. During this last exchange, Eppie had sent a text and Tink had immediately received one. Interesting, since they rode together.

Sure enough, just as Janessa said, "But—" Tink interrupted. "Hey, y'all. It's been fun, but I need to get home. I've got a pair of comfy shoes I'm hankering to slip on." She flashed a big grin Emmy's way.

"Me, too," a couple of others agreed, and the group dispersed with hugs.

"You ready?" Emmy asked. She was going to drop Maggie off at the salon to get her car.

Maggie pointed toward the ladies' room. "Gotta make a pit stop first."

"Meet you out front." Emmy hurried to catch up with Janessa, probably with a few last words of wisdom to impart.

All the talk of boyfriends and husbands, and especially Emmy's last analogy, had pushed Jeff to the front of Maggie's mind, a place he was never too far from. Being with him made her feel as if she was wearing platform stilettos—surprisingly comfortable, dangerously high and sexy, but they put her in a constant state of terror that she'd lose her balance and fall.

As she opened the restroom door, a warmth gushed from her, and her first thought was she'd started her period. A split second later, it hit her she shouldn't be having a period.

She rushed into the stall. "No. Please, please, please," she whispered as panic squeezed her insides. The sight of blood in her panties caused the world to spin around her. She leaned against the door, holding onto the hook she'd normally use for her purse, trying to wrap her brain around a plan of action when it was yanking her in other directions.

It might be nothing. I've been on my feet too long today. Get to my car and call Dr. Donovan.

She donned a pad from the machine on the wall and pinched her cheeks to bring some color to her deathly pale complexion then went to meet Emmy.

"Wow." Emmy was leaning on her car, and she glanced at her watch. "You must've met somebody and had a quickie."

Maggie forced a smile. "It's not Veterans Day yet." Buckling into the passenger seat, she focused on calm breaths.

Emmy's mouth was moving ninety-to-nothing about Janessa's situation, and Maggie managed to get through the short distance by only adding an occasional "Uh-huh" or "I know" in response. She'd said her "See you tomorrow" by the time Emmy's car pulled to a stop beside hers.

She opened the door and stepped out as a searing pain shot through her back. "Oh!" The next one gripped her from the front, doubling her over. She threw out a hand and caught herself on the seat on the way down.

"Maggie! What's wrong?"

"Help me." She ground out the words through the pain.

Emmy flew around the car and lifted her into the seat. "You having appendicitis? What is it? I'm taking you to the hospital." She fumbled, trying to get the seat belt over Maggie's hunched body. "Oh, to hell with this thing."

Still slumped in nauseating pain, Maggie pointed to her purse as Emmy got back in the car. "Get my phone and call Dr. Donovan. Tell her I think I'm having a mis-miscarriage." A sob accompanied the word.

Emmy's startled look spoke volumes, but she calmly did as she'd been instructed. Maggie recognized the pain, so similar to labor, and used the breathing techniques she'd learned when she was pregnant with Russ.

"Bleeding and cramping?" Emmy asked, her voice gentle as she held Maggie's hand firmly. Maggie nodded, and Emmy made the confirmation back into the phone. "Okay," she said before hanging up. "She's meeting us at the hospital."

Maggie tried to control her crying, knowing the tension only made things worse. But the whimpers kept escaping.

Emmy rubbed her back with one hand, trying to

console her. "It's going to be okay, Maggie Russell Wells Gunther Russell. Just hang on. Everything will be okay."

Maggie shook her head. "It's not going to be okay, Emmy. I'm losing Jeff's baby." A gut-wrenching spasm shook her body, loosening the sobs lodged in her throat.

She cried all the way to the emergency room.

"Damn!"

Jeff reached for his phone with one hand and the remote with the other, keeping his eyes glued on the TV as the Charger quarterback made his run down the field with the ball and a Rams player in hot pursuit.

"Run!" His voice echoed back to him as he hit the mute button. Reluctantly, he paused the game. He'd waited too long for the Chargers to score in this game, and he wasn't about to miss it now.

The piano arpeggio ring tone got louder as it made its second loop. At the last second, he looked at the caller ID and answered with a surprised smile.

"Mags!"

"Um…oh…no, Jeff. This isn't Maggie. It's EmmyLou Creighton. I'm using Maggie's phone."

"Hey, EmmyLou." Emmy's voice didn't hold its usual energy. In fact, was it shaking? And why was she calling from Maggie's phone? The thoughts shot through his brain in a split second and brought him out of his seat. "Is Mags okay?"

His heart stalled at the sniffle on the other end. "Tell me, damn it! What's happened to her?"

"She's...she's okay. She's sleeping."

The hand Jeff wiped down his face left a sweaty trail. If this was one of those high-school throwback best friend calls, Miss EmmyLou was about to—

"It's the baby, Jeff. She...lost the baby." Her voice ruptured on a sob as his knees gave way, and he landed back in the chair. "I'm so sorry," she whispered.

"She had a mis—" He'd heard correctly, and there was no use making her say it again. He ran a hand down the back of his head, massaging the muscles that had tightened into iron bands. "But Mags is okay?"

"Yeah. We're at the hospital in Paducah. They did a D and C...or something like that...to, you know... make sure everything was...was cleaned out...so she wouldn't get an infection. They're keeping her here overnight."

"And how is she...taking it?"

Emmy's breath did a quick triple catch. "I've never seen her so upset. Much worse than when Zeke died."

"I'm coming out there," Jeff said, more to himself than to her.

"Rosemary and Eli are gone, and she didn't want me to call Russ." Emmy's voice grew a little stronger. "And she's probably gonna be pissed at me, but she was going to call you tomorrow, anyway."

"You did the right thing, Emmy. I appreciate it." Jeff pushed from the chair again and started to pace, thinking aloud and trying to keep his mind from sliding quickly into the mire of grief. "I'll have to call Dad and get him to cover for me, and then I'll find the quickest flight out."

"Okay. Yeah...well...I really am sorry, Jeff. I didn't know...she hadn't told me." He thought he detected a note of hurt in her tone.

"We were going to tell Russ together when he came home at Thanksgiving. We wanted him to be the first to know, so we were sitting on the news until then."

"That's y'all's business," she said quietly. "You don't need to explain. I...uh...want to get back in there with her. I'm out in the hall right now, so..."

"Yeah." He found himself nodding even though she couldn't see him. "I'll get there as soon as I can."

"'Kay. Bye."

Jeff's pacing had carried him out onto the balcony. He did an about-face and strode back into the living room, thumb poised on the button to call his dad. But his hand began to tremble. The tremor moved up his arm into his torso and then spread throughout his whole body. The air compressed in his lungs, not moving in or out because the airways were closed by the muscles tightened around them. His hands found the back of the couch, and he leaned his weight against them, fighting for breath.

It released in a rush, bringing with it the upload

of grief and pain that he'd kept suppressed during the telephone conversation. *The baby...gone.* He managed to keep his sobs silent—neighbors were close and everyone kept their balconies open—but the tears flowed. He didn't try to hold them in. He needed to let them out now, so they didn't show up as he explained the situation to his dad.

He gave himself the time he needed to get everything under control, and then he pressed the button on his phone.

His dad answered on the first ring. "Hey. What's up?"

"I need to go to Kentucky for a few days, and I was wondering if you could cover for me?"

His dad loved when he could be in charge at the dealership again, so Jeff wasn't prepared for the long pause. "Look, son. I don't mind working, but if you and Maggie are trying to work up a case again for each other—"

"Mags just had a miscarriage, Dad." His voice quivered, and he swallowed. "She was pregnant with my baby. That's what she came out here to tell me last week. But I just got a call that she's in the hospital. She lost the baby."

"Oh, Jeff. I...I don't know what to say. This is quite a shock."

"I know. Maggie and I got together when we moved Russ, and she got pregnant...again. We were both happy about it. Were trying to work things out. But...now...I need to be with her, Dad."

"Of course you do. Go. Stay as long as you need to." Sorrow weighted his dad's words.

"Thanks, Dad. You'll tell Mom? And…and Chloe. I've already told her a little about Mags and I." His heart squeezed in his chest.

"I'll tell them. Call and let us know how Maggie's doing."

"I will."

"And, Jeff…I'm sorry, son. That's tough."

"Yeah. Thanks. I'll call you."

They hung up without saying goodbye.

Jeff roamed the condo, breathing deeply to calm his nerves before he called the airlines. His aimless wandering took him to the bedroom balcony and fresh air. A particularly bright star drew his attention, and he raised a finger to "touch" it. "Goodbye, little one," he whispered. "Your daddy will always love you."

It twinkled in response.

Turning back into the bedroom, he called the airlines to book his flights, not stopping with Nashville, but making arrangements all the way to Paducah's small Barkley Regional Airport.

Making arrangements to get there as quickly as possible.

Mags needed him.

CHAPTER TWENTY-TWO

A CLEAN BUT discomforting antiseptic scent burned Maggie's nostrils and the back of her throat as she woke up slowly to a room half-lit in blue. She was partially sitting up with the head of her bed raised to a forty-five-degree angle. A couple of seconds of edgy *Where am I?* wove through her mind before she remembered the hospital...*the baby.*

The heavy weight of grief pressed on her shoulders and slumped them forward. As her head bowed, a dark figure to her right caught her eye.

She turned her head to find Emmy asleep in the chair beside her, looking horribly uncomfortable with her neck bent to an extreme.

"Emmy," she whispered, and her friend's lips moved, though her eyes didn't open. Maggie's mouth and throat felt like she'd been sucking on a green persimmon. It took effort to work up enough saliva to swallow. "Emmy," she repeated. It came out louder but only as a hoarse croak.

Emmy's eyes fluttered open, and she winced as she reached up to massage her neck. "Hey, you." She stood, letting the blanket she'd thrown over her sink to the floor as she leaned on the bed rail. "I thought you'd sleep all night."

"Could you get me some water?"

"Sure." Emmy scurried to the cart pushed against the wall and poured a cup from the plastic pitcher. The clock above her head read 2:48 a.m. She stepped back to the side of the bed and handed Maggie the cup, eyes squinting with concern. "How you feeling?"

"Sad." Maggie took a sip from the straw. The icy water filled her mouth, and she held it there for a few seconds, rehydrating the parched tissue before letting the liquid slide down her throat.

Emmy's cool hand stroked the inside of Maggie's arm with what should have been a comforting gesture.

Although Maggie felt no comfort...no consolation, she managed to make eye contact and utter weakly, "Thanks." She took a few more sips and then set the cup on the nightstand within easy reach.

"You should go back to sleep." Emmy's gentle hand moved to Maggie's forehead, brushing some hair away from her eyes. "Want me to let the bed down?"

Maggie shook her head. She wasn't sure she could get back to sleep—a lot of things were pressing on her mind—but she would have a greater chance if she were alone.

"I'd rest better, I think, if I knew you were getting a good night's sleep. Go on home, Emmy."

Emmy gave a long blink, obviously fighting sleep. "I'm fine in the chair. You might need something."

"All I needed was a drink, and you got me that." She pointed to the cup. "If I need anything else, I'll ask the nurse. But I'll be fine. I'll call you in the morning when I find out what time they're releasing me, and you can take me back to my car."

Emmy leaned heavily on the bed rail. "You shouldn't drive tomorrow. You'll still be groggy. We'll leave your car...or..." She paused, her face tightening like it always did when she was debating whether or not to say something.

Nothing you say can help.

"We'll figure out something," she finished.

Maggie pushed the button to let the head of the bed down some, though not all the way. "I'll be able to sleep now. Go home. I'll see you in the morning."

Emmy nodded and then covered her mouth as it stretched in a wide yawn. "Yeah. I need to sleep in a reclining position. Call me as soon as you know what time you're getting out?"

"I will," Maggie promised.

Emmy slipped into her sweater and adjusted the shoulder strap on her purse. Then she kissed two fingers and pointed them Maggie's direction. "Love you," she whispered. Her chin quivered on the words.

Maggie nodded, unable to speak. She closed her

eyes and listened to the sound of Emmy's high heels tapping their way down the otherwise silent hallway.

She would have to call Jeff as soon as possible, though that could wait until she got home. It was sure to be an emotional conversation, but at least she wouldn't have to face him during it.

A heavy breath shuddered in her chest.

Our baby girl. Gone.

She rested her hand on her midsection, as she'd done so many times in the past three weeks since she'd learned she was pregnant. *You were right here.* She pressed a little, and a groan emerged as though it had been under pressure. "How can it be possible you're not there anymore?" she whispered, verbalizing her anguish. She didn't wipe away the tears, wanting to feel them...needing to feel anything except the emptiness in her tummy.

Grogginess overtook her, a blessed sensation she welcomed. But it seemed only a few minutes later that sounds filtered into her consciousness again. Talking and noise in the hallway. The *swish* of her door opening brought her to full consciousness. She squinted against the full sunlight of morning as a nurse's aide carried a breakfast tray into her room.

"Good morning." The cheerful young man nodded and placed the tray on the cart with her water pitcher. The chair beside her groaned as if giving up a weight, and a person appeared in her periphery.

She turned her head and let out a startled gasp. "Jeff!"

"Hey, Mags." He leaned over the rail, filling her vision. Rumpled shirt. Scruffy whiskers—at least a day's growth. Red-rimmed eyes. "Emmy called me last night," he offered by way of explanation. His eyes scanned her face and then returned to hold her gaze, and she saw the reflection of her own sorrow.

"She was a girl," she said softly, and watched a silent tear trace a path down his cheek.

HE'D NEVER FELT so helpless.

Maggie's arms were around his neck, clutching him like a drowning person would a piece of driftwood. Her tears soaked through the shoulder of his shirt as her sobs shook them both, rattling the resolve to be strong that he'd built through the long night.

More than anything, he needed to hold her, needed to feel her heart beating against his. But his awkward posture as he leaned over the bed rail only allowed connection from the shoulders up, depriving him of that assurance of life he so desperately needed at the moment.

"I'm sorry." She moaned the words, and he wasn't sure if she was speaking to him or the baby.

He smoothed her hair and pressed his lips against her temples. "It's okay."

"It's *not* okay." Her muscles clenched with anguish. "It'll never be okay."

A nurse walked in, the question in her eyes

evident. He shook his head, and she left, closing the door behind her.

"I fel—felt so good." The top of Maggie's head bumped his chin as she tried to speak between the sobs racking her breath. "I was try—trying to stay in shape. I—I must've done too much."

"You didn't do too much, Mags. These things just…just happen." He loosened her arms so he could move back and look into her eyes. He cupped her wet face in his hands as her tears continued, drenching his fingers. "It's nobody's fault. No one's to blame."

She jerked away from him, turning her face to the opposite wall, squeezing her eyes—and mouth—closed. He took the moment to wipe his face on his sleeve.

He continued leaning on the rail, but she didn't turn back. He reminded himself not to make demands—give her whatever she needed, which for the moment appeared to be silence.

He sat down and waited, biting his tongue as the silence became deafening.

In the early days, there'd *never* been silence.

Finally Mags rolled back and put the bed into a seated position, her breath softening into a normal rhythm. "You've been up all night." Her tone was listless.

"I caught a red-eye to Nashville. Got there around three. The flight coming here left at five forty-five and was less than an hour." He paused, but she didn't respond. "Emmy met me and took me to get your car."

She focused on the wall in front of the bed, never glancing his way. "You shouldn't have come." Her chest lifted and fell in a deep, resigned breath. "Nothing you can do here."

Thank God for the internet. During the layover in Nashville, he'd had plenty of time to research the emotional impact of a miscarriage and recognized Maggie's reactions as normal for many women.

"This is where I need to be," he answered.

She looked at him, then...and he wished she hadn't. Her swollen eyes, bloodshot and glittering with tears, and her skin bearing huge red blotches didn't make him flinch—but the steeliness in her gaze did. She gave him a hard look—one he'd never seen from her. It was the look of a woman who has suffered much and has become practiced at quickly erecting a protective wall. He'd learned the look from Chloe—had seen her use it often, though never directed at him—and that's what frightened him most.

He had no idea how to break through it.

"I don't need you here." The dullness in her voice had left as quickly as it appeared, replaced by a sharp edge, which sliced through his heart.

"Maybe not, but I'm here, anyway."

"I don't *want* you here," she said more emphatically.

Jeff was caught in a snare. How did he handle

this without coming across as overbearing? Maggie shouldn't be alone right now no matter what she thought. And all she had right now was him, like it or not.

Emmy had gotten no sleep at all, while he'd at least dozed a couple of hours on the plane. Eli and Rosemary were away. And Russ was out of the question. Above all else, this was where he needed and wanted to be.

"I need to be here for me, Mags." He met her gaze with an open heart. "I'm grieving for our daughter, too."

Her armor fell away, and her face contorted in a pain so deep it gripped his heart and wrung it like a wet rag.

She erupted into tears once more, rendering him helpless yet again.

SLEEP WAS MAGGIE'S only escape. Thankfully, it came easily and often throughout the weekend as the aftereffects of the anesthesia and the physical trauma metabolized slowly from her body. Perhaps she should've resisted it more, forced herself to face longer periods of consciousness. But facing longer periods of consciousness meant facing longer periods of Jeff—and *that* she couldn't handle. She felt too much when he drew near. Her heart ached with sadness and loss, and guilt festered deep in her soul.

She much preferred the numbness.

Every time she woke, he was there, hovering,

wanting to hold her, encouraging her to eat something he'd prepared. She was suffocating in his nearness, afraid if he held her too long, she might break completely apart.

By Monday midmorning, the stupor had left her. She resolved to get up and start moving—and get rid of Jeff. She showered and washed her hair, even put on some makeup so she didn't look so ghastly. She'd had to start over twice as thoughts of the baby brought tears, which smeared her mascara. But eventually she looked normal enough to fool Jeff into believing she was better.

"Wow, look at you." He propped the mop against the kitchen cabinet and came toward her with a tender smile that caused her eyes to sting. She blinked hard several times. "How you feeling?"

"I'm going to be okay." That wasn't a lie, although she wasn't exactly sure when it would come to pass. Years from now, she *would* probably be okay.

He rubbed a damp hand down her arm. "Are you hungry? Can I get you something?"

"I think I can eat." She was pretty sure he wouldn't leave until she ate, so she would force something down and make certain it stayed there. "But you go ahead and finish what you're doing. I can fix it myself."

He nodded, obviously pleased with the progress she'd made so quickly.

She eyed the contents of the refrigerator—a chicken casserole, a large bowl of homemade beef vegetable soup, a sack from Starnes Barbecue in Paducah. Jeff had been busy. She ladled some of the soup into a bowl and stuck it in the microwave for a couple of minutes. "Do you want some?" She reached for another bowl, but he shook his head.

"I had an omelet for breakfast. It filled me up."

She set the bowl on the table and got a spoon. Her stomach tightened as she lifted the spoon to her lips, but she forced the small amount down. It was delicious, with chunks of tender beef and barley—and it made her want to gag.

Jeff finished mopping and sat down at the place next to her. His hand reached out to cover her left one. Her right one, which held the spoon, trembled so violently she sloshed it back into the bowl. She pulled her hand from beneath his. "Don't, Jeff. Please don't touch me."

He looked like she'd slapped him, and her heart throbbed. She stood up quickly and moved away to lean on the counter by the sink, needing space to breathe, fighting back tears.

"Don't pull away, Mags. Please." He came up behind her, laying his hands softly on her shoulders. "We'll get through this together."

"Stop it." She twisted away from him and backed out of his reach. "No more. I've been through enough." The numbness was gone. Every fiber in her body swelled with anger, frustration, pain and sorrow. "If I'd never let you back into my life, I wouldn't be going through this now."

"I'm sorry." He held his arms out, and she rounded the table to put it between them.

"No. Don't say that. I'm not blaming you, Jeff. I'm blaming my damn weakness for you!" Her voice rose louder, but she didn't care. "I told you...I lose myself in you, and now, I've lost so much more than just myself. I. Can't. Do. This." Her hand curled tightly into a fist and beat her chest, punctuating the words that had to come out. "I can't keep putting myself through the agony that comes every time we connect." She stopped to catch her breath, and Jeff opened his mouth. "No!" She rammed a finger in his direction. "You don't get a say-so in this."

"Like hell I don't." Jeff's hands clenched his hips in his not-backing-down stance. "You pussyfoot around the word as if you're afraid of it. You call it a weakness for me. Damn it, Mags, you *love* me. *Love.* This is about two people who love each other. Who ought to be together. Ought to be married."

"Don't bring up marriage to me again." God, she was suffocating, gasping for air. "Ever," she croaked.

"I love you. You love me. We were brought back together for a reason—"

"And now that reason is *gone*." The last word gurgled on a cry of anguish, and she didn't try to stanch the tears. "Russ is grown and well on his way to being on his own. There's no reason for you and me to ever have any interaction again. We're done. Forever this time."

"Mags…" Jeff's fingers buried into the hair at the top of his head.

"Please, Jeff." Her heart was cracking, crumbling into little pieces. She lowered her voice to a plea. "Pack your things. Go back to California, and let me put what's left of my life back together."

The misery in his eyes would torment her for days to come, she knew, but she didn't flinch.

It was all part of this devastating loss.

She wasn't sure why the miscarriage happened—what she'd done to cause it…or deserve it—but there must've been something.

Jeff turned away and went upstairs to get his things.

LATE MONDAY WASN'T prime time for the business traveler, so Jeff managed to easily book a flight for that evening. Maggie took him to the airport in Paducah—a forty-five-minute drive of excruciatingly quiet torture, even though so much needed to be said.

What was the use? She was in no shape to hear anything he had to say, and the things he wanted to say bounced from too flimsy to too overbearing.

Neither were right.

He had her heart…she'd admitted that. He simply wasn't someone who could make her happy.

Was that even possible…for the person you love most in the world to be the same one you made the most miserable?

He spent the time in the air replaying the dilemma in his mind. But by the time he'd reached San Diego, he was no closer to a solution.

He pulled his luggage into his bedroom, not stopping at the bed even though exhaustion was begging him to lie down. He went to the balcony and scanned the sky for his baby girl's star, longing to glimpse a symbol of hope to combat the despair banging on the door of his soul.

No stars—all drowned out by the fake light that men use to try to find their way through the world's darkness. Not even a moon tonight. It had moved on to shine on other people—other lovers who would appreciate and understand the significance of its glow.

Turning his back on the world outside, he crept back into his bedroom, undressing as he went, letting his clothes stay where they fell.

He jerked back the covers and crawled into bed, praying for sleep…with no dreams.

CHAPTER TWENTY-THREE

ELI PRESSED THE button to turn off the book he and Rosemary had been listening to and pointed to the blue sign welcoming them back to Kentucky. "Won't be long now."

"Home's going to look good." Rosemary reached her arms over her head and stretched the stiffness out of her back. She'd been so enthralled in the audio book she'd hardly moved for over a hundred miles. "But give me a couple of days, and I'll be ready to go again." Relaxing back into the seat, she marveled at the change in the trees since they'd left. Everything had gone from summer green to autumn red and gold in less than two weeks. "We've got some tales to share, don't we?" She rolled her head toward the driver's seat again. Her neck muscles moved easily, all the tension that had locked them in place two months ago was gone.

Eli's smile sent a wave of warmth through her. "Be sure and share all our sex adventures with Sue Marsden, too. It's time I got back my Casanova reputation."

"Pfft. You old coot." She shook her head and

rolled her eyes. "You haven't been a Casa since the Nova was a new model of car."

"That so?"

"That's right." She tilted her head coyly. "But be nice, and I just might mention how well you handled your big rig." That garnered a laugh from him, which egged her on. "Yeah, I heard all you men talking around the campfires. These motor homes are just another phallic symbol to you guys, aren't they? Y'all stand around boasting about who's got the biggest and the best equipped. And you make fun of the guys who pull in and park with those little bitty rigs." She held up a hand and spread her finger and thumb about an inch apart.

"Better quit talking dirty like that, or I'll pull 'er over and haul you back to the bedroom and have my way with you again." He threw a thumb over his shoulder.

The suggestion sent a scamper of excitement down her spine. He'd done exactly that a couple of days ago somewhere in the middle of Texas. "Promise?" she taunted.

He faked a shudder. "Whoo! It's good to have my Rosie back."

"It's good to be back." She blew a kiss his direction.

They'd stayed at a campground an hour south of Nashville last night, stopping earlier in the day than they'd planned. It wouldn't have been a bad drive to come on home, but neither of them was overly anxious for their first vacation to come to an end. But now, the closer they got to home, the more excited she grew to see the trees on their own front lawn.

"You given any more thought to full-timing?"

She'd done a lot of thinking about it, actually. Every campground they stayed in had more than a few couples their age who'd sold their homes and taken to the road.

"Honestly?" She watched his face, bracing herself for his show of disappointment. "I don't think it's right for me."

He wrinkled his nose. "Me, neither."

Her cheek muscles relaxed again. "But I wouldn't mind wintering in Arizona—"

"Or Florida," he suggested.

"Anyplace warm," she agreed.

"And we could go north during the summer. Maybe even explore Canada. Take three months to visit Alaska."

Rosemary's head whirled with the possibility of seeing places she'd only dreamed of.

"Spring and fall in Kentucky, and summer and winter wherever our hearts' desires take us? Heady stuff, Rosie."

"The desire of my heart is wherever you are, Eli." She held out her hand, and he let go of the steering wheel long enough to squeeze it three times.

I love you.

He winked at her and let go, turning his satisfied

smile back to the road. "Heady stuff, Rosie—just like I said."

A particularly spectacular sugar maple tree shimmered fiery red in the sunlight. Maggie's yard was full of sugar maples—they must be in full glory right now.

"Did you tell Maggie we were coming back a day early?"

That Eli's thoughts coincided with her own no longer surprised her. They'd been together so long, sometimes they even finished sentences that the other started. "No, I didn't want her fretting if we decided to stop somewhere tonight. I'll just run over and surprise her when we get home."

Looking back over the past couple of months, Rosemary realized she'd been hard on her daughter. The things Eli said about Jeff and Maggie needing to be together weighed heavy on her mind. She wasn't sure she agreed with him. But if Maggie's future turned out to include Jeff Wells, Rosemary would just keep her mouth shut…which shouldn't be too hard considering her jaw muscles were already aching from being clenched merely at the thought of it.

MAGGIE SQUEEZED THE steering wheel, breathing in through her nose, out through her mouth. She'd come this far—she could hold it together one more mile.

Thank heavens, the woman had been her last

client of the day, because when she excitedly announced she was pregnant with her second child—*a baby girl*—Maggie had almost lost it on the spot.

Somehow she'd managed a smile and congratulations, but it had taken every ounce of grit she held in reserve. Now she felt depleted...and defeated.

She just wanted to get home and crawl into bed... and cry. God, she'd done a lot of that lately. One minute, she'd be fine, and the next an emotional wrecking ball would slam into her, demolishing her facade, revealing the empty room inside.

"Your hormones might be all over the place for a while," Dr. Donovan had warned. "And your emotions might follow along."

"You think?" Maggie murmured to the dashboard.

The past week had been one of the strangest of her life. She was so, so tired, yet sleep would slip from her grasp in a matter of only a few minutes. So, instead of resting as per the doctor's orders, she spent most nights wandering around the house in a kind of stupor—spending inordinate amounts of time in Russ's room doing nothing. She'd just sit, drawing some comfort by telling herself she'd protected one child enough to see him to adulthood, which always led to chastising herself for not being able to do it again.

Eating seemed unnecessary as she never really experienced hunger these days. Oh, she could sometimes get down a half sandwich that Emmy thrust upon her, or a bowl of soup, but nothing tasted good. Nothing tasted at all.

People asked if she'd lost weight, and it would run through her head that she'd lost a hundred-and-seventy-five pounds—the combined weight of the baby and Jeff. Sometimes she felt as though she carried the weight of the world, and sometimes she felt empty inside, like her heart and everything else had abandoned her along with Jeff and the baby.

Of course, Jeff hadn't abandoned her this time—she'd pushed him out of her heart and locked the door. When she'd nod off, succumbing to exhaustion, it was he who came tapping at the windows, the thief who stole her hours of rest.

She made the turn into her driveway, moving slowly to take in the changes in her yard since this morning. The green had disappeared from the maples. They'd donned their autumn finery, thumbing their noses at the oaks, which were only beginning to wrap themselves in their dull brown cloaks. As she pulled into the garage, the large white ash at the far side of the house caught her eye, and the sight broke her heart.

It was bare—all the leaves it had given life to and nurtured and clung to so tightly had broken loose and were whirling away on the breeze.

The poor mother ash could do nothing but watch them go, her branches waving goodbye.

Maggie's fragile heart broke open as she sat in the garage, too tired to wrestle with the weight of the car door yet. She braced her arm across the steering wheel and, leaning her forehead against it, emptied her soul of its misery, knowing it was a temporary fix but unable to stop the tears despite their futility.

A cold breeze slapped the side of her face.

"Maggie? What in the world's wrong with you?"

Maggie saw the blurred image of her mom standing beside her with the driver's side door opened wide. Maggie shook her head.

A hand touched her back softly at first, but then shook her, as if Mom was trying to wake her up. "Has something happened to Russ?"

"No," Maggie croaked. Leaning back, she brushed her sleeve down her face.

"It's Jeff, isn't it?"

Maggie heard the accusation in her mom's tone, and she paused to think on that before she spoke, staring at the rakes and shovels hanging on the wall of the garage. "No, it's not Jeff, and you need to stop blaming him." She answered slowly…and honestly, turning her head to meet her mom's hard glare directly. "It's me. It's always been me."

EVERY MUSCLE FIBER in Rosemary's body contracted at her daughter's answer, and her blood turned to ice. "What do you mean, it's you? Are…are you ill?"

Please not my baby, too. We just got through Eli.

Maggie shook her head. "No." She scrubbed her hand down her face, obviously fighting to stifle the sobs, which visibly shook her chest. "I'm not sick."

Rosemary waited. If Russ was okay and Maggie wasn't sick, she could be patient.

Her daughter leaned over and grabbed a handful of tissues from the box on the floor of the passenger side. She pressed them against her face, blew her nose and then took a gulp of air. "Let's go in," she said at last. "I have some things I need to tell you."

The cryptic tone shot another round of apprehension through Rosemary's system, and she started to tremble. Maggie hadn't confided in her in years. If she was doing it now, there must be something bad going on. She stepped back out of the way, noticing the gauntness of Maggie's features, and reminded herself her daughter had said she wasn't sick.

Was it the salon? Business always looked good when she dropped in, but was that a true indication?

"I thought you wouldn't be home until tomorrow," Maggie said, and the vacant tone sent a chill down Rosemary's spine.

"We made better time than we expected."

A light flicked on, and the garage door started its descent. "Did you have a good time?"

"Wonderful." Rosemary was in no mood to talk about the trip right then. The garage door hit the floor with a dull thud that reverberated in her stomach.

They made the rest of the journey to the house in silence.

Maggie was a persnickety housekeeper, so the sight of even a few dirty dishes sitting on the counter caused Rosemary's jaw to drop when they entered the kitchen. A bowl of cereal that looked as if it hadn't been touched sat next to the sink along with the cereal box—opened—and a carton of milk.

Maggie gave a heavy sigh as she walked over to the sink and proceeded to pour the contents of the bowl and the nearly full carton down the drain. "Sit down, Mom," she said over her shoulder as she turned on the water and flipped on the garbage disposal. "I want to start at the very beginning, so this may take a while."

The beginning of what?

Rosemary took a seat and clasped her hands on the table to quell her trembling.

The grinding stopped, and when Maggie turned off the water, the kitchen went eerily quiet for a few seconds before Maggie spoke. "I was pregnant with Jeff's baby, but I miscarried last week." Her voice wobbled its way through the sentence.

The information dropped into Rosemary's brain like a stone from a skyscraper. It traveled through her head and stopped in her throat before finally making its way to the pit of her stomach. She squinted in disbelief. "Maggie?" She tilted her head. "You had a miscarriage…last week while we were gone?"

Maggie nodded, her chin quivering on the breath she drew.

Rosemary stood and approached her daughter slowly, unsure of her own stability at the moment.

But her arms found their strength when they encircled Maggie, who wept softly against her shoulder.

She couldn't hold back her own tears, either— those spawned of sorrow for her daughter and guilt she hadn't been here during this sad time. "How far along were you?"

"Eight weeks. DNA tests determined she was a girl."

"Oh, precious." Rosemary rocked her daughter back and forth, smoothing her hair, patting her back, trying to console the inconsolable. "I'm so sorry I wasn't here for you. So, so sorry."

"There's nothing you could've done."

"But I could've been there for you." Panic jolted through Rosemary's system. "Were you alone?"

Maggie's head shook her shoulder. "Emmy took me to the hospital. They did a D and C and kept me overnight. Jeff was there when I woke up."

"Had you already told him?"

Maggie's sobs ebbed to sniffles, and she pulled away to sit down. "Yeah. He knew. That trip to Vegas…I didn't actually go. I went to California to tell him I was pregnant."

A flicker of irritation flared in Rosemary's stomach. "How could you not have told *me*?"

"Jeff needed to know first. And we planned to tell Russ together when he came home for Thanksgiving, and *then* everybody else."

The logical progression made sense and allowed Rosemary to ignore the petty jealousy burning in her belly. "Was Jeff okay? I mean, how did he take the news?"

A flicker of a smile played at Maggie's lips and her eyes took on a faraway look as if focusing on something over Rosemary's shoulder. "He was wonderful. Excited. He wanted me to move out there. Asked me to marry him."

Marry him? Again? Oh, dear Lord. Rosemary bit her tongue.

"Of course, I couldn't. He got trapped into marriage with me the first time. I couldn't do that to him again."

"I wouldn't call it entrapment." *But apparently Jeff did.* Anger prickled her skin at the thought.

Maggie shrugged and her eyes drifted back to Rosemary's, locking in place. "He was really upset about the miscarriage and very sweet and supportive. He tried to take care of me, but I didn't want him to. I just wanted to be alone." She squeezed her eyes shut. "I was horrible to him. Wouldn't let him touch me."

"That's understandable. You were grieving."

Maggie opened her eyes, and her face contorted with pain. "He was grieving, too," she said softly. "And I wanted to hold him...wanted him to hold me. But I couldn't." She ran her fingers through her hair and squeezed the roots. "He said he loved me..."

Rosemary's breath stalled in her chest. "He said that...*after* you lost the baby?"

Maggie nodded slowly. "Asked me to marry him again, too. He said we were meant to be together."

Oh, for heaven's sake. Could they still be in love after all these years? The air in Rosemary's lungs quivered as Eli's words from the campground surfaced in her thoughts...as they had so often the past week. *I'm afraid she'd turn back to Jeff,* she'd said, and Eli had replied, *Maybe she needs to.*

"Do you still love him, Maggie?"

She heard the fear in her mom's tremulous whisper, and she didn't want to scare her, but she was determined to come clean about everything. "I've never stopped loving him. Never will."

"But Zeke..."

"Was a substitute...and a poor one, at that." It was time her mom knew the truth about Zeke, so she shared it in as few details as possible, all the while watching her mom's jaw drop farther and farther at the shocking truth behind the man.

"I can't believe you never told me any of this." Her mom pressed a palm against her forehead, looking as though she were trying to keep the vast amount of information from exploding out of her frontal lobe.

Maggie spread her hands on the table, surrendering the truth. "It was just another failure."

"Life is full of failures, Maggie. If you're not failing, you're not trying. And if you're not trying, you're not living...you're simply existing"

Her mom's words struck a chord, and something thrummed deep inside her. "For years, I've felt like I was living through Russ. And then, I was around Jeff, and we were dancing and playing golf, and…" The rest was obvious. "And then I was pregnant, and I had this wonderful new life inside me, and she made me feel alive." She was all sobbed out, but a lingering tear ran down her cheek. She dabbed it away with a napkin. "And now, she's gone and Russ is gone and Jeff is g—" Her voice broke. She finished with a shrug.

"I can't believe I'm saying this." Her mom's eyes darted around the room, and her chest rose and fell on a sigh. "But if you and Jeff still love each other, why can't you work this out?"

"We have fifteen hundred miles separating us for one thing. And we both have businesses to run."

Her mom's voice was quiet. "Those are excuses, not reasons. What is it that really keeps y'all apart?"

"I'm not me with Jeff, Mom." Maggie groped for the right words. "I'm an extension of him." Her mom squinted, head tilted in question, and Maggie tried again to explain. "I wouldn't have danced in Chicago or gone with anyone else on the spur of the moment to Lake Geneva." Her mom's eyebrows rose in surprise. "Yeah." Maggie gave a sheepish grin. "That's where we were when you called to tell me about Dad's surgery." She dismissed the subject with a wave of her hand. "But, I wouldn't have invited him to stay with me on my own. He talks me into doing things that aren't me, they're him. I get lost in him. And no way would I have considered facing the crowd at the park. I was acting like him, not me."

Her mom leaned back and closed her eyes, and when they opened, they glimmered with unshed tears. She shook her head. "You're wrong, Maggie. Those things he talks you into? The things you do that you attribute to his influence? They're exactly what you would've done before..." Her voice trailed off and she swallowed.

"Before what?" Maggie's heart paused.

"Before Russ."

Her heart did a double beat to catch up.

"You were right when you said you've been living through Russ for years. Eighteen years to be exact. But not always. You were the most fearless child." Her mom pressed a fist to her lips, giving a chuckle that was nostalgic and sweet. "Lord, you were into everything." She shrugged her eyebrows. "You weren't afraid of anything and you wanted to try everything, which, of course, is the reason you got pregnant at nineteen. But after Russ came along, it was like somebody flipped a switch on you. You were so protective of him...and, now that I think about it, probably terrified something would happen to you and take you away from him. You were convinced nobody else could take care of him like you did." She pointed her finger. "If you remember, that's why you started the salon. You didn't want him in a day care…wanted him right there with you all the time. Since the day he was born, Russ was your whole life. Yet, in one short week, Jeff managed to bring out the old you—the courageous you who wasn't afraid of facing life head-on."

Maggie propped her elbows on the table and leaned her head into her hands, massaging her temples while the truth of what her mom was saying sank in.

But what about Jeff's control over her? No doubt, he had a strong personality. But if she'd done the about-face her mom said she had, he would've been grappling to understand what was happening to the woman he loved…would've been trying even harder to bring it all under control. And if she'd been suddenly facing a new side of herself that was afraid of everything, they would most definitely have been at odds.

He hadn't been trying to change her. He'd been trying to *restore* her to…*to my old, real self.*

The lightbulb moment brought a few seconds of respite before the pain of what-might-have-been placed a vise grip on her heart. She sighed. That was all water under the bridge now.

"I see what you're saying, Mom, and I think you may be right," Maggie said at last. "And I think I would've been the same way with this baby."

"I doubt that." Her mom shook her head. "Age changes us. We get older and wiser. We learn from our mistakes and finally realize which ones weren't mistakes, after all." She leaned closer. "Like Jeff, for instance. Why don't you call him?"

Maggie's stomach somersaulted at the suggestion. All those things she'd said to him the last time they were together made her heart ache all over again. "I've put him through enough."

"Would you mind if I called him?"

Maggie tried to blink the incredulity from her gaze. "Yeah, I would. We've said everything that needs to be said. The only thing that could make this any worse would be for him to think I've gone running to y'all again like I used to, trying to gang up on him. That never should've happened in the past—and it certainly shouldn't happen now."

Her mom's mouth tightened around the edges. "I'd like to apologize for all the bad things I've said about him over the years. And I'd like to tell him I'm sorry about the baby."

"Send him a card." Maggie pulled out her phone. "Here's his address."

Her mom keyed the information into her phone and then placed it on the table, absently drawing figure eights on the screen. "So why were you crying in the car? Because of your baby? Because of Jeff?" she asked softly.

"My last client told me she's pregnant with a little girl. It made me sad."

Her mom came over and knelt down in front of her, taking her hands. "And it will for a while. It's all part of the grieving process, remember? First, disbelief and denial. That's followed by anger and guilt—where you are now. You're mad at life's unfairness…that no matter how hard we try to control it, some things are out of our control."

Maggie shuddered. "That's it exactly. Why does *she* get to have a little girl, and I don't? Why did my baby leave me? Was I not good enough?" The quiver of her chin vibrated in Rosemary's heart.

"That's the anger and guilt talking. You know you're a good mom. Look at Russ." She brushed the hair from Maggie's eyes, and Maggie leaned into the gentle touch, realizing how much she'd missed it. "Life's full of mysteries. Some we solve, some we don't. Give yourself time to get to that acceptance stage, sweetheart. It's there. You just have to move forward to reach it."

Maggie stood, pulling her mom to her feet and into the first real hug they'd shared in what felt like a lifetime.

It was a small movement physically, but emotionally it moved her a giant step forward.

CHAPTER TWENTY-FOUR

"TELL YOU WHAT." Rosemary put her hands on her hips and looked around, innocently easing herself between Maggie and the table. "Go wash your face. Change your clothes if you want. I'll clean up in here, and then we'll go to my house and I'll fix us some supper."

Maggie threw a glance toward the dishes left on the counter and shook her head. "I can take care of it, Mom. I don't want you cleaning up my mess."

"I want to help." That wasn't a lie, although her conscience pricked at her double meaning. "And, anyway, your dad and I want to tell you about our trip." She gave a soft swat to her daughter's bottom. "Go on. You need to eat. It'll be good for you to get away from your thoughts for a while."

Maggie hesitated but finally gave a relenting sigh. "Okay. I won't be long." She started toward the front of the house.

"Take your time," Rosemary called after her. "We're in no rush."

She waited until she heard the footsteps fade into the bedroom before she grabbed the phone Maggie had left on the table. She pulled up the contacts and, to her relief, found Jeff's information still open. Quickly, she punched his number into her note app and then put the phone back on the table exactly where it had been.

The phone call would have to wait until later… sometime when she could be alone.

Whistling a happy tune, she moved over to the counter to start cleaning up her daughter's *other* mess.

JEFF GLANCED AT his phone but didn't recognize the number coming in. He hit the ignore button.

"You shoul' take tha," Chloe chided. "Somebody migh' nee' you."

"Shh." He waved her to quiet down. "Whoever it is can need me after Rudy makes his touchdown." No matter how many times he saw this movie, Rudy's touchdown never failed to get him *verklempt*. He didn't want to talk business over the phone with tears in his voice. Besides, whoever it was didn't leave a voice mail, so it couldn't have been too important.

"How's Maggie?"

"Shh!" Even the mention of the woman's name made his heart hurt. "We don't talk anymore. Her choice."

"You shoul' call her an'way."

"How 'bout saving the advice until the movie's over."

His phone vibrated again. Same number as before.

"Damn it!" He heard Chloe's delighted chuckle as he paused the DVD. "Hello?" he barked into the phone.

"Um…hi." The voice on the other end was hesitant and female, and he felt a twinge of guilt at his bad manners. "Is this…um…Jeff Wells?"

The voice solidified in his mind, causing the beer he was drinking to solidify in his stomach. "Rosemary?" Oh, God, had something else happened to Maggie? He shifted to the front of his seat.

"Yes. I didn't think you'd recognize my voice." She gave a nervous laugh, which lowered his anxiety level a bit.

"That western Kentucky accent's quite prominent. And it's only been a couple of months since we spoke in person." Had it really been only two months? So much had happened…

"Well, the reason I called…"

Her hesitation made him want to scream. Why in the hell *had* she called?

"Maggie told me about the baby, Jeff. I'm so sorry. I see what a terrible loss it's been for her, and I'm sure for you, too."

Except for the initial conversation after he'd arrived back home, he and his parents hadn't discussed the baby again. And, even though the subject hurt, it was comforting to speak of her out in the open. "Yeah. It was—is—bad. Healing takes time." He cleared his throat. "How is Mags?"

"Well, like you said, healing takes time. She's on her way, though, I think."

"Glad to hear that."

Chloe's eyes were wide, and she tilted her head. He gave her an I-don't-understand-it-either shrug.

"I…also…want to apologize for the way I treated you at the hospital, and—" her heavy sigh sounded in his ear "—and for how unfairly I've treated you over the years."

"That's kind of you, Rosemary, but you don't need to—"

"Yes, I do. I've bad-mouthed you for eighteen years, putting every bit of the blame for your and Maggie's troubles on you, when I was as much a part of the problem as anybody, and I'm sorry."

Her confession rendered him momentarily speechless, but there was no time for response, anyway.

"I stuck my nose where it didn't belong and always took her side against you. It wasn't fair for me to do that…to you or her."

The sincerity in her voice touched him. He waited to make sure this was an official pause before he answered. "Well, you've surprised the hell out of me, Rosemary. This really wasn't necessary, but I do appreciate it. Thanks."

"You forgive me?"

"Yes. Certainly. Apologizing takes a big person."

"Good…" There was another longer pause. "Because now that you understand I have only the best intentions for you and Maggie both, I'm going to stick my nose back where it doesn't belong."

His teeth clenched with instant annoyance. How could he have been so stupid as to think she was actually offering a sincere apology? "In that case, I'm hanging up now." He ground the words out. "Nice talking to you, Rosemary." He lowered the phone, thumb on the cancel button.

"Jeff!" Her shout blasted over the line. "Please don't hang up yet. You and Maggie belong together!"

Chloe's eyes had grown to the size of saucers, but now she narrowed them into a look that was fierce and feline. "Don' hang up," she whispered, piling all her emotion into that final *p*.

Jeff slowly lifted the phone back to his ear. "I'm listening."

SHE'D GOTTEN HIS ATTENTION, and Rosemary took it as a good sign.

"I won't keep you long," she promised. "But there are some things I want to be sure you're aware of."

"Such as...?"

"Such as the fact Maggie still loves you. Just this evening she told me for a fact that she loves you and always will. Now, I don't know if she's told you the same thing, but those words hold a powerful message if you'll hear them with your heart."

"Maggie and I have acknowledged we still care fo—"

"It's not just 'care for,' Jeff. It's love, straight up, pure and simple." She pounded the word, hoping to crack his thick skull with it.

"Whatever it is, we've acknowledged it's still there. But we also know it's illogical to try to build a relationship when we live so far apart. We both have businesses to run, and neither of us can afford to continue flying back and forth."

"She said the same thing, and I told her those were excuses, not reasons."

"They're viable truths, Rosemary."

"Maybe." She didn't want this to become an argument. "But love finds a way."

His laugh had a sharp edge. "And apparently it has. What seems to have worked well for the past sixteen years is keeping our distance. It's when we're together that things don't go so well."

"They must go *fairly* well." She met his sarcasm head-on. "She's gotten pregnant by you *twice*." Oh, Lord! Had that comment overstepped the bounds?

Apparently not. His answering chuckle sounded lighter. "I appreciate what you're trying to do, Rosemary. Honest, I do. But…did Mags tell you I proposed to her?"

"Yeah. And it shows you're an honorable man. You wanted to do the right thing for the baby."

He spoke again, his voice quieter. "But I asked her twice. Once before and again *after* we lost our baby."

"I know. She told me that, too. And that's what makes me believe y'all need to be together."

"Yeah, well, she didn't see it that way. She claims she loses herself in me. Isn't herself—"

"Yeah, yeah, yeah. Is just an extension of you." Rosemary let out her breath in a sigh, shaking her head in frustration. "I've heard it already, and, pardon my French, but I think it's bull hockey. She doesn't *lose* herself in *you*. She lost herself in Russ." She reiterated the speech she'd already given Maggie. "Those things she claims you talk her into were easy to talk her into because they brought out the old Maggie—the *real* Maggie—the one who got pushed out of the way once she became a mother and started being so extra careful about everything."

"Did you tell her that?"

"Yeah."

"And how did she take it?"

"She admits I'm right."

"That's scary."

Rosemary laughed. He really was easy to talk to, and she just might be making some headway. "But Maggie also says she's caused you enough heartache and grief, and that she's not willing to do anything that might lead to more of the same."

"Which is why you're the one calling instead of her."

"Yes."

"Did she know you were going to call me?"

"Not exactly."

"What does 'not exactly' mean? Did she *ask* you to call me?"

His incredulous tone indicated her meaning had gone foul. She wouldn't have him thinking Maggie had come running to her to take sides again. "She would probably have a heart attack if she knew we were talking."

"Oh," he said, thoughtfully pausing before continuing. "Damn, Rosemary, I'm sorry. I should've asked before now how Eli's doing."

Rosemary felt the smile break onto her face. "He's great. Better than he has been in years." At least, some parts of her life were back to where they should be.

"Good. And you enjoyed the trip in your motor home?"

The question took her aback…but, of course, Maggie would've told him all about that. They were traveling when he was here last. "Fantastic," she answered. "What a wonderful way to travel. Fun and comfortable, and no flying involved. Suits me—well, actually both of us—to a T."

"I'm glad it went well, and you had a good time. But…back to my question. So, Maggie doesn't know we're talking?"

"No. I mentioned I wanted to call you, but she told me not to. Said y'all had already said everything that needed to be said."

The pause on the other end made her regret her words. She felt the mood shift as surely as if he'd been standing right there with her. "If she feels that way—" tension sharpened his tone "—then I think you and I have nothing else to say, either."

No! Crap! In desperation, Rosemary plunged wildly into the one topic she was certain would keep him on the line. "Look at Russ…how he turned out." She spoke rapidly. "Y'all may have changed a lot over the years. But those changes haven't necessarily been bad or…or even things that should keep you apart. You've both grown up and learned to deal with problems in an adult manner. You've worked together to raise a son who's about the most perfect young man on God's green earth—and I'd say that even if he wasn't my grandson. It took a lot of cooperation for y'all to make that work. But you did, and that tells me there's a foundation for happiness there if y'all would just start to build on it again."

"Russ is my proudest moment—" His voice broke, and the sound cracked her heart. "But he seems to be the only thing we can get right."

"And you would get plenty of other things right if you get back together, give it another chance." She hoped he took that as the encouragement she intended and not as an accusation.

"Maggie's made it clear she's not interested in trying again. Not with me, anyway." Rosemary recognized the defeat in his voice because she felt it, too. "I appreciate that you called, Rosemary. And I do believe you're sincerely trying to help and not just butting in. But I think we're done here, don't you?"

"I suppose." She was fighting back tears of frustration, but she wouldn't cry, not yet.

"And when Russ comes home for Thanksgiving, give him an extra tight hug from me, would you?"

"I will, Jeff. It's been nice talking to you."

"You, too."

"Well, goodbye, I guess."

"Bye."

Rosemary slunk back toward the house, hoping Eli was absorbed enough in his TV show not to notice she'd been outside for a while.

He'd be pissed if he ever found out she'd called Jeff.

And Maggie would be livid.

Well, too bad. Desperate times called for desperate measures. And, to her way of thinking, Maggie and Jeff were desperation personified.

CHAPTER TWENTY-FIVE

MAGGIE STEPPED OUT of the motor home into the chilly mid-November air, carefully juggling her hot tea, phone and paperback. The weather was so unpredictable in Kentucky in November. One day could be warm enough for shorts and the next cold enough for gloves.

This one fell somewhere in the middle. The jeans she wore gave just enough cover to her legs and the steaming cup warmed her hands.

Several more campers had pulled out today, leaving the campground nearly empty. Only she and four other RVs remained. The entire place would be closing down December first, and her Dad would come get the motor home and take it back to Taylor's Grove. But for the next week, it would be here if she and Russ wanted to camp a bit while he was home.

She suspected he might. Maybe he'd even want to go tomorrow as soon as he got home. He loved being on Kentucky Lake as much as she did.

Dragging her chair down to the edge of the water, she settled in to watch the flocks of Canada geese passing overhead in their race south. Romantic creatures that mated for life, they held a special place in her heart.

"Lur-erk!" She bellowed a honk like her dad taught her when she was eight. Thirty years later, she could still get the attention of those in hearing range. These weren't, and her call went unanswered.

She watched until she lost sight of their V formations, which reminded her of arrowheads all pointing the same direction to some great unknown. Always forward—never back.

Back was never an option.

This day had been a duplicate of the one before and the one before that. Gray water meeting gray sky, thin gray clouds muting a setting sun. Nothing that required focus. A dull, peaceful canvas that allowed her thoughts to travel wherever they wanted.

Mostly they traveled to Chicago and San Diego.

She'd thought her mom was way off base when she suggested they leave the motor home at the lake after their last camping trip and let Maggie use it as a getaway on her days off.

Who needed a getaway when they lived alone?

But Mom had been proved right…again.

Getting away from Taylor's Grove and the house and the memories and the loneliness had been a good thing. A wonderful thing.

Silent time with no distractions—time to reflect on the changes in her life the past year. Time for her soul to heal and fill with peace as she let go of the negative and began to, literally, count her blessings, touching her thumb to her fingers in silent enumeration.

Foremost in the things she counted was Russ, eighteen and in college, making it on his own. She'd allowed his age, coupled with her widowhood, to convince her she was old. But blessing number two—the baby—proved to her otherwise. Although still there, grief took up a much smaller area than it had previously and acceptance filled in the surrounding gap. And with that acceptance came the acknowledgment that she was much younger than she allowed herself to think. She could still get pregnant. Her body still brimmed with hormones…with life—enough to create more life. Getting pregnant a third time certainly wasn't in her plans, but knowing she *could* brought thanks to her heart.

Blessing number three. She touched her thumb to her middle finger—her dad's health. She'd lost the baby, yet another precious life had been restored. Grief and joy commingled. Neither existed without the other. The never-ending cycle.

Never ending was a fitting description for other things, too—like blessing number four. She made herself speak the name aloud. "Jeff." Then she breathed in through her nose and out through her mouth to ease the pain that still lingered. If she said his name often enough, maybe it would become commonplace like *water* or *food*. But right then, she craved him more than the other two.

God, she loved him.

But she'd made the decision to push him out of her life and cut off any contact. And he'd respected her wishes at last—finally relinquishing control.

That accomplishment sounded better in her head than it felt in her heart.

During these weeks of silence, she'd found her strength again, both mental and physical. She would move forward now like the geese, accepting the unknown with courage, grace and dignity.

She closed her eyes and took a deep breath—finding once more that place of inner peace, accepting that the ache deep in her soul would always be there as a reminder of all she'd lost.

Only then could she be truly thankful for all she had.

An explosion of sound came from nowhere. Her eyes jerked open to the sight of a flock of Canada geese, low and directly overhead. She sprang from her seat and honked, laughing as all seven tilted their heads and answered.

Seven.

One was without her mate.

Had he died? Or had they gotten separated by life's uncertain circumstances? Maybe he was waiting patiently at the end of her journey, watching the sky, positive she would find her way back to him.

The thought stirred a yearning at some primal depth, causing Maggie's heart to explode into a wild rhythm that pushed blood to every part of her body. Her arms and legs and fingertips and toes tingled with the lively certainty she, too, could soar if she would only spread her wings and have faith.

The flock disappeared, obscured by the treetops, but she continued staring at the sky where it had passed. This path was different from the one the others had taken, and the image of the V-formation arrowhead imprinted on her brain.

It pointed the direction she knew her heart lay— west toward the sun. Toward California and Jeff. And, despite the cloudy day, her vision was crystal clear—she and Jeff together forever.

Was it still possible to make the vision a reality?

Perhaps. But it would take her head and her heart agreeing on what some people would find absurd.

Moving forward in her life actually meant the same as finding her way back.

THE CLUB HEAD connected with the golf ball, and Jeff heard the satisfying *ping*, confirming he'd hit the sweet spot. He watched the tiny orb soar upward then down in an arc so perfect Tiger Woods would've been proud to have made the shot. Sure enough, it landed exactly where he'd aimed—at the top of the rise on the green—and then started rolling down, gathering speed, curving with the lay of the land until it found its way to the edge of the hole and disappeared inside.

An eagle—two under par on a tough par five hole. A rare occurrence among amateurs.

He stalked toward the hole to retrieve his ball,

trying to work up some excitement. He should feel proud...elated even. He should have dinner in the clubhouse and brag about the shot. He should give Maggie the credit because the damn woman had him so damn frustrated he'd crushed the first damn shot of the hole, sending the damn ball farther than any damn drive he'd ever made.

Damn it!

He penciled his score into the box on the scorecard and thrust it and the ball into his pants pocket. For weeks, his conversation with Rosemary had played on a continuous loop in his brain.

She told me for a fact she loves you and always will.

She loves you...always will.

Love finds a way.

Where was the way? Wasn't the fact they *hadn't* found a way proof in itself that love doesn't have the best sense of direction?

He shoved his pitching wedge into his bag and got back in the cart. Despite the score he'd just earned, the mood to play had abandoned him. Well, honestly, he hadn't been in the mood to play in the first place. He'd thought the game would get his mind off Maggie, but it hadn't worked.

Nothing worked.

He followed the cart path and was nearly back to the clubhouse when his phone vibrated in the holder.

The caller ID flashed *Russ*. Finally something to brighten his mood!

"Hey, son."

"Hey, Dad. How's it going?"

He'd been granted the chance to brag a bit, after all. "Couldn't be better." Certainly an exaggeration, but he didn't want to let on anything was wrong. "I just got an eagle on number twelve."

"Wow. Impressive."

The words were correct, but the lack of enthusiasm put Jeff's nerves on edge. Of course, they didn't have to go far to get there. They'd been hovering on the edge for over a month now. "Yeah, well…um, is everything okay at school?"

The long pause said it all and brought the hairs on Jeff's arms to attention.

"You know I'm going home tomorrow for Thanksgiving." Russ's voice was pulled so taut Jeff felt the tension in his own neck.

"Yeeeah?"

"Well…" Another pause and then words rushed out. "I've decided I'm not coming back. I mean, since I don't have my car up here, I'll have to come back and get the rest of my stuff, but—"

"Whoa! Whoa, whoa, whoa!" Jeff fairly shouted, garnering angry glares from the people putting on the green he was passing. "Wait just a minute," he said to Russ, and then stomped on the pedal to quickly get to a place where he could talk. The next fairway was empty, so he pulled under some trees and stopped the cart. "Now." He fought to keep his voice calm. "Tell me what's going on."

"I'm moving back home, Dad." Russ's voice trembled.

"Why, son? What's happened?"

"I...I just don't like it."

He couldn't remember Russ ever saying those words before. The kid had always been the easiest person to get along with. What in the hell could've brought this on? "I understand that Chicago's really different from Taylor's Grove, Russ, but you can't—"

"Yes, I can, Dad." The harsh tone was one he'd never heard, either. "I'm grown now, and I can do what I want."

That attitude lit the fuse on the keg of dynamite Jeff had been sitting on since Rosemary's call. "Now you listen to me, young man—"

"I don't have to listen" was the angry retort. "I'm going home tomorrow. And I'm staying."

"Talk to me. Tell me what's happened." Jeff waited for an answer. It came as three short beeps. "The little shit hung up on me!" Jeff exploded, and hit Redial, listening to it ring. No answer. He waited a few seconds and hit it again. No answer. He jabbed the pedal with his foot and raced back to the clubhouse. A wide-eyed attendant who met him didn't ask any questions as he brought the cart to a skidding stop. Jerking his clubs from the cart, Jeff threw them over his shoulder and stormed to his locker, where he tossed them in and slammed the door.

He was almost back to his car when his phone rang. He answered without looking at the caller ID. "Hello." It was a harsh statement, not a question.

"You've talked to him then." Maggie's voice, her tone matching his own.

"Yeah. What in the hell is going on?"

"I have no idea. He hung up on me, and won't answer when I call him back."

Jeff detected hurt in her voice. Well, he sure as hell didn't feel hurt. He was mad. Pure and simple.

"I guess I'll find out when he gets here," she said.

"*We'll* find out." He stressed the word, a plan of action already formed in his mind. "I'm coming out there, Mags. We've got to talk some sense into him before he loses his scholarship." The thought of that happening made Jeff's jaws tighten to the point of pain.

"Oh…" He heard her discomfort.

"Don't worry. I'll get a hotel room."

"No. Don't do that. Stay here." Her voice quivered, but he couldn't tell much from her tone.

Was she pleased? What did it matter, anyway? Right at that moment, he didn't give a rat's ass. Parenting took precedence over everything else.

"Okay," he halfheartedly agreed, knowing he'd book a room, anyway. That way she'd truly have the choice, and he wouldn't be forcing her into anything. He reached his car. "But I can't talk now. I'm mad as hell, and I've got a shitload of stuff to take care of before I leave."

"I understand," she said. "I'll see you tomorrow." She was gone.

He climbed into his car and gave the steering wheel a swat with the palm of his hand. "What in the hell else can go wrong?" He sat there a minute, breathing deeply, then he leaned forward. "Please don't answer that," he said with a glance through the windshield up at the sky.

CHAPTER TWENTY-SIX

THE ALARM SIGNALED someone was coming up the drive. Maggie glanced expectantly out the window. As she'd hoped, it was her mom's car with Jeff in the passenger seat. She threw on the sweater lying on the back of the chair and hurried out to meet them.

Jeff was out of the car in a flash, worry etched into the crease between his brows. He looked older than he had two months ago, though still the sexiest guy she'd ever known. No salutation was uttered. No hug. He simply stepped toward her, took her arms in his hands and rubbed them gently up and down. His touch caused her heart to bounce hard in her chest like a ball thrown against a brick wall.

"How is he?" he asked.

She gave a one-shoulder shrug. "Silent. I've never seen him like this."

Her mom popped the trunk but didn't get out. "So he's not said anything?" she called through the passenger door Jeff left open.

Maggie stepped over to the car while he retrieved his luggage from the trunk. "Not yet."

"He will." Her mom gave her a reassuring smile.

Jeff's hand pressed the small of her back, its warmth seeping through her sweater and the knit top below. She breathed easier now than she had in the twenty-four hours since Russ's call.

"Thanks for picking me up, Rosemary." Jeff leaned down and gave a small wave. "You saved me the money and the hassle of dealing with a rental. I'm grateful."

"Happy to do it." She made a shooing motion with her hand. "Now, go straighten out my grandson."

Maggie nodded and closed the door. They held off going inside until her mom's car made the turn around and headed out. Then she turned to Jeff. "I'm glad you're here," she said honestly, though not giving away the depth of emotion she felt.

Jeff searched her face, his gaze lingering for a fraction on her mouth and then moving up again to lock with her eyes. "Me, too," he said.

She intertwined her fingers with his and filled him in as they made their way through the garden. "He hugged me really tight when he got off the train and made chitchat, but as soon as I mentioned school, he sulled up like a possum."

When she opened the door, the house was pulsating with the beat of heavy metal music originating from the second floor.

Jeff grimaced, his eyes rolling toward the ceiling. "No indication at all of what's wrong?"

She shook her head, reluctantly letting go of his

hand. "He went upstairs and locked himself in his room as soon as we got home. He's been there ever since."

They passed through the kitchen and great room, and Maggie dropped her sweater onto a chair as they passed. Then they continued down the hall toward the front of the house, where they simultaneously came to an abrupt stop. Their eyes met.

Her bedroom was to the right, the staircase to the left.

An excruciatingly awkward moment passed, her pulse throbbing to the beat of the drums overhead while her breath stilled in her chest.

Jeff's grimace deepened. "I know you said I could stay here, but I got a room in Benton. I thought you could take me into town later."

He didn't want to stay with her.

Maggie's heart sank with a thud, but she managed a nod. "Okay." She glanced around—anything to break eye contact so he wouldn't see her disappointment. "Do you, um…want a drink first? Or a minute to catch your breath?" She wasn't sure how he was being affected, but the room felt ten sizes smaller than normal to her.

He shook his head and ran a hand through the top of his hair and down his face. Then he gripped his hips with both hands. "No, I want to talk to our son."

She led the way up the stairs, and when they reached Russ's room, she would almost swear she could see the door vibrating from the sound waves buffeting the other side. She knocked lightly. "Russ?"

No answer.

Jeff stepped up and pounded with his fist. "Russ!" he shouted. "Get over here and open this door now."

The music stopped and footsteps shuffled their direction. The door opened and Russ's sad puppy-dog eyes greeted his father. "Hey, Dad."

"Hey, son." Jeff pulled him into a hug, and Maggie's heart shattered under the onslaught of emotion.

Jeff loosened his grip and stepped back, tilting his head toward the staircase. "Downstairs." It was an order, not a question, and Russ slunk by them, imaginary tail between his legs.

Maggie followed, with Jeff bringing up the rear. The silent procession made its way down the steps and to the great room where Russ flopped unceremoniously into a chair.

Maggie sat on the couch and, without hesitation, Jeff sat down beside her in a show of solidarity. Her breath shuddered in her lungs at his close proximity.

Jeff dove right in. "We're all here to talk like adults, and that's what we're going to do. We won't tolerate any sullen, childish behavior. Is that understood?"

Russ nodded. With his head lowered, his eyes shifted between theirs, making direct contact with both.

Jeff leaned back, turning slightly in Maggie's

direction and resting his arm across the back of the couch behind her. He held his other hand out, giving Russ the floor. "You start."

"IT'S JUST NOT what I expected." Russ shrugged, looking miserable. "I thought living in the big city would be great. I mean, I love San Diego. But Chicago's not San Diego. I miss my friends, and I miss home."

Memories of those same feelings squeezed Jeff's heart. Murray, Kentucky, had been a far cry from the city and culture he'd grown up in. "A move like this takes time to adjust to, son," he said gently. "It's natural for you to miss your friends, and, of course, you're going to be homesick. That's all part of growing up. But you make new friends. You're not having trouble with that, are you?"

Russ shook his head.

"And remember..." Mags entered the conversation. "Most of your friends aren't here, either. They're away at school, too. Do you talk to them? Stay in touch?"

"We talk some." Russ scooted back in his chair, a bit more relaxed.

"They'll be home this week, too," Mags said. "Invite them over for Taco Tuesday. We'll fix tacos and y'all can play pool like you used to. It'll help you see that though some things have changed, other things remain the same."

Russ nodded, but the way his Adam's apple

bobbed as he swallowed hard told them they hadn't touched on the real problem yet. Jeff wasn't surprised. Russ had spent summers in San Diego, away from his friends, his entire life, and had never suffered homesickness. That it was rearing its head now seemed off. "But that's not what's really bothering you, is it?"

Russ leaned forward again and rested his elbows on his knees. His fingertips pressed together and apart in a push-up motion. Jeff recognized the gesture—the same one he used when he was agitated. "Everything's just a lot harder than I thought it was going to be," he said. "The competition on the team is tough. I mean, really tough. And the classes. Man, they're so hard!"

"College is hard, no doubt about it," Jeff agreed, trying to be supportive.

"And high school was really easy for you," Mags added. "You didn't have to study much, and now you're having to develop study habits."

Russ crossed his arms and flopped back into his seat. "But I don't like having to study all the time. I'm either on the golf course or studying. I never get to do anything fun. I want to go someplace easy."

Jeff could hardly believe his eyes...or his ears. He wasn't sure where this chuck-it-all behavior came from, but he sure as hell didn't like it. He opened his mouth and stretched his tight jaw muscles before he spoke. "You don't just leave school in midsemester because it's hard. You figure out what you have to do, and you do it."

Russ rolled his eyes. "I *have* figured out what I have to do. I have to quit. It's not fun. It's hard. I want out."

"Russ—" Mags began, but the speech rushed out of Jeff's lips before he could stop them.

"You do not quit something simply because it's not fun or it's hard." Jeff surged to his feet, slapping the fingers of one hand against his other palm. "Giving up is not an option when it comes to the important things in life."

Russ came to his feet then, too, meeting Jeff's gaze full on. "You mean, the important things in life like marriage, Dad?" His voice was quiet, but the edge was sharp and it sliced Jeff's heart wide open. "Or is that one of those throwaway things it's okay to walk away from?"

The punch from his son's words landed hard in his gut and knocked the breath from him, rendering him speechless for a moment.

How could it be that the silence in the room was so much louder than the earlier music had been?

He coughed to make some room around the piece of heart lodged in his throat. "Russ, your mom and I…" *What?* What could he say to make his son understand that no matter how much you love somebody, sometimes you have to give them up, let them go? Especially when the entire premise sounded absurd, even to him.

A warmth moved through him, and he became aware Mags was standing beside him...had slipped her arm through his and pulled it close against her. When she reached out and took Russ's hand, Jeff watched the tension ease in his son's face. "Russ, your dad and I have made mistakes, and we admit that." Her voice was gentle yet firm and unwavering, and she intertwined her fingers through his. God, her hand felt wonderful. "But we want you to learn from our mistakes. Quitting is not an option. Maybe at the end of the semester or the end of the year, if it comes to that. But not in the middle. Now tell us what's really going on."

Russ's eyes welled with tears. He blinked fast in an effort to hold them back and then his shoulders slumped in surrender. "Nothing's ever been this hard for me. I'm afraid of...of failing. Y'all... and Grandma and Grandpa...and all my high school teachers. Everybody'll be so disappointed."

Jeff laid a hand on his son's shoulder and squeezed lightly. "Are you failing? Really?"

"No. Not yet."

Maggie's hand twitched, and Jeff met her eyes, read the relief.

"But I feel like if I let up for even one second, it'll all blow up." Russ swiped his hand down his face. "I've got two papers due when I get back and a test coming up soon, so I don't even get to enjoy my time at home. I'm so tired I feel like I could sleep the entire week."

"Then the first thing we need to do is let you get some rest." Maggie cradled their son's cheek in her palm. He closed his eyes and leaned into it briefly. "You can't think straight or make any kind of decision when you're this exhausted." She shot Jeff a meaningful look before she went on. "Go crawl into your own bed, leave the music off and just rest. Sleep as long as you want. Tomorrow, we'll revisit this and look at it with fresh eyes. Okay?" She raised a questioning eyebrow toward Jeff and he nodded.

"Good idea," he said.

Russ took a long deep breath. "Okay. That sounds great actually."

Jeff patted his son's shoulder as Maggie kissed his cheek, then together they watched him climb the stairs, feet dragging with exhaustion.

"He's going to be fine," Maggie said as soon as they heard the door upstairs close. "When he got whiny like this as a little boy, I always knew he was just overtired." She dropped his hand and rested hers on her hip, absently touching her other hand to the base of her throat. "I could use some fresh air. How about you? Want to go for a walk?"

He nodded. Anything would be better than standing within arm's reach of the woman he loved and feeling a million miles away.

THEY SPENT THE first few awkward moments roaming around the front yard, shedding their anxiety about Russ by discussing the abundance of walnuts still hanging on the branches and the Indian corn stalks and pumpkin display she'd put up as decoration.

The sun had dropped below the trees, adding an additional coolness to the air, when Jeff finally came to a standstill, shoving his hands into his pockets and looking her directly in the eyes. "How are you doing, Mags? I mean…are you still doing okay?"

She started to cross her arms but caught herself and instead slid her fingers into the back pockets of her jeans. "I'm fine. I've been resting, not pushing myself too hard. It's given me a chance to work through the grief. You?"

He nodded. "Chloe's been a great counselor. I feel almost normal again. I mean, the pain's always going to be there…"

"But it's bearable," she finished his sentence, and they shared a sad smile.

"Exactly."

"Jeff." She dropped her eyes for a moment to catch the breath that eluded her when his gaze was so unflinching. "I said a lot of things I regret the last time we were together."

"Let's not rehash any of that, Mags." His eyes closed in a long, tired blink. "Rosemary said you told her we'd said everything that needed to be said. Let's just leave it at that."

Maggie winced at the thought of her mom and Jeff having such a conversation. But she should've realized they'd fill the time in the car from the airport with *something*. "I don't *want* to leave it at that." She was determined to at least apologize. "I said things I didn't mean, lashed out at you when you were being wonderful. I'm sorry."

He shrugged. "It's okay." He backed away from her at a quick pace and turned toward the driveway.

She caught up with him, grabbing his arm and jerking him around to face her. "It's *not* okay." She ground the words out through clenched teeth. "I said I regretted letting you in my life, and that's a lie. I don't regret you in my life. Not the first time. Not the second. Not ever. No regrets."

Jeff held up his hands in a surrender pose and shook his head. With a purposeful stride, he stalked back toward the house.

"Where are you going?" she called.

"I'm going to get my luggage," he answered over his shoulder. "Go get your car. You're taking me to Benton."

The sledgehammer pounding in Maggie's chest told her with absolute certainty if she let him go this time, it would be the end.

No more chances. No going back.

She took off at a run, beating him to the steps and blocking his way. "I'm not taking you to Benton. I want you to stay here."

JEFF DID AN about-face and ran his hand down his face, swiping it across the back of his neck, which had broken out in a sweat at Maggie's words. "No.

I won't do that to Russ. It will send the wrong message, and the poor kid's stressed enough with everything else going on." He walked a few steps away, then turned to her. The love he saw in Maggie's eyes gripped his insides and squeezed.

"Maybe it could be the right message—that we're trying to work things out."

Jeff's brain whirred as he tried to figure out exactly what she was saying while still keeping his heart at bay. *Trying to work things out?* What in the hell did that mean? Reconciliation? Back to being exes with benefits? They couldn't allow themselves to get caught up in the emotion of the moment again. Not with Russ's trust in them at stake.

"No. I don't mind telling Russ we still care for each other. That much is true. But leading him to believe we're trying to reconcile, and that it's only a matter of time before we're back together is just setting him up for disappointment. I won't have it." He ran his fingers through his hair and scrubbed his face, then settled his hands back on his hips. Despite the cool breeze, he was burning up.

"But maybe we *can* get back together." She walked toward him, hands on her hips, mirroring his stance.

"Don't say anything else, Mags. You're forgetting that I'm overbearing and a control freak—"

"I know. Which means you try your hardest to take care of the people you love and keep them safe."

"Which *means*," he continued what he was going

to say before she interrupted, "I'm not willing to try to make a long-distance relationship work. I want you with me—all the time—or not at all."

Her arms folded across her chest. "You want marriage."

Damn! This was like walking a freaking tightrope with no safety net. Say the wrong thing and lose her forever. But the only way to keep his balance was to tell her the truth, so he gritted his teeth and laid it out. "Hell, yes, I want marriage! I want a wife…a real family life. Not love that comes around like shiftwork or any of that exes-with-benefits crap."

She dropped her arms and took a step that brought her up against him. Her eyes were big and luminous as she scanned his face. "Then marry me, Jeff."

His heart jerked to a stop. "You're asking me…?"

She caught her upper lip between her teeth and gnawed for a moment before she spoke. "Since you were here last, I've been having this recurring dream where you've talked me into riding this motorcycle. It's exhilarating and I'm going fast, but headed toward a canyon. You keep telling me I can make the jump. I go off the cliff, suspended in midair, and then I realize I'm all alone. You're nowhere around…and that's when I wake up."

She reached for his hand and pressed it against her cheek. "Last night, I didn't wake up in midair. I made it to the other side. You know who was there?"

He shook his head. "You," she said. "You were waiting there to catch me…had been there all along."

His heartbeat hammered in his ears.

"I want to be your wife," she said softly. "Become a real family again. So Jeff Wells…will… you…marry…me?" Her expression was dead serious, not even a glimmer of a smile.

Everything he'd dreamed of was being offered in her eyes—everything, that was, except a real solution. He shook his head. "I can't move to Kentucky, Mags." The jagged edges of his emotion scraped his throat. "I would love to, but I have too many people depending on me, and I just ca—"

Her finger touched his lips and silenced them. "I want to sell the salon and the house. I want to move to California and be with you. I've given this a lot of thought. I can help your mom with Chloe, so your dad can go back to work as much as he wants, and in turn you can have some time off."

He shook his head again, heart pounding now with wonder and fear. They were so close to happiness, yet still so far away. "I can't let you do that. It's not fair for you to give up everything."

"Well, let's get one thing straight." One of her eyebrows rose. "You don't *let* me do anything. I'm not asking your permission. I do what I want, and this is what I want. I'm not *giving up* everything, Jeff. I'm *getting* everything."

"Oh, God, Mags…" He gathered her into his

arms, and she relaxed against him. Nothing had ever felt more wonderful, more perfect...or more right.

She leaned her head back and his mouth found hers with a kiss he never wanted to end.

But she eventually pulled away and leaned back again, though remaining in the confines of his arms. "Is that a yes?"

"Yes, ma'am." He answered her smile with one of his own. "It's a definite yes."

ROSEMARY ANSWERED THE phone before the first ring was completed. "Hi, sweetheart."

"Grandma!" Russ's voice was breathless with excitement. "You won't believe this, but Mom and Dad are out in the front yard kissing! I looked out my bedroom window, and all of a sudden they were in this lip-lock. Ew! I mean major, movie-like kissing."

A rush of joy spread through Rosemary, warming her from head to toe, and she danced a few steps of a jig in the middle of her kitchen. "Oh, I'm so glad."

"You are? Did you know anything was going on between them?"

"I've had my suspicions."

"This is just un-freaking-believable." His laugh brought a chuckle to her lips, as well. She could picture that beautiful smile of his beaming across his face.

"Now, don't get your hopes up too high till you've talked with them," she said. "Find out what's going on."

"It's not *getting* my hopes up, Grandma," he said quietly. "My hopes have been up since I was three."

Her breath caught on his words.

"Uh-oh, they're coming in. I'm gonna go talk to them. Love you!"

Rosemary took a deep breath then, feeling the air flow deeper into her lungs than it had since...she couldn't remember when. She reached into the cabinet and retrieved two glasses and a jar of Emmy's finest.

If ever there was a fitting time to celebrate with moonshine, tonight was it.

CHAPTER TWENTY-SEVEN

"I DO."

Maggie spoke the words calmly and quietly, despite the excited pounding of her heart. Jeff's face broke out in a smile that was repeated in Russ's face just beyond his shoulder. She felt herself beaming, never before so full of happiness as she was at that moment.

Jeff raised her hand to his lips and kissed the gold band he had placed there—the same one he'd placed there all those years ago.

Emmy sniffled behind her.

"Then, by the power vested in me by the Almighty Creator and the Commonwealth of Kentucky—" Pastor Sawyer raised his hands over their heads in a gesture of blessing "—I now pronounce you husband and wife."

"Again," Maggie added, and Jeff winked at her.

"Still," he whispered.

"You can kiss your bride on the lips now, Jeff."

The small gathering in the pastor's study laughed as Jeff did just that, but Chloe let out a loud "Yay!"

Russ was first to pull them into a three-way hug,

and Maggie thought her heart would burst with joy. Next came her parents, then Jeff's mom and dad, Chloe and Faith.

Emmy was last. "Whooee!" she yelled, livening up the room as she pulled Maggie and Jeff into a hug that rocked back and forth as if they had a musical accompaniment.

And perhaps they did—Maggie certainly heard music flowing from her soul.

"Maggie Russell Wells Gunther Russell Wells!" Emmy shouted the name with exuberance. "You've come full circle!"

"And the circle stops here." Jeff's arms came around Maggie's waist from behind, and he nuzzled her ear.

"Yes, it does," Maggie agreed. She held up her left hand, proudly displaying the gold band. "Maggie Russell Wells Gunther Russell Wells is the only one that has the perfect ring to it."

* * * * *

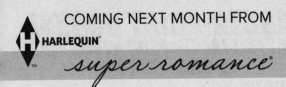

COMING NEXT MONTH FROM

HARLEQUIN

super romance

Available May 5, 2015

#1984 THE RANCHER'S DREAM
The Sisters of Bell River Ranch
by Kathleen O'Brien
Grant Campbell abandoned a life to follow his dream of breeding horses. He has no regrets, until he gets temporary custody of a baby and turns to Crimson Slayton for help. He's secretly attracted to her, and being so close makes him long for those other dreams he left behind...

#1985 ONE MORE NIGHT
A Family Business
by Jennifer McKenzie
Grace Monroe makes plans. Not only as a wedding planner, but in her own life, too. She knows what she wants—and how to get it. Everything changes with Owen Ford. Owen is charming and carefree and nothing Grace is looking for. Even so, something about him tempts Grace to give him just one more night...

#1986 CATCHING HER RIVAL
by Lisa Dyson
Allie Miller's life is a little crazy. She has a newly discovered twin sister, she's been working hard to launch her PR business and now her heart's decided to fall for her biggest rival. Jack Fletcher is a gorgeous complication that Allie has no time for— she *should* be trying to steal his clients, *not* his heart!

#1987 HER HAWAIIAN HOMECOMING
by Cara Lockwood
When Allie Osaka inherits half ownership of a Kona coffee plantation, she has one goal: sell the estate and travel the world. The only obstacle is Dallas McCormick, her not-so-silent partner. Irresistibly drawn to the sexy foreman, Allie must decide whether or not she's willing to come home—for good.

YOU CAN FIND MORE INFORMATION ON UPCOMING HARLEQUIN® TITLES, FREE EXCERPTS AND MORE AT WWW.HARLEQUIN.COM.

HSRLPCNM0415

LARGER-PRINT BOOKS!
GET 2 FREE LARGER-PRINT NOVELS PLUS 2 FREE GIFTS!

HARLEQUIN

super romance

More Story...More Romance

HSRLP13RR